Cryptogram

... because the past is never past

T0159483

Cryptogram

... because the past is never past

Michael Tobert

COSMIC
EGG
BOOKS

Winchester, UK
Washington, USA

First published by Cosmic Egg Books, 2014
Cosmic Egg Books is an imprint of John Hunt Publishing Ltd., Laurel House, Station Approach,
Alresford, Hants, SO24 9JH, UK
office1@jhpbooks.net
www.johnhuntpublishing.com

For distributor details and how to order please visit the 'Ordering' section on our website.

Text copyright: Michael Tobert 2013

ISBN: 978 1 78279 681 7

A CIP catalogue record for this book is available from the British Library.

Design: Lee Nash

Printed in the USA by Edwards Brothers Malloy

We operate a distinctive and ethical publishing philosophy in all
areas of our business, from our global network of authors to
production and worldwide distribution.

Acknowledgements

It has taken what feels like several lifetimes for *Cryptogram* to reach its final form and, in the course of these, I've had more help than is decent. I am most grateful to David Lorimer for steering me through the scientific and medical evidence for the fundamental nature of consciousness and to Chris Given Wilson for pointing out the literature on the Cathars and the Inquisition, particularly *Montaillou*, Ladurie (Penguin, 1980). For matters scientific and technical, I would like to thank Pascal André, David O'Brien, William Whelan-Curtin and Zach Williams. For the title, Peter de Wolff. And for the text, so many thanks to so many people: Roger McStravick, Max Wolf, David Christie, Jason Taylor, Antonia Brown, Julio Martino, Vanessa Neuling, Helen Coyle, Charles Macgregor, Howard Goldfinger, Anna and Andrew. Without their astute comments, *Cryptogram* would not be what it is. Andy Duff has been my writing buddy throughout, my sounding board and the person who fills me in on all those essential things which I prefer to overlook. Madeleine has scrutinised every draft with a penetrating eye, and always come up with inspiration and ideas – nothing quite like having a writer in the family! Natasha has read more than her share and – in writing as in life – told it to me as it is: a wonderful gift. Finally, I can't forget Katya (10), who is never far from the action.

To Goenkaji

In this country is a snake which devours its own Self. It prepares by not eating for two years. Once it has fasted to such an extent that it is too weak to hunt, its appetite–by an act of Divine Cruelty or perhaps Retribution–returns. So feeble is it at this point that it can only satisfy the voracious cravings of its stomach by ingesting its own flesh. It begins with its tail. The first mouthful immediately makes it feel better. Its health and vitality improve. How nice is this tail, it thinks–so I surmise–and takes another bite. In this way, it advances along itself. However, the more it eats, the less beneficial the process. This is true, in particular, when the snake reaches its stomach. In consuming this, it consumes both the source of its cravings and the means to satisfy them. Whereupon, or shortly afterwards, it dies. Travellers coming across such a creature in its final hours may wish to breathe in the vapours which it emits. These are said to be extremely beneficial to human health.

From 'Travels in Unknown Kingdoms', Francis Smythe, (London, Robinson and Sons, 1903; first published 1830.)

Northern Europe, Mid-21st Century

Polotti

After the world turned sour, polotti came into being as the poor man's pool. It is a strange game. The polotti table has no uphol-stered cushions and no baize to cover it. It is just wood: table top, three-inch sides. And, like all things natural, it's unpredictable. Balls never roll precisely as the novice – even as the hustler – expects. Instead they drift and slide and come off the sides each time different by fractions.

This is so even for the table into which Jimmy Sands has worked years of daily beeswax, rubbed it, sniffed it, smoothed it, placed his cheek on it in the only act of love this bone-hearted curmudgeon has ever been known to exhibit. (This lasts until they find Jimmy hanging from a beam, after which his table never has the same care again. This is still a long way off.)

Now the burnished wood gleams even under the dim bulb overhead, and Stephen is bent over it as if in prayer. He sniffs its beeswax through the hall's prevailing odours – the acridity of ersatz tobacco, the vaporised sweat of the drinkers – and, lacking any other god, gives thanks to Jimmy. 'Thank you, O Jimmy,' he silently intones, 'for this table which you have given us.' This is all part of Stephen's act, part of his hustle.

Stephen turns his head sideways, taking in his audience: drinkers, mostly, and those placing bets. Close to him, neither drinking nor betting, are his friends, Rokas and Suzanna. They give him eye-smiles, silent whispers of encouragement. *Friends*: such a thin word, Stephen thinks, no meat on it at all – but what other word is there? Not quite *lovers*, not yet. He straightens. He is playing a man who was in the hall when they entered. The man watched him on the table missing shots and said, 'How about it? 50 eurars a game?'

Rokas is lounging on a chair placed out of cue distance. His legs protrude forward and his back and arms so overwhelm the sticks beneath him that he looks as if he has lost the support of invisible wires, like a pantomime giant abandoned from above by a puppeteer with aching arms.

Don't think, just because Rokas is lounging, he isn't paying attention. He is paying attention, all right. When Stephen is *on*, no-one looks away, not even Rokas, who knows nothing about polotti. And Stephen is *on* this night. He often is when he's hustling: the need to dangle on the brink of losing spices his blood and daubs a sheen of channelled calm on his forehead, around his mouth and, most of all, about his eyes. To those, like Rokas and Suzanna, who know him, it is this not-quite-angelic aura which is the giveaway, the sign that he'll pull it off, that the moment when it all comes apart in his hands is not now, not yet.

Suzanna sits next to Rokas. She is not a watcher of games, doesn't enjoy their twists and turns and tortures, and doesn't watch polotti. At this time – it is before the game has been cleaned up – not many women do. She is here on a whim. 'Why don't I join you?' she'd said to Stephen and Rokas, linking arms with them as they'd set off that evening.

She knows she is a burden to them, someone who has to be both protected and pleased. This knowledge laps at her pleasure in being here and stiffens her. And because she does not yet feel comfortable where she is, she does not look around at the drinkers and the gamblers and smile at them as she would have done were she elsewhere. Instead, she keeps herself apart, sitting on her straight-backed wooden chair as if she is sitting on an island with an empty sea all around and not a fish in it – and, if there had been, it wouldn't have dared to flap onto the beach and say hello.

This stiffness is not in her nature. It makes her uncomfortable and she wants to be rid of it. So she lets herself observe the masculine coarseness of the place, its smells and its smoke and the sounds of men around her in all their swagger and bravado. So she sees, for what it is, the harsh and jagged undertow of the hall. And, gradually, by seeing it, she softens and is herself again.

Stephen circles the table. He adds to the polish of its burnished wood with the heel of his hand, joining his molecules to it and taking some back into himself. In this way, Stephen absorbs the table and its secrets. Often, when he's hustling, he can do this – it's his special skill – but polotti is a special case; it doesn't mean all other secrets open up to him.

Stephen has clichés to follow; he is a hustler and the dictums of the hustler's script have been rehashed time and again since hustling began. Therefore, as the script prescribes, he takes the man slowly, while the watchers, drinks in hand, and their hangers-on, move close and the side-bets ratchet up. The man can play all right and he doesn't think he's come to lose, so there is in the game that necessary fraction of uncertainty which is beyond Stephen's ability to control. Both men sense it, and this is felt also by those who have money on one man or the other. And the eurars stack.

Stephen, leaning over the abyss which he himself has created, needs thirty off the last shot of the last game to steal it. He will let the struck ball linger on the burnished wood and make it off three corners. Forty. Maximum. He will turn to the crowd and hold his arms aloft. Who doubts me now?

Who doubts me now? Stephen knows who doubts him. He always knows. He feels the doubt in his gut; he feels it in his mind. He draws back the cue and finds the secrets of the table drained away and nothing left but froth. Stephen stops. He can't play the shot.

He puts down the cue, turns to the man and says, 'Look, my friend, I don't want to take your money. Let's call it quits. Cancel all bets between us. An honourable draw. What do you say?'

The man hoots his derision. The crowd cat-calls. Rokas and Suzanna swap questions across the eye-waves.

'Okay, if that's how you want it,' says Stephen to the man and to the crowd. 'Okay, so this is it then,' he says to himself. He picks up his cue, prays to some greater god than Jimmy, and makes the shot. 'Ha!'

Luck? Magic? Is there really something deep within, some beneficent genie come up to save him? Not even Stephen knows.

The crowd cheers. Rokas and Suzanna sit silent, not entirely sure what they have seen. They look for explanation in the other's eyes but find only what is in their own: a sort of wonder, a sort of disbelief. And fear: fear is in there somewhere too, fear for their friend and of the abyss over which he lingers.

After the last ball has disappeared into the only remaining pocket, Stephen laughs, peels off a ten eurar note from his winnings and gives it back to the man as if it's charity. When Stephen is *on*, it doesn't make him nice.

The man doesn't like it. He bridles. He hasn't come to the hall to be humiliated. Not him. And how did he end up losing anyway? Was there cheating? There must have been; that last shot was impossible. He's been diddled, he's been done, and he aches to get his own back – aches to replace the injustice that curdles his guts with a greater distraction: with his fists on Stephen's face. This ache is about to overwhelm him when Rokas, noticing the man's internal monologue, his rising colour, climbs out of his chair. Like some awakened force of order, Rokas assumes the man's cue, assumes it in a way that has finality creamed into its every lacquered pore: that's it, game over, I'll play now.

The man, and all of those watching, are suddenly aware of what had escaped them when he was lounging in his chair: that Rokas is a cut above them all. He is taller than the tallest of them, his feet are flatter than any of theirs, his eyes more benign. The man in the shadow of the giant steps back – an involuntary movement, what else can he do? – and mustering what dignity he can, slinks away.

Suzanna smiles. As if Rokas would strike anyone! She joins the two men by the table and stands between them. 'You'll get yourself hurt one of these days,' she says to Stephen. 'There'll be a back alley some time, and they'll get you then.'

'You think I can't look after myself?' asks Stephen, putting on his most harmless smile, his baby smile which sits on his wide-boned stubbled face like innocence on the face of a dictator.

'You didn't have to rub his nose in it, that's all. Being nice costs nothing.'

'Oh, is that so? Well, maybe it does, and maybe it doesn't.' Turning to Rokas he says, 'Let's play. I'm in the mood. A eurar to make it interesting.'

Rokas dips into his pocket, pulls out a coin and hands it over. 'Here. For when you win.' He picks up a ball, rolls it over the polished wood and watches it wander down the table. It hits the board on the right and slides off. 'I'm not even sure I know the rules.'

'Two players, one cue ball, 10 balls, 10 pockets, one ball per pocket, more sides you touch, more points, fewer the pockets remaining, higher the score. You keep playing until all the balls are gone. Pot the cue ball and the game is over, just as you'd expect. Simple. You start.'

'Why don't I play, too?' asks Suzanna. Playfully, she engages Stephen with her eyes. Tilting her head a fraction, she smiles enquiringly. And in her smile and also in her eyes, are other questions half-articulated and half-understood: by him, by her.

Stephen looks around. The drinkers have gone back to their drinking. Jimmy Sands is watching from the bar, disgruntled. 'I suppose you could,' Stephen says. 'Do you know how?'

Suzanna steps closer. 'Show me,' she says. She looks up at him, amused.

'Here,' says Stephen. 'Rest the cue on your thumb and forefinger… like so.' Trespassing cautiously on what he wishes was his, and with Rokas looking on, Stephen takes her hand and forms it. He passes her his cue. 'Now, hold it loosely in your other hand and let it run forward. Got it?'

'Yes, I think so,' says Suzanna. She places a ball in front of her, top-spins it twice around the table and drops it in the bottom pocket. She laughs. 'My stepfather taught me. He had a farm, three sons and a table.'

'And there was me about to give you odds,' says Stephen.

'My turn,' says Rokas. He picks up the cue, tosses it like trivia from hand to hand, crouches over it so that it disappears somewhere beneath him and then stands up. 'You two play. I'll watch.'

The opening game goes unnoticed. During the second, some of the drinkers, out of curiosity, wander over. During the third, they place their bets. Rokas holds the money because, although no one in the place has seen him before, they don't think he looks like a runner. Rokas writes it all down on squared paper he finds behind the bar: names, amounts, who against whom. 'One at a time. Slow down,' he says.

They want Suzanna to win, of course. They've seen Stephen play and know she doesn't have a prayer – but who doesn't cheer for the three-legged dog, the little guy, the no-hope hopeful who hangs in there though he's taking a pounding? So those who can't bring themselves to bet against, or who've got long odds, root for her. The rest keep silent, made mute by the money they stand to gain.

Ten black balls, one white cue ball. Wide pockets and any pocket will do: but room in each for only one ball. First pocket, one point, second two... More sides, the higher the multiplier, up to four.

Suzanna is a clean striker of the ball, familiar with the spins and how to move the odds in her favour. But the opening exchanges go against her. She doesn't know the table and Stephen is fresh from it. It doesn't faze her. She plays the easy balls. She listens to the wood, opens herself to its resistances and its surrenders, lets its whisperings lodge... because Suzanna knows what years of playing against her step-brothers has taught her and what few there have the wit to imagine: that polotti is a woman's game, that what it demands is patience not presumption, give not take, intuition not certainty, respect not power. The game can't be controlled; it is too close to the garrulous edge of chance for that.

And Suzanna has one other thing going for her. Stephen isn't *on* any more. How can he be *on* as he was before? Everything has changed. He isn't hustling now; so now he can't ride the moment, can't let himself be pulled along by polotti's wild horses. And what's he left with? Her. She's what he feels: feels her in the rustle of her shirt as she moves within it, in her smell, in the wood itself. She is all about him – but not as opponent: as a different kind of presence for which polotti is a sideshow. Somewhere within him he suspects that he will win nothing if he tries to win, perhaps even if he wants to win. But, also, out of habit and of pride, he doesn't want to lose, can't let himself lose – and so is caught, pulled in opposite directions by forces he can neither put into words nor reconcile as they roil his stomach. Therefore he plays stiff polotti, polotti of the conscious mind, average, ordinary, inadequate and Suzanna starts to catch him.

The crowd love it. Even those with money on Stephen start to cheer, as if in that moment and against all sense they are able to shrug off their scummy self-interest and back… what?… the impossible?… the uplifting?… love?… life? Who knows what, but every time Suzanna bends over the table, coyly tugs at the edge of her skirt, whispers her blandishments to the ball as it rolls, their cheers rise louder.

By the fourth game, Suzanna is 50 points behind – but she is beginning to make the angles, get the multipliers. In game six, she makes pock 8 off three sides, 32 points, and pocks 9 and 10 off two – 89 in three balls. She looks across at Stephen and sees he is feeling it, sees the cross-tug of emotions on him, sees him fighting the twist but not knowing how to shrug it off. Should I miss a few, she thinks. She plays with the thought and lets it pass on by.

No. Let him work it out for himself.

After that 89 in three balls, it's over. Mopping up remains, but she knows, he knows, the watchers know: it is done. When she pots the last ball to finish it, a straight shot into pock 10, nothing fancy, Stephen says, 'You played well.' But he doesn't go over and kiss her as on another day he might have done.

Instead, he goes to the bar and orders the beer which everybody knows Jimmy brews himself. The drinkers make a space for him and he sits there in silence, mouthing his beer and his confusion in equal draughts. Suzanna and Rokas stay by the table and don't say much either, quiet as people are after they've seen something out of the ordinary and don't quite know what to make of it.

After a while, Rokas says, 'Well, we could play, you and I, though I won't give you much of a game.'

Suzanna spots the black balls and hands him the cue. 'You never know,' she says.

Rokas takes aim. He drives the cue forward but tugs it on the down-stroke so that it hits the cue-ball with a slicing action left side. The ball slews across the wooden surface and finds its way, unimpeded, into a side pocket. 'Oh. That's your game, isn't it?' he says.

'Try again. Let the cue flow.'

Rokas tries again, strikes the ball dead centre and sends it up and down the table at crazy speed. Suzanna reaches across and catches it. 'Try again.'

Suzanna watches him hitting balls, watches him getting the feel of what works and what doesn't, how the ball rolls over the wood. Occasionally she makes suggestions, but mainly she is content to sink into her own thoughts.

She looks across at Stephen by the bar, at the stiffness in his bearing, how ill at ease he is, how gawky almost, and she regrets what happened when they played. She would like to reach out to him and pass her hand over the stubble on his cheek and the hairs on the back of his neck, just so she can take the stiffness out of him – though she knows he wouldn't allow it. More than anything what she wants is for Stephen to be again as he was when potting that last ball against the man: beyond effort, beyond desire, both vulnerable and invincible all at once. That was the best of him, she thinks, the impossible best. Should I have let him win, she wonders. He'd have been happier if I had. Would I?

Beside her, Rokas continues to hit balls. He is immersed in what he is doing, aware of nothing else around him but the small details of technique, rhythm, cue speed, angles and all the game's other unpredictable intricacies. Suzanna watches him as he hits one ball after another up the table, to the side pockets, up the table again, hard, soft, side-spin left, side-spin right – and she feels that his concentration excludes her, is perhaps intended to exclude her.

'What are you thinking about?' she asks.

He looks up. 'Thinking about? Not much. Why? What should I be thinking about?'... as if she might have a nugget of polotti truth to pass on.

'Oh, nothing, you're doing fine.' She smiles at him, a smile which allows him to carry on, sanctions his own exclusive world. She thinks, Rokas does what he does because he is Rokas and Stephen does what he does because he is Stephen. When you boil it right down, how little my life changes theirs. And then an extra clause tacks itself on: or theirs mine.

This she hates. She dismisses it with a wave of her hand, rejects it utterly – and, from nothing but an empty ache within her, conjures her own dead son. He'd be 14 now, she thinks, old enough to play polotti. He could be standing here, right next to me, taller than me, I expect – but I don't suppose he'd want to play with his mother.

Stephen comes over. 'I'm going,' he says.

'Wait up,' replies Rokas, 'we'll all go.' He puts down his cue.

'I'm getting better, by the way. Next time, I'll be ready.'

They leave, all three together as they came, except that the evening at the polotti hall with its small victories and defeats has wearied them, and Stephen especially.

The night is clear, the stars bright and their thick coats too thin to keep out the cold. The cold bites through them and down to their teeth. Suzanna links arms with the two men and they walk like that for a while, but it is a mechanical sort of a walking with no rhythm in it and no harmony and, after a while, Stephen stops to untie and tie again the lace of his boot. When he straightens, he doesn't take her arm. He walks separate then and so do they.

They pass the town's only jazz club and read the sign outside: *Coming soon, One Week Only, Corny Kelleher, the Best in the West!* The words slither snakelike from top to bottom, surrounding in their coils the image of Cornet Corny himself, the black Irishman, lazing, one arm on *Week*, one toe on *West*.

On Prior Street, daubs of dull light attach to the rooms above where the street-watchers by their windows look down or move about like shadows. Stephen, glancing up, sees a man and a girl in a yellow dress, standing. The man smiles as they walk beneath and pulls the girl into his side. Stephen turns away, not wanting to be reminded of what he does not have.

The neon of the boarding house for the down-and-outs holds out against the dark, half its letters disappeared. *B....IN.*, it reads. On the corner, through the iron surrounds of the police station, a dim blue. Here and there, a footstep in the gloom, a shout from a street over, intimation of life among the shadows, but the palpable crowds are gone. They are alone.

Silence in the pavement air, disturbed only by their footsteps: Rokas' flat carthorse feet plodding as if he was ploughing up Prior Street, Suzanna's trippity-trap on her half heels and Stephen, half on the pavement and half off it, peg-leg-Joe limping alongside.

Stephen moves into the road, giving the pavement over to the two of them.

They pass a few lightless shops: a baker's which will be starting the morning's bread soon enough and a second-hand shop: clothes and books, life's basics. Suzanna stops and peers into the window, seeing if there is anything she can make out. The darkness defeats her.

They turn in silence into Hetherington's Pike, a winding lane which connects Prior Street to Stanley Street where the trams run down to the station and a stop or two further on.

No-one speaks. No one has words to say. Silence wraps itself around them like skin. Silence patrols their borders and none of them can break out, none can find words which might allow them to come together at a place less lonely. To move out of silence into speech seems like a betrayal of what is real for the sake of nothing more substantial than the tawdry analgesic of chatter.

Yet this silence numbs them, and Suzanna most of all. It is too lonely, its distances too great.

They are between one bend and another of this winding lane when five men come out of a fold in the wall and stand in front of them. They are edgy, hungry pack animals, cowled and threadbare. Rokas puts his arm around Suzanna and brings her close. Stephen moves in to her other side. She is what they will fight for if it comes to it.

One of them, older than the rest, advances, his hand outstretched, rubbing a thumb and forefinger together. 'It be your folding people we is wantin bros, your freddly eurar bills, then we be outta here. No problemo.'

Rokas towers over them all. 'How much are you boys hoping for?' he asks.

'Everyting. Every little ting.'

'Everything! Now, that's a lot,' says Rokas amiably. 'Everything's the sort of amount that can get you into trouble.

Why not just ask for as much as you need and then we'll give it to you and we can all be on our way?'

The man sighs. 'Everyting, big fella, everyting… please. You observe how I say *please*, being as being polite is polite. It be like dis, see, what we don't use right now, we put by for later, I'm speakin here o, you know, stocks, investments, dat sort o ting, mebbe a little penthouse on Prior Street, you get me. Me and ma bros here, we is collectors sure, but also in-vest-ors. So deposits please, and I'm tinking particularly here o' – he turns to survey Stephen – 'you. We hear polotti been kind dis evening.'

Stephen says, 'It's true, I did make a little money tonight. Worked hard for it, though.'

'We also brother. We is workin hard. Don't you tink dis is work?' The man pulls out a jackknife, the tool of his trade, moves it from hand to hand.

Stephen shakes his head, tuts his teeth. 'Producing a thing like that before you've got a feeling how the balls are rolling! Risky. Very risky.' He pauses, as if contemplating. 'I tell you what, though,' he says in the manner of a man with his arm around another's shoulders, 'I'll go easy on you: 100 eurars, risk free, cash in hand, that's what I'll give you just to say goodbye, au revoir, and no hard feelings. How about it?'

'Take it,' says Suzanna. 'Please, it's generous. It's the best you can do. Take it. I don't want to see you hurt.'

'You crazy!' says the man. 'We aint discussin! I is workin here, not playin aroun wiv you all. So, game time is over, my bruvs, everyting you have.' The four others step closer to their leader jerking upward knives of their own and grinning as if by way of punctuation.

'You sure we can't persuade you?' says Stephen. 'You really want to go ahead with this?'

'Shut it right,' the leader answers, turning from Stephen to Rokas and back again. 'Give us your loolah and we is on our way toot sweet or even faster.'

Stephen shrugs and head-butts the man on the bridge of his nose. As he staggers back, Stephen takes from his coat a sock with a polotti ball inside and smashes it against the man's knee. He collapses instantly. Rokas roars, a roar from deep within himself, and his roar bounces off the walls of that narrow and winding lane and the four men turn on their tails and fly like chickens foxed in a hen coop for the next bend in Hetherington's Pike.

Stephen's first kick is instinct. His second is out of anger. His third comes from deep, and has in it everything within him that is unresolved. He feels the crack of the man's rib run through his toes.

'Get up,' he commands.

The man struggles to his feet and, wrapping his arms around himself as if to hold the air inside, limps away. Stephen follows and, when the man turns to face whatever else is coming, Stephen reaches into his pocket and, out of pity for the man, but most of all out of pity for himself, gives him 800 eurars, all that he has.

'These are hard times,' he says.

Stephen watches the man in his pain and pride straighten and turn and somehow get his broken bones away, clear of Stephen and the Pike, so that somewhere else he can scratch out another day and perhaps another after that.

For several moments, Stephen appears to follow his flight – but the world about him has vanished, driven out by memories of a life not so very different except that he had a uniform then, the red and blue of the Porphryian Academy, and crazy Barney beside him to take the knocks. He is dizzy with the recognition of it: himself then, himself now, those poor men, the awful circularity. He throws himself to the ground, curls up like the about-to-be-born and sobs.

His pain vapourises, rises up and is breathed in by Suzanna and Rokas who, out of love, make his pain their own, embody it as they cannot help but do with their own scarred mementos, until they too have to come to ground. They kneel beside Stephen and cover his body with their own, Suzanna on one side and Rokas, on his knees, from the other – so that anybody, regarding them, as I do, from some ethereal elevation beyond, might wonder what this mound was in the middle of Hetherington's Pike and think perhaps of a tent pegged out as shelter for the lost.

Friends

Rokas and Stephen sit at a corner table of a bar. Is this before or after the game of polotti, the winning and the losing, the kick and the crack of ribs and the lying down in the lane, all three of them tented out? It is before. Time is tricky[1].

The bar is downtown, off a winding alley between main streets and not much frequented except by men who spend most of their days inside it. The bar is where they first met soon after Stephen arrived in town. They still like to drink in this bar even though they both now work for Porphyrian and have the money to drink elsewhere.

An amiable silence is between them, the sort of silence there often is between friends who forgive sufficient of each other's sins to dispense with the need to cover them over. Stephen has his elbows on the table and is scratching his hair. He is scratching to get at the headache beneath, a layer of dull pain that lies just below the skin and bone at the top of his head. He looks up and sees Rokas watching. Steady eyes meet squint.

'Bad night?' asks Rokas.

Stephen tries to remember, shakes his head non-committally.

'Does she have a name?'

Stephen scratches again. A vision of Suzanna comes into his head. He discards it as best he can. 'Angie,' he says.

'And?'

'Crazy. Drinks like a Slav. I'm getting too old for this.' Stephen picks up his beer and downs most of it. Wipes his lips with his sleeve.

Rokas laughs. 'Angie. Details please.'

Stephen's head hurts too much to reply. After a while he says, 'Give me a moment, and I'll see if I can come up with something.' Then he says, 'Worth it, mind you.'

'The hangover? Angie?'

'Yes, Angie.'

'What did you talk about?'

'Hmm, good question, what did we talk about?... We talked about Porphyrian.'

'Ah, him.'

'She says it isn't crime which defines society: crime is the same everywhere. What defines society is punishment: who metes it out, how much, in what form. She says we are all defined by Porphyrian.'

'Did you tell her you worked for him, what you do for him?'

'Did I? Maybe. No, I don't think so. I will though. Definitely. Without a doubt.' Stephen manages a smile. 'Another beer?'

'I'll get them.' Rokas signals. The barman comes. Rokas raises two fingers, moves them gently sideways between Stephen and himself. 'So you'll be seeing her again?'

'Yes.' Stephen is silent, remembering. 'You know, Rokas, I think she could be the one.'

'That's great. I'm pleased for you.' When the beer comes, Rokas lifts his glass. 'To you, Stephen, much happiness.'

'One step at a time... mustn't get ahead of myself.'

'We should all do something together, me and Suzanna, you and Angie. I'd like to meet her.'

* * *

The best café in the town has a high, ornate ceiling with fractured angels puffing wind or kisses out of corners, and warrens of old bullet holes.

Stephen arrives early with Angie. She is a Nordic type with skin the colour of white wave-tips on the break. She knows he hopes she'll make a good impression on his friends. 'I will be a good girl,' she promises. 'Best behaviour only.' She sits with her back ruler-straight. Her legs are crossed, her hands folded on the hem of her skirt, her lips a pretend-prim.

Playfully, Stephen kicks the underside of her seat. 'Okay, okay, just be yourself then,' he says and they're both laughing as Suzanna and Rokas join them.

There are smiles all round. Introductions. Stephen says, 'The manager is Austrian, or his parents were, or his grandparents. Something like that.' He turns his head across the empty tables in search of Georg, who is upon him before he turns back. 'We've come for the cake,' he says.

'Ya,' says fat, laughing Georg, for whom cake is a totem of his beneficent ancestry, 'cake is vot keeps me young.' He pats his embonpoint with satisfaction and smiles, his eyes shining behind the rising hills of his cheeks. 'I bring you cake and my good tea, ya?'

'Ya,' they all say in unison, also smiling.

And once they've eaten and wiped their mouths with almost-pink paper napkins, Angie takes it upon herself to hold court. She picks out subjects from the air, holds them up like a magician with his props, and flashes them before her audience, now you see them, now you don't: books, gossip, guns, Porphyrian's Spring Clean[2], still much debated. Sometimes she behaves like a professor, sometimes like a lost child.

'How long have you all been friends?' asks Angie, drawing breath.

'Well, Rokas and I are almost brother and sister. Almost. Not quite, thankfully.' Suzanna laughs. 'Stephen and Rokas met when Stephen first came to town, that's a few years ago now. And I met Stephen not long ago, in a bar, though Stephen likes to say he's met me before. He says this because he's a bit mad, but I'm sure I don't need to tell you that.'

Both women look fondly at Stephen. He thinks, how similar they are, they could be sisters. He turns from one to the other and decides they aren't similar at all. A different look altogether. And he knows which of the two draws him in, no contest, which holds his heart. He doesn't know how, or from what hidden part within him he reaches this understanding, but he knows it's final. He's like a man who's bought himself an impulsive present and wonders if he can take it back. He knows that sooner or later he will.

Angie catches the understanding on his face. She takes it into herself and retreats, the show over.

The three friends exchange commonplaces among themselves until Suzanna, tiring of this, angles her chair away so that she can be alone with Angie. The two women talk quietly. Presently, Suzanna asks her about her family. 'I was brought up by my father,' Angie says. 'I had a child when I was eighteen by a man who I never saw after our first night.'

'Where is your child now? Is someone looking after him?'

'Oh, no, he's dead.'

'I'm so sorry,' says Suzanna. 'Forgive me, please, I had no idea.' She stretches out and places her hand on Angie's arm.

'It's okay. It's been a while now. I don't mind talking about it.'

'How did he die?'

'He was walking with his grandfather and they were caught in cross-fire. A shoot-out between arms dealers, or their gangs.'

'Porphyrian?'

Angie nods, says nothing, doesn't need to. Acceptance of the inescapable.

Suzanna turns away from it. 'Do you think you'll want more children?' she asks.

'Oh, I don't know. We'll see.'

The women now talk as if behind a high wall, just the two of them, and Suzanna tells Angie of her life on the farm and her own lost son and of her birthmarks and other intimate things.

The men wait, content at their exclusion.

Suzanna interrupts their silence. 'Do you ever think of having children?' she asks them.

Stephen says, without hesitation, 'Yes.'

'You'll make a terrible father,' Angie tells him.

'Will I? Why? How do you know?'

'Some men are lovers, some are fathers. You are a lover, my darling, always will be. Nurturing is not in your nature.'

'And you, Rokas, what do you think about having children?'

Rokas considers the question. He says, 'Men and women come together and make new bodies. But where do these babies get their souls, do you think? Whose souls do they inherit? Where has mine come from? Where will it go when I die?'

Suzanna turns away. Such evasion, she thinks, such heartless evasion and, if she was at home with him and not in this café, she knows she would cry.

Stephen sees her turning away and understands that his friend will lose her. No touch on the table, he thinks, poor Rokas. And then? Then a familiar image brightens behind his eyes: she and him, together: an image from somewhere deep or from the surface layers of rank opportunism, he doesn't know which.

Stephen keeps his images to himself.

Suzanna

When that rain which is on the cusp between rain and snow – neither one thing nor the other, but cold and biting – smacks into Suzanna's face, she thinks of home and that feeling in her stomach of not knowing which side of the cusp she wants to fall, whether the peace of defeat is better than the war which never ends.

She'd have been softer if her father had lived. He died of a fever as soon as he'd done his bit, and her mother never forgave him. He was the village doctor so, according to her, succumbing to the fever was an act of desertion. 'Of course he could have lived if he'd wanted to, but some men just don't want a family. Not your fault, my sweetie, don't ever think that.' That's how her mother talked, one thing twisted round another, and no end to it.

Her mother went on about her father so much that she kept him alive for both of them. It was how Suzanna came to love him. She held him up to the light of her mother's complaints and thought what a sweet gentle man he must have been for her to hate him so. Her poor dead Dad – if she'd have been him, she'd have deserted too.

Then there was 'the evidence of his sins' as her mother called them: two birthmarks on the inside of Suzanna's left and right thighs, each resembling a baby, one brown and healthy and the other splashed dark red with scar tissue around it as if it had been removed dead from a fire. When she sat and looked down at her legs, the two babies seemed to gaze at each other across the divide as if both, the dead and the living, yearned to be in each other's arms. Suzanna didn't know what the babies signified but she imagined they were important somehow, that perhaps, in their own strange way, they were a gift, perhaps even, as her mother seemed to think, something her father had left her. So the babies existed in her mind as well as on her thighs. When she was older, they sometimes came back to her as a sudden thought: oh, maybe this was the baby who died or maybe the dead baby could have lived, if only…

She wanted to know how her father gave her these babies. She asked her mother.

'How! By leaving me. By leaving us. The womb is sensitive. It remembers its violations and leaves a stripe on whatever it carries.'

She understood *stripe*. 'Are these babies my stripe?'

'What else could they be? Do you think they're the mark of the Devil?'

'What is the Devil?'

And, sighing, her mother told her: Heaven and Hell, good and bad, black and white. When she'd finished, she sniffed: so that Suzanna understood that the scars may be hers, but the pain of them was her mother's and that her mother would bear this pain bravely. Her mother had a good line in torture.

Even so, the more the torture, the more Suzanna grew to like her two baby birthmarks. They proved she had a father and that he'd loved her so much he'd left her these remembrances.

He'd also left his piano: for her, she supposed, since her mother didn't play. Suzanna played it every chance she got. She practised and she practised and each note she played, she played for him. Not only for him. Since she lived in a world of opposites – Heaven and Hell, good and bad – also to show her mother whose side she was on: though this Suzanna didn't understand, not fully, not then, except in some buried place too deep for her to get at.

She practised day in day out, a little girl sitting on her stool. She had two plaits which she learnt to do by herself, and she sat up with her back straight and her forearms at 90 degrees. The piano would lead her somewhere, she knew that, and somewhere was better than where she was.

The notes swarmed from her fingers like locusts in search of plenty. Her mother couldn't read their message – perhaps she didn't want to – so the locusts crawled all over her, nibbling as they went. It's only music, her mother said to calm herself, and Suzanna doesn't play badly.

She tried talking Suzanna out of it, suggesting she should spend more time with the children in the village. When that didn't work, she held her hands over her ears. 'Please,' she said. *Please* brought her respite for a time, but the appeal to pity can only be used sparingly. Suzanna's piano was moved to the boxroom which was hardly big enough to hold it and the door was kept shut.

One afternoon: Suzanna behind the closed door improvising, her mother in the kitchen marking the exercises of the village children.

'Stop,' her mother called. 'Can't you see I'm working.'

Suzanna recognised the tone. It went straight to her stomach and gassed it. But Suzanna knew she couldn't stop, couldn't surrender.

'Now!' her mother yelled. 'I don't want to have to come in there.'

Suzanna kept on playing. She may even have played louder. Footsteps stamped towards her, God knows what her mother was wearing, hobnail boots probably. She flung open the door and crashed it against the wall. She put both her hands on Suzanna's shoulders, close to her neck, and shook her back and forth so that her plaits waved in the air as if there was a hurricane and Suzanna thought, this is it, it won't be long now, when she strangles me it will all be over.

Suzanna stopped playing. She had to. She grabbed the frame of her stool as tight as she could. The stool had metal arm-supports and on the side of these were decorative loops which made perfect hand-holds for her little hands. She clung on. She clung on so tight she couldn't be dragged off and, in the end, her mother stopped. Stormed out, slammed the door. 'No tea for you, tonight, young lady. From now on, you look after yourself.'

After that, she did. Looked after herself, made her own meals, did her own clothes. She didn't mind. We won, Dad, didn't we?

Soon after her fifteenth birthday, her mother married a farmer. He had three sons around her age. She gave them names out of her school story books, commonplace names that made them no better than she was. She called them Tom, Dick and Harry, because they were all one to her, and she continued calling them that even when they weren't.

Her mother brought all their furniture and belongings to the farm, everything except the only thing she cared about. The piano was left in the house, abandoned on bare boards, so alone it was all she could do not to cry. In front of William, the new husband, her mother said to Suzanna, 'Look, let us sell it for you. You can keep the money, buy something for yourself, or save it for when you're older.'

Suzanna sat on her stool, held its frame as if her life depended on it, and with her back straight and her eyes to the front, told William that this piano had been her father's, was now hers and, if it was sold, she'd go with it. William went back to the farm and returned with a trailer hitched to his tractor. He and the boys got the piano on it and took it to the farmhouse. None of them said a word, but she thought this was the nicest thing that anyone had ever done for her.

She enjoyed living in the farmhouse. She had her piano and the boys had a polotti table. They often played together. The boys liked to put their arms round her, pretending to show her this bit of technique or that, but it wasn't long before she could beat them all, no trouble.

But the piano was her enduring love and she played as much as she could. It turned out that William liked music. She didn't suppose he'd heard much in his life, being out there on the farm. When she was playing, he'd sit on a chair across the room with his elbows on his knees and his head resting on his hands. She thought at first he was asleep, but he wasn't, he was listening.

When she stopped, he'd lift his head and say, 'That was nice, play some more if you want to.' So she did. She never minded playing.

Her mother didn't say anything at first, but then one night she came to Suzanna's bedroom, put her face close to hers and hissed, 'I've been cheated once by death. I won't be cheated a second time by you.'

'But... ' Suzanna began, but by then the door had closed on her.

Her mother must have spoken to William because after that he didn't listen to her playing any more.

When there was no school, Harry, the youngest of her step-brothers, spent his days with his friends in the village. Tom and Dick worked with their father in the fields. It was her job to bring them their lunches. Because they each liked different things, she used to wrap them in different cloths so they would know whose was which. William's was wrapped in a green cloth, Tom's in red and Dick's in blue.

They were tired after a morning's work so she didn't disturb them with chatter. She just sat down quietly somewhere and waited until they'd finished. Then she collected their cloths and containers and took them back to the house. She often found messages in the cloths. William's was always respectful, thanking her for his lunch, showing his appreciation. Tom's was straight to the point, suggesting all sorts of things which sometimes made her smile and sometimes made her blush. Dick's was written with words of reverence as if to an angel or a distant goddess. And Harry wasn't any better. When he came back from the village in his short trousers, he'd fling whatever he was carrying on the floor and kiss her full on the lips. Usually they fell around laughing.

She liked all this. She was happy for the first time in her life. She felt wanted, part of something other than just herself. She felt she had a family.

One day, her mother announced that she had to go to a

meeting in the town. All the teachers in the villages had been summoned. She would be away for five days. She asked William to come with her. 'I can't my love,' he said, 'I have carrots to pull.'

'But the boys can do that surely? It's our one chance to see the town together. We could take the tram up Stanley Street. I hear that's quite a sight.'

'I hear that too, but I can't leave the farm. Without me, who knows what the boys will get up to.'

'Will you be okay?' she asked them.

'We will,' they all replied.

On the first night after she went, Suzanna was woken by a body next to hers and a hand passing under her nightdress. The hand was rough and calloused. She turned and looked into the eyes which were watching her and saw nothing in them but a question: no insistence, no demands, just a wondering. She thought, how much pleasure can he get from my mother and one night what's the harm for all he's done for me, and she reached out and drew him close.

On the second night, what she saw in the slits of the adolescent eyes that were staring down at her was desire. She smiled and met his passion with passion of her own.

On the third night, the hand that passed under her nightdress was the soft hand of a supplicant. It travelled across her body as if trespassing on holy ground and she took him to her out of adoration.

On the fourth night, she felt a kiss on her lips as she slept. She opened her eyes. 'You too?' she said.

'Yes, I'm old enough don't you think,' and he guided her hand down his stomach where his young life rose to meet it.

'Yes,' she said, 'you're old enough,' and she made love to him out of the joy of being young together.

Why? When she thinks back, she believes she understands. Was she shutting her eyes and pretending that all this was being done to her, and what could she do, a poor helpless girl alone in that house? No, it wasn't like that. She was 16, she knew what she wanted. And it had been so natural, like a consummation of everything they'd given her, a mingling of love, nothing more. Or not much more. Revenge against her mother was in there somewhere, but it was buried then, a feeling that throbbed down below rather than a thought lying out on the surface. At 16 you are not aware of these things as you are when you're older – though, even now, she can't say she knows why she does all the things she does, and she's 30 and getting older by the day.

When her mother came back from the town, she felt the heat in the air and knew that something was up. She wanted to make Suzanna pay for it and she did, putting her to work and never taking her eyes off her. Suzanna didn't complain. Didn't even blame her. Didn't need to, because what was buried deep, but sending up its vibrations nonetheless, was her victory, her torture of the torturer.

Everything has its price – she found that out soon enough. After two months, she knew she was pregnant. She also knew she couldn't have the baby. A baby needs one father not four, and she was too young to be a mother.

She went to see an old lady who lived outside the village, half in and half out of the forest, whom the villagers said had tribal blood in her from way back.

The lady offered Suzanna a powder.

'What is it?' she asked.

'It is ground from the scales of a snake. It will help you.'

Her bony hands mixed the grey grindings into a glass. Suzanna shut her eyes. Some things are best done with eyes shut, because open they let in the whole tangle of consequences, all the *if thises* or *if thats*, which are too knotted to be unravelled. So, seeing nothing, she drank the powder and prayed that it was now all over with.

After four months, she was still carrying. She didn't mind. In fact, she was happy. She thanked God for rescuing her from what she had tried to do. She wanted the baby now, wanted him more than she'd ever wanted anything. Her baby.

She told William she was going to live in the town. He held her and gave her money. He cried. When she left, the boys hugged her one by one and said beautiful things to her, but what the words were precisely she couldn't remember. What her mother said to her, she couldn't forget. Her mother leant forward as if to kiss her and, instead, whispered in her ear, 'Don't come back.'

Suzanna went to stay with a woman who had a flat on Prior Street. She liked her from the start and soon came to love her. The woman was called Helen.

Suzanna told her everything that had happened because she wanted it all out in the open. No secrets. 'Was it incest?' she asked.

'No, my little swan,' Helen said, stroking her hair. 'It's unusual, four fathers and all of them related, but no blood lines have been compromised. No reason why your baby will not be strong.'

The baby was a boy. He was fine and healthy and Suzanna kissed him and fed him and fussed over him like no baby had been fussed over before. After a week he caught a fever and died. She nearly died too, of grief and blame, both. She knew it was her fault, that somehow it just was. Sometimes she thought it was her mother's final revenge and no more than she deserved. Sometimes she thought this was the message of the baby scars on her thighs and that his death had been her destiny all along. Once, when her bitterness overwhelmed her, she even blamed her dead father and the fever he'd died of. 'Just like him,' she cried out to the corpse she'd long since buried.

A voice came back to her from beyond the grave. 'No, I died because you went to an old woman and drank a powder. I can take a hint.'

Among the Cathars, Languedoc, Mid-13th Century

A girl is sitting. Two men are watching her, a third is taking notes. One addresses her, says, 'Suzanne?' She is darkly complexioned, long-necked, has a simple elegance. Her back is against a stone wall but she doesn't let it take her weight. At the question, 'Suzanne?' a light flares in her black eyes. It flickers like fear. She does not know what is to come. She wonders if this scene – herself, the inquisitors, the man taking notes – will be all she'll ever have. She feels it isn't possible, she is too young.

The First Inquisitor speaks again. 'Suzanne, tell us how you became infected.'

To which she responds with denial. 'Infected? Nothing has infected me.'

The Inquisitor sighs gently, the indulgent father. 'Very well.' He pauses, immersed in thoughts of his own. Finally, almost inaudibly, he speaks again. 'The truth: how it wriggles, how it tries to escape, as if it wants us to think it is only comfortable in dark and hidden places.' He pauses, looking down at the greying hairs on his hands. Then, his voice rising, he says, 'We must search it out. We must listen for it, my child. We must have patience. There is time enough.' Again he pauses, letting the silence around him weigh heavy on the girl who wonders as to her fate. 'I would like to hear your story,' he tells her at last, 'from the beginning, or in the way you wish to tell it, and, as for circum-locutions, trips to this or that, however far removed, well, I am going nowhere. I am a patient man. My patience is legendary. Everyone round here knows that.' He waves his arm airily in the direction of the gallery. 'I once listened to a man talk for three months and during that time I said no more than yes and no and how interesting, but…?'

'What happened to the man?' asks Suzanne.

'The man? Ah, his tongue was cut out if I remember correctly and then he was burned at the stake.'

'You tell me this and yet you expect me to talk?'

'Oh, you will forget. They all forget. Such is the pleasure you will feel as you give up your secrets, it will drive out all thoughts of life and death.'

The Inquisitor settles comfortably in his chair. Beside him, but a little further away, a second inquisitor is scratching his thinning hair and smiling a thin smile. As suggested by their relative positions, the two men are not equals: one is the master and one the apprentice. It is the apprentice's first appearance in court and he is older than he should be. He intends to make a favourable impression. He scratches again and retracts his long legs under his chair as if wishing to kneel.

By the wall of the courtroom, seated at a desk, a scribe waits with quill in hand, poised in case a word should fall, like a heron beside still water waiting for fish. He has sat thus for so many years that his back is hunched. It is unlikely that he could straighten it even if he wished to do so.

Suzanne watches the men who watch her. She ponders the arguments for and against. There might, she thinks, be safety in silence. If she keeps her mouth shut, what can be proved against her? But, then again, perhaps her silence will be seen as guilt. She does not know. She does not know the assumptions on which this court is based. She does not know the law which underpins it, if law there is. And if she is to be taken, come what may, then perhaps she should tell her story. What is there to lose? And isn't her story no more nor less than herself? Her thoughts, her actions: are they not her? Should she go out mute, as if she has never existed, without making so much as a scratch on the records?

A small cough clears her throat. The scribe's head inclines an imperceptible inch closer to his parchment. The court is all ears.

'My father owned a house. We were a large family. People came to visit.'

'Was it a large house?'

'Large enough, I suppose, for us anyway. Not as large as yours, sir, I imagine, you being a man of the Church.'

The Inquisitor seems amused. He lets his chin rest comfortably on the first fat fold of his neck as if accepting the dig. He smiles an encouraging smile and says, 'A house, large family, visitors – sounds like a good place to grow up.'

'I was happy then. We all lived together, my father, my mother, my uncle, my brother and my two sisters. Oh, and my old grandmother too.'

'Did she sit in a corner all day long and have bony arms?'

Suzanne laughs. 'Bony arms as brittle as twigs, but she didn't sit in a corner. Outside, in the sun, with two old friends.'

'And not a tooth between them, I bet.'

'One each. One on the left side, one in the middle and one on the right. We called them the three toothies, but only among ourselves.'

The Inquisitor rocks back and gurgles pleasantly among the layers of his chins. 'Sounds like my grandmother, God rest her soul.' He crosses himself. 'I suppose as we approach the end, we all come to look the same. Dust to dust.'

'Yes, but she was alive on the inside, right to her last moment.'

'I hope she didn't die alone. That would have been sad for her.'

'No, she wasn't alone.'

'Who was with her? Family? Friends? Visitors?'

Suzanne is suddenly wary. She knows she is being led, but she doesn't know where. In her eyes, caution. 'We were all there, her family that is, and people from the village.'

'And your uncle, the priest, would have administered the sacraments, I'm sure.'

'My uncle was away.'

'Ah, so no priest, no last rites. Did nobody intercede on her behalf?'

She is silent.

'Tell me,' continues the Inquisitor, 'after a person dies, what do you think happens then?'

'I think what the Church thinks.'

'Which is?'

'That the soul of a good man goes to heaven.'

'And what of the soul of a bad man?'

Suzanne says nothing.

'I've heard it said,' admits the Inquisitor confidentially, 'that the soul of a bad man jumps into the first body he can find, so that in his next life he can make a better job of escaping the toils of the Evil One. What do you think of that?'

Silence.

'Well, answer this then, Suzanne. Who decides the future of a man's soul? Is it God or man himself?'

'I don't know, sir,' says Suzanne. 'I am only a village girl. What is the teaching of the Church?'

A certain admiration creeps into the face of the Inquisitor. He understands now that this case will take time. He lets his body relax, lets it accept the implications of the days and weeks to come.

'When last I heard,' he says, 'it was God who did the deciding, but who knows what the next Pope will decree.' He laughs and notices with satisfaction how the girl's eyes soften. 'But enough of all these church details,' he says. 'Tell me about your family, how you live.'

'We keep animals, sir, mainly sheep but also cows and pigs. And outside the house, we have a yard full of chickens.'

'Is it your job to collect the eggs?'

'Mine and my sisters.'

'And your grandmother, when she was alive, told you how to do it, I'm sure.'

'She cackled worse than the hens.'

'Yes, that's what grandmothers do, especially those with no teeth.'

'One tooth, sir, in the middle.'

'Yes indeed, one tooth. And how many teeth does your uncle have?'

'He has them all, at least I think so.'

'Yes, I've heard that. He is a handsome man, I'm told. Quite a man for the ladies.'

'He is a priest, sir, as you know.'

'Ah yes, so he is – and quite a one for the ladies.'

A murmur arises from the half-empty gallery.

'The women of the village seem to like my uncle, if that is what you mean.'

'And you, do you like your uncle?'

The Inquisitor lets the innuendo hang. He has no idea of its validity and doesn't care – widening the angle of attack, sowing confusion; such diversions (if diversion it proves to be) never hurt. He notes with satisfaction that Suzanne doesn't answer, her neck bowed in silence. Hmm, I wonder, he thinks.

He shuffles his papers. He is in no hurry, none at all – for if there is one thing he has learnt in all his years, it is that no man, whatever he may care to imagine, is free from the desire to destroy himself. Not even he, the Inquisitor – ah, how he has battled to keep it under. Certainly not her. To draw the dagger, to cut her own throat, all she needs, all anyone needs, is a little time among the echoes of self-reflection – and an inquisitor who knows his trade.

A smell of leather and hard riding overwhelms the first blossoms of spring. Steam rises from the hot urine of the horses, and from their flanks. The great men have just arrived, perhaps five minutes ago, and are now in the courtroom, talking with drink in hand and one foot on the rear of a servant who struggles with

their boots. On the cobbles of the courtyard their horses whinny and stretch or bend their necks over a water trough. They also are attended: by grooms with oat bags and brushes.

The great men – the duke, the bishop – and the lesser – the courtiers, the lower orders of cleric and the men of trade – have come to see the work of God be done. Besides, there has been a whisper, a salacious whisper it has to be said, and they wish to ensure fair play all round.

All of them, great and small, sit in their seats and wait. Nothing happens. They begin to fidget. Time marks its own passing by silence. The tick tick of the turning world is heard only in their minds. Finally, the greatest of the great men makes a remark to the man sitting behind him. This man nods energetically and leaves. When he returns, it is with a message. The First Inquisitor is ill. He dined last night on quails' eggs and believes these might have been the cause. Eyes turn downwards and towards the Second Inquisitor.

The Second Inquisitor has developed a tic around his mouth. Presumably he's always had it, but sometimes he is able to keep it under control. Not today. Today, the irreconcilable dragons within, the red and the blue, are at war and the battle is there for all to see: the cheek and corner of the top lip, left side, flashing at the moon, flashing at the great men who look down from the stalls expecting a show.

The Second Inquisitor feels this expectation like a weight. Where is the First Inquisitor? What is keeping him? Why is everyone staring? Suddenly it dawns on him. This is his moment, his chance. He draws breath. His twitching stops, gone completely, or at least for now. He rises to his feet and all those in the court gasp. See how tall he is! Has there ever been a man this tall?

He is a hard man to label, this lofty though lowly Inquisitor. Does he not relish the terrible power of the Church, its absolute truth, its taste for blood? Certainly – why else does a man

become an inquisitor? And yet he has a tic, an irritating seed of doubt that has lodged in his upper lip. Who knows – does he – how far its roots have spread? Appropriate then that this gargantuan enigma is called 'R', because R is a letter which has still to grow into a name.

R begins to raise a finger. Those watching imagine that the finger will come to rest on his head and scratch. They are wrong, surprised. It continues rising, up, up, and points as if at the moon. His reach is immense and the girl, Suzanne, sitting on her chair, seems suddenly to be in range. Does he intend to strike her? She thinks he might – see how she draws back, raising her forearm to her face to defend herself. See how the great men in the gallery above sit forward in concentration.

The show has begun.

'You have a brother,' says R. His finger still points upwards and seems now at odds with the mundane nature of the words he has just uttered. What is the finger doing? What is it for? At what is it pointing? It seems that drama has turned suddenly to farce and, as if to demonstrate the point, a titter comes from the gallery above. R swings round: a reflex, this swinging round, this staring back – a gesture of defiance that has its origins in who knows what – but perhaps, in this case, unfortunate. He finds himself looking into the eyes of the bishop. Was it the bishop who tittered? He doesn't know. Somehow he manages a smile. Not a convincing one: in fact, such are its inherent contradictions that the smile is grotesque, but it is a smile just about sufficient to satisfy the conventions. The bishop is amused, highly amused, judging by the look on his face. He knows now he will see a show although perhaps not the show he came to see. He doesn't mind.

R's arm drops to his side. 'You have a brother,' he says, and the words come out gently.

'Yes,' says Suzanne, 'I do.'

Silence.

R, not having expected that he would be leading the interro-

gation, has not prepared his line of attack. He wonders what questions the First Inquisitor would ask. 'Tell me about him,' he demands finally. With this he sits down, gets up, moves to the First Inquisitor's chair and sits down on that with his feet stuck out hugely in front of him. His eyes dart around; he is not sure if this chair is for him.

There is laughter in the court. The duke bellows, the bishop smirks, and the butcher, the baker and candle-maker, taking their lead from their betters, are engulfed in hilarity. Suzanne does not laugh. She looks at the Inquisitor and understands that she is not the only one who is on trial. She feels a moment of sympathy but knows better than to show it. Sympathy from her to him! He would kill her with his bare hands.

She looks down. She registers the approach of large feet and the command which falls upon her: 'Tell us about your brother!'

'Yes, sir,' she says meekly. Meekness, even if it is put on, is all she has; it's the best she can do.

'My brother is a year older than me, and my sisters are all younger. As a child, I looked up to him. When he was 12, he left our house and went into the hills where our sheep were.'

'But he came home, didn't he? You saw him often. He didn't... '

There is a commotion at the back of the court. The First Inquisitor enters. A servant supports him. He walks into the courtroom and bows to the bishop and the duke. 'Forgive me, sires,' he says. 'It is sometimes a mistake to rely on the sureties of the well-intentioned, even in a matter as small as an egg.'

'Word reached us,' says the duke. 'Are you now fully recovered? You look a little pale.'

'Thank you, my lord. I had intended to spend the day in

reflection, but no sooner was I on my knees than I felt the Lord calling to me, reminding me that His work remained to be done.'

'Ah, yes indeed, the Lord's work is never-ending. It is good to have you back, but you need not have worried. In your absence, your assistant has been demonstrating a style all of his own.' The duke smiles.

'How good of you to say so,' replies the First Inquisitor, bowing slightly. With a finger, he summons the Second Inquisitor who comes towards him, bent at the waist, with his hand scratching in the remains of his thinning hair.

Just as I was getting into my stride, the Second Inquisitor thinks to himself, is he trying to trap me? Why? What is his game? and the Second Inquisitor reminds himself to take care. The left side of his top lip rises and hangs for an imperceptible moment. Then it falls back, hesitates, rises and falls once, twice, three times in quick succession.

'Tell me what I've missed,' says his superior, settling fatly into his chair. 'Ah, I see,' he says after a while, 'you think the brother is the weak link. Perhaps. But it doesn't matter. The chain can be broken in so many places.' Dismissing the Second Inquisitor with a wave, he turns to Suzanne. He approaches her. 'Your brother went into the hills... '

'My brother, yes, in the hills... ' and Suzanne, in that moment, sees parched rocks and, there, a man behind a boulder, pursued, men on fast horses. She starts. She gasps. 'Run, Stefan,' she shouts, 'run,' and the word escapes, jumps from that landscape and enters the courtroom.

'Run? Did you say run?'

'Did I?' She holds a hand to her mouth.

'Is your brother... is Stefan in danger? From whom? Why should he run? Tell me. Perhaps I can help.'

Suzanne looks at the fat Inquisitor and wonders what he knows. 'Stefan... no. I just had a picture in my mind. A daydream, nothing more.'

'But it frightened you, didn't it, my child? Dreams when they come, whether by day or night, can be frightening. Tell me what you saw. You will feel better.'

'No, sir, thank you, sir, it was nothing really.'

'Oh, I doubt that. Your brother in the hills. Run! you said. You shouted it out, so he was hiding, so he was about to be caught, perhaps worse, perhaps killed, and hardly older than you, Suzanne, a young man with his whole life ahead of him. Why would anyone want to kill him?'

'I don't know, sir. He has done nothing wrong.'

'But they do want to kill him?'

Suzanne says nothing.

'Where is he now? In the hills?'

Again Suzanne says nothing.

'On the run?'

Suzanne looks up at the First Inquisitor and sees sympathy in his face. Kindness. The face of a father. She yearns to trust him, to tell him everything he wants to know. Ah, if only she could… If only her own father were here today. He would know what to do.

The Inquisitor watches the girl. He understands how he is perceived. It is one of his skills. 'Where is your father?' he says. 'Why is he not in court? At a time like this, a father should be with his daughter.'

'My father is dead, sir. He died last year. He caught a fever.'

'Oh, I am sorry to hear that.' He indicates to a porter to bring a glass of water to the girl. He waits while she drinks. 'So your father is dead, and your brother is in the hills and you are all alone in this court. Is there no-one else who could be with you? Your uncle, where is he?'

'My uncle is a priest, sir. He does not feel he should be here.'

'Does not feel! What sort of man is this? Does not feel! Does not wish to be associated with someone who is infected perhaps. Or is he afraid, this uncle of yours? Are there sins of his own for which he should be fearful?' The Inquisitor stares down at Suzanne.

'I can't say, sir. My uncle is a priest. He knows the word of God.'

'I hope so, my child, I truly hope so... but in the meantime he leaves you in this courtroom all alone and without support.'

'I am at your mercy, my lord.'

'Well then, I shall be merciful where your uncle is not. I shall appoint a defender for you. Someone who knows the ways of this court. Someone who will put your case for you. Would you like that?'

'Yes, sir, thank you, sir.'

'Very well, I shall appoint... ' – he looks around the room and up into the gallery where the bishop and duke are transfixed by the spectacle, amused by the breach of protocol, mired in specu-lation about the motives of the Inquisitor, a man of vast experience – 'I shall appoint... you' and his arm stretches out and its finger points and the Second Inquisitor gasps.

'Me!' exclaims R. 'Me? How can it be me? I am trained to prosecute.'

'Then regard this as part of that training. The good prosecutor must also know how to defend. I appoint you. Defend her.'

R sags as he sits. He doesn't know what this means. He has never heard of such an appointment before. Doesn't it go against all precedent, all common sense? What trap is the Inquisitor setting for him? If he defends her well, will the Church thank him or condemn him? If he defends her badly, will he be castigated for his incompetence? R starts to sweat. He takes out a handker-chief and mops his forehead.

'So, go, take your chair, sit by the suspect. Your loyalty is now to her. Perform to the best of your abilities.'

'Yes, sir,' says R and moves across the courtroom. A buzz follows him and settles around his shoulders. His lip begins to jerk once more and, in his stomach, he feels a knife-point twisting.

✝

'You told the court that your father died last year. We are sorry to hear that.' The Inquisitor pauses and lets his eyes close as if in consideration of this man he did not know. When he continues, he says, 'But I believe you still have a mother.'

'Yes, sir,' replies Suzanne.

'That is a mercy, at least. But I don't see her here in this court. Does she not love her daughter?'

'She does, sir, I believe.'

'But not enough to be here today?'

'She is away. She may not know what has happened to me.'

'Away? Where? Since when?'

'She has been away for some weeks. I believe she is trying to find my brother.'

'Your brother who has run away?'

'My brother who has gone away.'

'Yes, gone away, thank you. And your mother has gone away also. Do you think she will return?'

'She will. She loves her family and she loves her village. She would never leave.'

'That is good to hear. A loving mother is the most precious thing a child can have. Don't you agree?'

'I do, sir.'

'Even more precious than faith in the wisdom of your Church?'

Suzanne hesitates. A chair scrapes on the floor. R imagines – though it is an imagining not without considerable misgivings – that it is now his duty to intervene. He has been instructed to defend Suzanne against the wiles of the Inquisitor, and so defend her he must. He unfolds, and adopts a position (palm of hand cupped beneath his chin, legs splayed wide apart) which he considers appropriate for what he is about to say. He coughs modestly. 'Love for the Church is an all-consuming love. As is love for a mother. I am sure that Suzanne, in her own way, loves each equally.' He sits down.

The First Inquisitor is amused by this display. He fights back an urge to interrogate R on the subject of mothers and the love he had for his own. He wonders what he might find. Instead, in self-denial, he says, 'Ah, so you are sure. Well, certainty is a great asset. But tell me, Suzanne, is he right to be sure?'

'Yes, sir,' replies Suzanne, not looking up.

'Good. Let us hope that the time never comes when you have to choose between them. But for now, tell the court about your mother. How old is she?'

'I believe she is 30 years old.'

'Exactly 30. Or perhaps a year less? Or a year more?'

'Perhaps a year more. Perhaps 31.'

'Well, that's good. Shall we agree that she is 31? Do you think that is right, as far as you know?'

'Yes, sir. That's what is said about her.'

'And you? How old are you?'

'According to my mother, I am 19.'

The Inquisitor smiles. 'Well, your mother should know if anybody does. So, if she is 31 and you are 19, she must have been 12 when you were born.'

'Yes, I suppose so, if you say so, sir.'

'Well, I believe that is what the arithmetic tells us. What does your champion say? Can he add and subtract?'

R jumps up. There is an expectant titter in the gallery. He says, 'She was 12. Not an uncommon age to have children in the villages, so I believe.'

'Indeed.' The First Inquisitor returns to Suzanne. 'And your brother. Is he older than you?'

'He is a year older than me, sir.'

'Exactly a year. Or closer to two?'

'One year I think, sir, as far as I know.'

'So your mother was 11 when your brother was born. Is that also common in the villages?' He turns to R.

'Not uncommon, I believe.'

'So, in the villages, they fornicate as soon as they are able?'

R notices an itch at the back of his neck and scratches it. 'I believe they do, sir.'

'And do they get married as soon as they are able, or is fornication sufficient?'

'Most of the women marry young, so I am informed.'

The First Inquisitor waves R back to his chair. 'And what about you, Suzanne? You are 19. Do you have any children?'

'No, sir.'

'Have you ever had any children?'

'No, sir.'

'You have never had any children? Are you sure?'

'Yes, sir.'

'It's just that I thought when we were questioning some of the other girls in your village, there was talk… ' – he exchanges glances with the keeper of the court record – 'but never mind. Who can know better than you about children you may, or in this case, may not have had. So no children?'

'No, sir.'

'Are you married?'

'No, sir.'

'No! I am surprised. A pretty girl like you.'

Suzanne says nothing. The First Inquisitor looks at her kindly. 'Please forgive me if I ask you why you are not married. I find it hard to imagine what could possibly be the reason.'

'I suppose nobody wanted to marry me.'

'Why ever not?'

'I don't know, sir.'

'Are most of your friends married?

'They are, sir.'

'To local boys or boys from outside?'

'Local mainly, or from the village nearby.'

'None left over for you?

'It seems not, sir.'

'It surprises me that your father did not arrange a marriage, as I believe is customary in your region? Did he at least try?'

'I don't know, sir. I don't think so.'

'But I must ask again. Why not? What was stopping him? You were 18 when he died. High time, was it not?'

'Nothing was stopping him, sir. He just didn't do it.'

'No, apparently not. But it's strange, don't you think?'

'I don't know, sir.'

'Were you present when your father died?'

'Yes, I was, sir. We all were, all his family.'

'Tell me please, if you wouldn't mind, what you can remember of his death.'

'Well, he had the fever, sir. I didn't see him much then. We were kept out of his room. We slept in the kitchen or in another room with the cows.'

'And when he died?'

'When he died, he was laid out on his bed and I helped my mother sprinkle water on his face.'

'You didn't wash him?'

'No, sir, that wasn't our custom.'

'I see. What else did you do?'

'Well, we cut his hair and his fingernails and kept them in a box in the kitchen. And my brother sat on the roof of the house holding a cross.'

'Did he? Do you know why?'

'For protection, sir.'

'Protection against what exactly?'

'Against the Devil, sir. We didn't want the Devil carrying off his soul.'

'Was it likely that he would?'

'I don't know, but just in case… '

'And why the roof?'

'Why? Well, because the Devil might fly over in the night.'

'Do you think the Devil did take your father's soul?'

'I can't say, sir.'

'Where do you think his soul went, if it didn't go to the Devil?'

'I don't know, sir.'

R fidgets uneasily in his chair.

'Was your uncle, the priest, present when he died?'

'No, sir, I don't think so.'

'But didn't you say that all your family were there?'

'Yes, sir, but not my uncle.'

'He is never there when needed, so it appears. Was anyone there to give your father the last rites?'

Suzanne pauses and thinks of the man who placed the Gospels on her father's head and consoled him with the words of a religion that did not require the intercession of priests or men such as the First Inquisitor.

'No one was there, sir.'

'He died unshriven then and came to the gates of St Peter bearing all his sins before him. Is that so?'

'If you say so, sir.'

'Ah, I do, I do. The poor man. Was he at least good in this life?'

'Yes, sir. He was a good father. He didn't beat me or do anything else. We always had enough to eat.'

'What did you do after he died?'

'We just went on with our lives, sir.'

'Yes, of course. What else could you do? Tell me, after your father died, where did you all sleep?'

'In the bedroom, sir, as before. It is better than sleeping with the cows.'

'Where did your mother sleep?'

'She slept where she always slept, sir.'

'With you?'

'Yes, sir.'

'In the same bed?'

'No, sir. I slept with my sisters in one bed, and she slept in another.'

'And your brother?'

'He slept in another bed.'

'In the same room?'

'Yes, sir.'

'And your uncle, where did he sleep?'

'There is a room above the kitchen. He sleeps there.'

'Why didn't your brother sleep up there with him?'

'My uncle wanted his own room. He is a priest.'

'Yes, I see.'

'What do you wear when you sleep?'

Suzanne hesitates. She doesn't know what answer is right and what wrong. She turns to R. 'What does he want me to say?' she asks.

R leans over to her and says quietly, 'You can tell him the truth. If you have done nothing wrong, the truth will protect you.' As R says this, his mouth twitches.

'We wear our shifts.'

'I've been to your village, you know,' says the Inquisitor. 'It's a nice place to live, I imagine, but how hot it is in summer. There was no wind at all when I was there. You might wear your shifts in winter, but not in summer, surely? You must take them off then.'

'Sometimes, maybe.'

'And did your brother sleep naked, also?'

'I suppose so.'

'How do you know? Did you see him?'

'I suppose I must have.' Suzanne can be seen to sweat. 'I don't know, sir. I can't remember.'

R, suddenly, is standing. 'But most families in the village sleep in the same room. And in the summer, they will sleep without clothes.' He pauses and then, as if in conclusion, blurts out, 'There can be no sin where there is no desire.'

'Thank you,' says the First Inquisitor looking up from his chair. 'You are quite right. No sin without desire. And nakedness does not imply desire. Not at all. Besides their mother was in the room with them, was she not? What better chaperone could there be? Do you wish to say anything else?'

R shakes his head and sits down. The bishop and lord above, by now attuned to the dramatis personae of this tragic comedy, look at each other in scarcely restrained amusement as, with convulsive jerks, R settles his feet.

✞

The landscape is sparse, pocked by outcrops of rocks, good for nothing more than light grazing. Periodically the rocks gather themselves and become hills. In the hills are deep caves, some of which were inhabited long ago: but no longer, except by men with something to hide.

Sheep watch and bleat in groups of twos and threes, and run off, shillying, when the riders approach. The riders are in no hurry. In this country they do not expect to find what they are looking for. They have been looking for weeks, but they are being paid. They think they would rather be riding the land than trying to make a living from it. Or hiding in it. They are of the same stock as the fugitives, but work is work.

The sun is now at its height. They dismount and walk their horses to an overhang of rock under which a small pool has formed. They presume the water has come from the cave. They drop their reins and take out some food – mutton, cheese and dry bread – from the bags strung across their saddles. They settle themselves down and eat. They drink from water canteens which they carry with them. One of them goes to the mule that has been tethered to the tail of the trailing horse and brandishes a leather wineskin. He takes a swig, returns to the group and passes it around. The wine that is produced in the valley is strong and it is not long before all are asleep.

For the woman and her son now trapped in the cave, the sleep that has settled on the men might be an opportunity. They could take advantage of the meal, the wine, the afternoon repose to tiptoe silently out. They could climb higher up into the hills where they would once again be free. They could if they wish take their hunters' horses. But while the opportunity is attractive, it is not without risk. Can they be sure that each of the men – there are eight in all – is asleep? Or if asleep, how soundly? Suppose a shard of rock were to come loose under their feet, might one of them wake? And what about the horses? Might they not neigh and alert the men, especially if they were being led away by strangers?

The son does the thinking; it is his terrain. Most years since the age of 12, he has, with others, driven sheep on these hills and passes. The son is now 20 and heavily bearded. His eyes shine brightly even within the gloom of the cave. He looks at his mother and makes her understand what he intends. Slowly, carefully, he walks deeper into the cave, away from the light and out of sight. His mother is anxious, unsure, but she is also a tough village woman. She takes the direction he has taken. That there will be some sound arising from their movement is inevitable but they hope it will mingle with the other sounds of the cave, the drip of water, the scurry of small animals.

The depth of the cave can only be determined by exploration, and exploration, or movement of any kind, carries risks. These they accept even though they don't know whether the cave ends a few feet from where they are standing and so makes escape impossible, or whether it winds for miles underground and comes out who knows where. It is what the son likes about the caves: that their ending is unknown, that there is no certainty there even is an ending – a shaft of light somewhere in the distance – waiting to be revealed. There is only the journey made with outstretched arms into a deeper darkness, to which surrender, as if into the hands of Fate, is the only option. It may be assumed then that each time the son lands his foot on rock he smiles.

His mother does not smile. Though she too holds herself in the hands of Fate, she thinks of the three daughters she has left behind and wonders how they are faring. She blames herself for leaving them. What has she achieved except her own safety? Has she made her children safer by her departure or put them at greater risk? And what about Suzanne, her eldest? How will she endure in the hands of the court? Riven as she is by the agony of hopeless caring, she conjures up the face of the First Inquisitor, whom she does not know, and in that moment when she sees his fatherly and beguiling eyes, her toe catches a loose stone.

The stone rolls across the floor, stone on stone, and the sound of it rolling and striking the rock wall is different in its nature to the other sounds coming from the cave. Mother and son stiffen in anticipation. A horse whinnies. The whinny enters the cave, bouncing off its uneven surfaces.

One of the men outside wakes up or perhaps was awake before. At any rate, he sits up. He looks about him, down into the valley and back into the cave. He sees nothing. He wonders if the sound he thinks he heard signifies anything at all. He reasons that whatever is in the cave, if indeed there is anything, must come out. Or if it doesn't come out, it will either die within or emerge somewhere, anywhere, in the surrounding country. He weighs up the risks of investigation against the fact that he is being paid for pursuit, as well as for capture. If capture is postponed, he will not be the loser. He settles back down. He can discuss all this with his fellows when the sun is lower in the sky.

Mother and son are now committed to finding another way out of the cave. They cannot return. If the riders know they are inside, they will wait for them. Or follow them. Neither mother nor son will give themselves up. Repentance comes at too high a price: a lifetime of whipping, of public humiliation and of the duty of denouncing friends and family. In the cave, with their life's blood still pumping and the prospect of escape before them, they do not contemplate repentance. Not yet.

Shapes rise up out of the deep darkness: boulders as unforgiving as church doors, aragonite prisms, amalgams of schist layered like thoughts and petrified forever. They persuade the mind to generate shapes of its own. The son thinks of his own son, still bathed in his mother's blood when he took him and snuffed the life out of him and hid him from the eyes of the world. He puts the fingers of his right hand to his mouth. For her, for my only love, what else could I do? He sees her naked, on her knees, hands clasping her swollen belly. She begs. Whatever I may say, promise me. And he had, had sworn to her that he would.

He sees also the smoke rising from the wood fire in which the tiny corpse was placed and understands that the same fate awaits him. He shudders. He contemplates a pyre of green, undried wood, its pricking heat, the first crackle of skin, the hours of slow incineration. He wonders whether those things the Perfect Men have told him of death and lives to come will be sufficient to sustain him through that agony. He wonders whether he has lived enough times to be brave.

He thinks again of the baby's mother and of their love which they had from the beginning. He remembers back to those lost, happy days when they played together, naked and inseparable, without care or shame. He remembers when she showed him the black hairs appearing on the cusp of her legs and when he came in his own hands and held them out to her.

They hear sounds: a stream seems to be running hard below them. In the distance is a louder roar, perhaps a waterfall. They do not hear the sounds of men behind them. They do not believe that riders have followed them into the cave.

Being underground, it is impossible for them to know the direction they are taking. The son has his hand on the cave wall but its twists are too numerous to enable him to map their course in relation to the land above. He tries to recall places in the surrounding country where he has seen water escaping.

They continue for some time. The sound of water is closer now and the rock on which they are walking is narrow. They are on a ledge. The son stops with his back to the cave wall. He allows his toes to feel for the point at which the ledge ends. There is not much to stand on, but he hopes it will be enough. The waterfall is close. He imagines the stream gathering itself as it approaches, but how far it is below them he doesn't know. He holds his mother's hand with his own and edges sideways. All seems to be well. They can't move quickly but at least they are moving.

His mother beside him is breathing hard. The journey is difficult but she is a village woman. She is strong. She knows how to endure. It is not her body which will betray her – but her mind is still busy with the faces of her children and yearns for a resting place for them all, a place they may never reach. She imagines the waterfall that she hears close by. She sees herself as a drop of water that has become separated from the stream and is now, in its descent, alone. Alone she falls, waiting for that moment of bliss when she will be reunited with all the other drops that ever were on the far side of the fall. When she lands, she knows it will be with a splash and she will be smiling.

So imagining, she smiles, but as she smiles, she trips – and her fall follows the path she has foreseen, only a moment behind, and it is exactly as she anticipated except that when she lands it is not with a splash. She lands on a rock and dies instantly, her body flung forward into the stream where it gathers speed until it reaches the crest of the overhang and drops like a stone into wild water below, from where it speeds away to become the dust she once was – while her spirit rises up to who knows where in search of whatever destiny is to come.

Her son has felt her hand come loose from his and heard her descent. He calls out in whispers against the noise of falling water and hears nothing in reply. He continues to shuffle along the ledge until it becomes too narrow, until there is no way out but down. He braces himself. He prepares. He puts his spirit in the hands of those who have a worthier claim to life than he does: the son whom he had to kill, his mother, his sister, the dead or soon to be so. He falters, and he jumps.

He is lucky. His guardians have looked after him. He lands in the stream. The current sweeps him down and over into the fury of the fall. He is tossed this way and that, the pressure of the water plugs his ears, his foot hits something and his leg crumples above it, his heartbeat hammers in his head – but he is alive, he can breathe and he knows that soon the current will slow. And in the joy of a life returned to him, he finds himself humming a tune. He lies on his back and laughs aloud, his mother, his leg, all cares seemingly forgotten; such is the power of the stream of life that it drives everything else out of his body and replaces it only with laughter.

The stream winds its way gently down and he with it. He senses a lessening in the gloom. He opens his eyes and a full white moon is shining on him. He lies in the shallows looking up in wonder and delight and only after several minutes does he become aware of eight men on horseback watching him. One of them calls out, 'Hello, Stefan, we've been waiting for you.'

The son says nothing. Then he asks, 'Do you have my mother?'

The men look at each other. With a sign, two dismount and walk back up the stream. One of them says, 'Don't be alarmed. If we find her, we'll take care of her.'

Northern Europe, Mid-21st Century

Rokas

Rokas was brought up by bears. So he believes. It's a belief he clings to in spite of the incredulity it engenders in others. Some beliefs are like that.

Rokas makes no secret of his supposed origins. He likes to relate them with a flourish, somewhat in the manner of an old traveller returning from foreign lands with tales of wonder, and the villagers gathered around him their jaws dropping.

Now he is with Stephen. Stephen has recently arrived in the town and the two men are becoming friends. They are in a bar of no distinction, drinking beer. Rokas has wiped the froth from his lips with the back of his huge and hairy forearm and his eyes have sunk backwards in their sockets as they review the events of days gone by. It is story time.

'I am,' he begins, 'human, though without the early associa-tions which human society might have provided. My first mother was a bear and for her care and love I shall always be grateful. I lived with her for a few years before I came to town. The smell of tree bark and raw fish still reminds me of those happy days. Here,' he continues, 'let me show you my bear walk.'

Rokas gets to his feet and lumbers flat-footed round the table at which they are sitting.

'You look like a gorilla,' says Stephen.

'The walk of a bear and a gorilla may seem similar to the uninformed, but that was definitely bear.'

'So, Mr Bear, why aren't you living with Mummy Bear now?'

'I left her when I was five. Approximately. It's impossible to be precise. I can't tell you why I left. Some deep genetic urging perhaps. Whatever the reason, I set out for the town with nothing more than long hair which came down to my knees, extremely long nails which were not ideal for urban life and some scraps of paper.'

'Scraps of paper,' interrupts Stephen, 'really?'

'Yes,' continues Rokas, 'scraps of paper. Obviously, I had no idea at the time what the words on the paper said, but this didn't stop me from understanding that these scraps of paper were the most important thing I owned. Which they were of course – they were all I had – but even had I owned other important things, these would have been the most important. I imagined they contained something of great value but whether they did or not I will leave you to judge.'

Rokas recites a passage from these scraps which he knows by heart.

' "*Down there, men and women are still in search of the meaning of life (or death). In order to find it, they look in all the wrong places. They send out probes. They send out rockets. What they discover is no different to what they already know: an amplification here, a wrinkle there, but essentially the same. At first their discoveries make them excited, which they take to be a form of happiness. Afterwards these discoveries make them feel as they have always felt: miserable. They don't know why this is. It is our job to drop hints.*" '

'I see,' says Stephen. 'I imagine you felt privileged to be trusted with this information.'

'Of course. Wouldn't you?'

'Yes, well, I suppose I might if I found myself in those circumstances. But what happened next? You've left Mummy, you're all on your own except for a few bits of paper, you're not exactly fashionably attired... What then?'

'Then?... Then a kind woman called Helen found me on the outskirts of town, hiding in the branches of a giant cedar. Sensing my needs by some form of intuition or remote reception, she laid out a bowl of succulent grubs at the base of the tree. Hunger presently persuaded me down and, after scooping up the first handful and belching generously (as was required in my culture), I found her voice oddly reminiscent of ancient memories and therefore comforting. She led me by the hand and took me to her house.'

'That was brave of her.'

'The first thing she did was bath me. She began with cold water, imagining (correctly) that anything else would have been alarming. Little by little, she introduced warmer water until, before long, I was lying back in the steaming tub singing staccato bear lullabies to myself. I imagined then that I would enjoy my new life and my new mother.

'Next thing Helen did was cut my hair and nails. Then she dried me and put me in some clothes she had. Soon I was just like other boys.'

'That I find hard to believe,' says Stephen.

Rokas ignores him.

'I was of course behind in my lessons and it took me a while to catch up. I quickly learnt that the many 'bear' things I knew – tree craft, rooting skills and suchlike – were of no benefit in my new surroundings. Consequently, I discarded them all, cast them aside like the traumatic memories everyone in my new world imagined they must have been. I devoted myself to my studies and before long was able to read what was written on the scraps of paper I had kept by me since the day my life changed. Reading, however, is one thing. Coming to a full understanding of what the words might mean is a task which continues to occupy me even now.'

'I imagine it does.'

'I was 16 when Suzanna came to live with us. We became brother and sister. Suzanna encouraged me to believe that my past was nothing to be ashamed of, that many children had been uprooted by Porphyrian's Spring Clean[2] and that not all were as fortunate as I in the circumstances of their early years. We spent many long hours together during which I tried to recall all that I had experienced. Suzanna understood that the task of separating what was real from what was imagined was an impossible one, but this didn't affect her willingness to listen. We discussed *mothers* at great length and I couldn't help feeling that, of the two of us, I had had the easier time.'

'I'd like to meet this Suzanna. She sounds interesting.'

'She is. She plays the piano beautifully. Our evenings together, with her at the keyboard and Helen singing in her velvet soprano, were of such purity that they moved me to a place where I could begin to make progress in the task I had set myself, the task of unravelling the meaning of my private papers.'

Rokas stops, looks at Stephen.

'Is that it?' says Stephen.

'I imagine you don't believe me.'

'My considered opinion?'

'Certainly.'

'It's a good story, no doubt about it, but apart from the obvious physical resemblance between you and Mummy Bear, I'm not sure I'm entirely convinced. The bit about being brought up by Helen is, I suppose, verifiable, but I'd say the remainder can be laid to rest among the rhubarb. Another pint?'

They drink in ruminative silence. 'Tell me about Suzanna, description please. I'd like to meet her.'

'And you,' demands Rokas, 'what's your story?'

'I knew my mother anyway.'

'Yes?' says Rokas.

'She died when I was 12. Left me to join the other scrap feeders washed up by the war. So I signed on for one of the Porphyrian *Academies*. Remember those? *Be part of the team, help the clean-up.* You'll remember the uniform – blue commando trousers, red flak jacket, blue and red trainers? I was a *Porphyrian Pup*, one of the first. Me, Barney and Fogarty, the old inseparables. Barney was the craziest. He was never going to keep his bits together. But Fogarty'll still be out there somewhere. If I ever go back to that town, I'll look him up, buy him a drink, say hi, Fogs, do you remember when.'

'So you were one of the *Porphyrian Pups*,' says Rokas. 'Well,

well.'

– That, and more, was then.

* * *

Now Rokas is 31. He works for Porphyrian. Working for Porphyrian is not unusual. Since Porphyrian owns everything worth owning in the town, the large and the small, the good stuff and the bad, everybody does. Even those who don't think they work for him, do. Even Suzanna, who plays piano in a bar, tinkles his keys.

But Rokas is mainstream. He designs guns. This is his job. His job, yes, but this does not mean he accepts the gospel of the Porphyrian Spring Clean and all its subsequent applications. Not at all. His values are his own and he insists on them. He designs guns only for self-defence: signature guns, voice activated, single shot[3].

Besides designing guns, Rokas also writes stories. If he had to rely on his stories for his daily bread, he would be dead of starvation. If he didn't write stories, he would be dead to himself, dead to the streams within which are compelled to seek out the light of day.

Rokas wonders daily as to the nature of these streams, these underground sources which provide the material for his stories. They intrigue him. Is it possible that they are mere concoctions of his mind, mere rearrangements of impulses and experiences already present in the six inches between his ears? This seems to him unlikely. Inadequate. He senses something more, some ability to receive, from out there, ideas which are beyond his own limited capacity.

He can't explain this. Or doesn't wish to. If asked what or who might be 'out there', he will only wave his hand airily and say, 'certain things are beyond our understanding'. This is prudent – popular disbelief in such matters makes explanation fruitless –

and Rokas, although a storyteller, is not a man who, these days, is given to explaining himself to the world. His eyes are turned inward.

Yet, though he may wave his hand airily and say, 'certain things are beyond our understanding', he feels within himself that he is edging towards the very understanding that he denies. Edging only, but still moving forward. And he has supportive evidence of a sort. He has those papers, scraps really, which were with him from before the time of his earliest memory. These scraps are, to him, endlessly intriguing.

He is rereading one of them now.

"Don't think it's going to be easy. It isn't going to be easy. You've no idea. What's it take? You tell me. It's not as if there's a shortage of evidence. We've had patients dying on the operating table, no heartbeat, no brain activity – file closed – coming back and telling the doctors what's on the hospital roof, where the nurses stored their teeth, who said what to whom – as clear a demonstration as you could wish that consciousness doesn't depend on a body. Then there's telepathy, psychokinesis, children who remember when they were their grandfathers, you name it. Doesn't make any difference – you won't believe the amount of scepticism that's down there. I mean, how many white elephants do you need in order to prove that not all elephants are grey? Anyway, look, thanks for helping. We really appreciate it."[4]

Because of this fragment and others of which it is a part, Rokas believes that he might be more the receiver of stories than the generator of them. He likes the thought of this, that he is somehow connected to consciousnesses other than his own. He delves for incidents that lend support to this possibility. Occasionally he finds them. Here is an article he has pinned to his wall. It is from *Nature*, September 2028.

"From the time the 'water maze' experiment was first set up in Australia, America, Britain, Sweden and Japan, rats routinely took 195 seconds to escape. Then, on June 20th 2028, a rat in Australia found a concealed short-cut and escaped in 58 seconds. On June 21st, a day later, rats tested in America, Britain and Sweden also escaped in 58 seconds. (Japanese rats were not tested because

*of a Shinto holiday.) The researcher who suggested that rats must have their
own social network wasn't joking."*

In spite of his feeling of being connected to some wider
consciousness, Rokas finds that, when he writes, he is unable to
escape the world in which he lives. Since this is the world which
Porphyrian has created in his own image, a world of guns and
death and all the miasma of lies and negotiation that naturally
attend it, he is troubled. Perhaps the world beyond, from where
these voices seem to come, is no different to Porphyrian's world.

This he doesn't want to believe. This he can't believe. How
would there be any meaning in life if those consciousnesses *out
there* were still embroiled in the same mess as poor souls like him,
if mankind's lives were continually repeating but not advancing?
No, he thinks, this cannot be. This must not be. Most likely, I am
not picking up the messages clearly. I must be mangling them,
polluting them with the dross of the day-to-day.

Rokas sets his jaw, takes up the story that lies on his desk,
reads it through and sets it aside for further consideration. It now
rests on top of a pile of stories, all, like this one, put aside. The
pile is badly stacked and the top overhangs the bottom by several
inches. It is surprising that it has not yet collapsed.

Rokas' first short story: Entanglement

Soldiers in columns criss-cross the city. Some are wearing red uniforms and some blue (though both have dragons on their sleeves.) Sometimes they stop, throw down their rifles, lean against a doorway or an old stone wall and reach into their bags for a smoke. They will smoke anything. The days of tobacco are distant memories for the older ones and no memory at all for the rest. Therefore they are not unhappy at the slicing heat that enters their lungs. They breathe it in and out, relaxing as they do so.

Sometimes a red column marches down a road hearing nothing but the sound of its own pipes and drums, when out of a side street comes a blue column which also hears nothing but its own deafening music. Both columns clatter to a halt, surprised that the enemy has come upon them unawares. An exchange of fire may then result but other outcomes are also possible. What happens depends on circumstances which are themselves a matter of chance or, if you prefer, destiny.

Each column may, to take a single example, observe the other in a silence broken only by the shuffling of boots and then, at a signal from the captains – a questioning nod from one followed by a reciprocating nod from the other – march backwards. In this war, the art of marching backwards has reached new levels of perfection. The enemy is always kept in sight. Backs are never turned. The discipline of the march is maintained by a single man at the rear (which has become the front) who alone faces the direction of travel. His task is to shout out 'left right left right', 'left wheel', 'right wheel', as the occasion demands. This man is known as the pilot or rudderman depending on the colour of his uniform.

The role of the pilot or rudderman is one of considerable responsibility and difficulty. He has at all times to remember that his left wheel is the soldiers' right wheel and, of course, his right wheel, the soldiers' left. Should he forget, the effects on the column are disastrous. The streets of this city are narrow and a column which marches backwards into a stone wall is at a considerable and frequently fatal disadvantage when it comes to responding to enemy fire. The fate of the pilot or rudderman out of step with his column, if he has not been crushed in the ensuing collision or felled by hostile ordnance, is more often than not to be burnt at the stake. The winters are cold in this city and bullets in short supply.

The columns of marching men do not have the city to themselves. People still live in it and go about their business. They have become used to ducking for cover, to shrugging their shoulders when the fruit or vegetables they have grown and brought laboriously to market are either shot to pieces or borrowed: a term used by the soldiery to imply that the object in question will be returned. In this war, the meaning of borrowed (like other words in common parlance: 'permanent' for example) has added an imaginative dimension somewhat beyond its usual borders.

After the shooting is over, the stall-holders put their trestle tables back on their feet as well as they are able, select such of their produce as is still edible and wait patiently for customers. What else can they do? And customers, they know, will come. Customers are always on the lookout for bargains, especially in a time of war, and an apple in which a bullet is lodged is, naturally, the subject of negotiation. There is plenty to be negotiated about: the nutritional value of what remains, albeit less than it was, and also the material value of the spent bullet – not much in itself but when beaten down, combined with others and refashioned, not negligible.

Often then, after a shooting, the market becomes a lively place, with the citizens shouting, laughing, waving their arms and behaving as if whatever has just occurred was no more than a shower, the necessary precursor to a blue sky and warm, soothing sunshine.

I was leaving the market one day when I noticed a girl walking some ten paces in front of me. She had attractive legs beneath a flowing skirt, wore a peasant's bodice that showed her to good advantage and, around her head, a scarf. In her wicker basket lay a swan whose long neck was draped over the basket's side and hanging down lifeless. Its eyes appeared closed. I am not speaking as an expert on swans. For all I know, swans might not be capable of closing their eyes. They might be lid-less. Even so, this swan seemed to have its eyes closed. It was to all appearances dead.

When the girl suddenly collapsed, I ran forward to see if there was anything I could do. Soldiers are not above (or below) knowing how to behave and, besides, they are used to dealing with collapse in all its forms. At my approach, the swan promptly revived, made a great honking noise, jumped out of its basket and stood with its wings outstretched and its beak pointing with intent in my direction. There was no doubting its animosity, especially as it now started to hiss violently.

A crowd gathered. Our city spawns crowds like a bog frogs. That there are individuals in the city there is no doubt – indeed we have seen them in the market negotiating with stall-holders – but individuals can also find comfort in the crowd, in being swept along, in surrendering (like a woman in the experienced arms of a powerful lover) to the loss of control. Not to mention safety in numbers. Not to mention that sheer nosey curiosity is easier in a group.

I addressed the gathering, provided reassurance ('It's okay, I'm a soldier') and suggested that everyone keep their distance, the girl needing air and the swan not to be trusted.

'Where's your uniform?' shouted one.

'If you're a soldier, how do we know which side you're on? Red or blue, which is it?' demanded another.

'Look,' I said, 'just now, it doesn't matter which side I'm on; there's a girl on the ground who needs help.'

The swan meanwhile began making short sallies in my direction and imbuing its hisses with an undertone which implied, at least to my ears, positive hatred. Such emotion in a mere bird struck me as strange. I took out my revolver and was about to shoot it when the girl woke up.

She looked around. She reached out to the swan and called it something intimate, like Mitty. It was so soft her call, I couldn't make it out, not precisely. Mitty – if such was its name – instantly quietened *down and I took this as my cue to move closer. The crowd dispersed immediately. It was only afterwards I realised, as I leant over the girl and put out my hand to reassure her, that I was still holding the revolver.*

Suddenly a shot sounded at close range and I heard a bullet strike a nearby market stall. I turned round and found myself looking at a man of about my age who was also carrying a revolver. It was of the same make and series as my own.

The guns in our city were supplied by an arms dealer with many chins who treated his customers with great civility. He supplied both sides with equal dispassion and seemed not to care that the customer of yesterday might be laid to rest by the customer of today. His reliance on new customers coming to his store (rather than on repeat buying by his old) did not hinder the expansion of his business. Those who remained alive were grateful and word of mouth spread quickly. The owner became a wealthy man directing, at the time of his death, a chain of thirteen stores manned by each of his thirteen sons, all of whom were conceived in a single year when he was in his prime and unattached to the woman who eventually became his wife.

I did not know if the man, now standing in front of me holding, as I was, a revolver, supported my side or the other. I did not rule out the possibility that he posed a threat. His gun, though pointing at the ground, might easily be lifted and fired in my direction: as quite possibly it already had been.

I told him, by way of alerting him to the fact that I was no pushover, that I was a soldier and asked whether it was his bullet that had struck the market stall. He replied that he also was a soldier and that it was.

'Why did you fire?' I asked.

'Why did you draw your revolver?' he replied.

I found myself unwilling to tell the truth, which was either that I felt myself in danger from the swan (which sounded rather weak coming from a soldier) or that I wanted to get to the girl without any interference from a dumb bird. In our city at that time, the casual murder of animals was looked on with less tolerance than the casual murder of humans. The murder of humans (if causing death in a time of war can be so labelled) happened on a regular basis for no good reason that anyone could remember (had there ever been one.) So instead of telling the truth, which I should have done, I said that the girl was an old friend of mine who had looked as if she was in need of protection.

At this point, the girl, who had been watching all this without saying a word, suddenly spoke. 'Ah, Petrusha, thank you.' This seemed to be addressed to me. 'And you, Sergei, thank you also. How good to find my two best friends with me now, a pleasure I did not expect.'

Since my name was not Petrusha (nor even Peter), I immediately doubted whether his was Sergei and, indeed, whether he was any friend of hers at all, any more than I was.

'Come,' she said, 'let us find a bar and drink.'

So we left, all three of us, or should I say four, the swan having resumed its position in her basket. We drank. One thing (as they say) led to another and before we knew it we were all in her bedroom.

We did not remove our clothes immediately. First we sat on her bed – there were no chairs and not much floor that wasn't covered by piles of pamphlets. I leant down and picked up the nearest one to hand. It was written in staccato imperatives urging the crowds to march behind the blue columns. 'Help us!' it read. 'Drive out the Reds! Fight for peace!' I dropped it and watched as it floated downwards and came to rest on another pile. I slid a pamphlet out from the middle of this second pile, taking care not to disturb whatever physical principles kept its haphazard structure upright. 'People!' it exhorted, 'the Blue Guards are exhausted. Help us to rid the city of their menace. Together we can build a better future.'

'Yes,' said the girl, 'I know what you're thinking, but I have one rule in this bedroom: no thinking. Remove the thought from your mind or leave immediately.'

Well, I don't know if you've attempted it, but it isn't easy to remove a thought once it has stuck in your mind. I did my best and she could see I was trying.

'Perhaps this will help,' she said and, standing up, took off her scarf,

throwing it onto the piles of pamphlets. She undid the clips in her hair. Her hands then went to the fastening on her skirt and we heard a faint pop indicating that the clasp had opened.

You will notice that I said 'we'. With good reason, for Sergei, like myself, was now sitting on the edge of the bed, transfixed, as I was. We had forgotten completely, or at least temporarily mislaid, all that had gone before: him trying to kill me, the red or the blue, and all the things, large and small, which up to then had been our preoccupation. We watched as her skirt fell to the floor and heard the rustle as she stepped out, the rustle which sounded in our ears and re-sounded in our imaginations.

The night was a night of sinuous contortion, of the blurring of edges and of identities, of advances and withdrawals; him, her, me, we criss-crossed the dark streets of our mutual city in a silence broken only by a gasp, a groan, a sigh.

Next morning, aroused by a noise that penetrated slowly and at first unrecognised into my sleep – it was the sound of hissing, a sound I confused, such was my state, with nothing more alarming than the running of the bath in my mother's old house in the country – I found my arm around Sergei and his around me. The swan was on the floor, its wings stretched out, its beak open. With undisguised animosity, it took a step forward. I reached for my revolver but found that it, like the girl, had disappeared.

Suzanna: moving on

Helen is her real mother, the mother she was meant to have. That's what Suzanna thinks. She doesn't believe that the good things which come to her are accidental – or the bad things either. She believes in a determining energy somewhere out there. She doesn't call this energy God. Certainly not God. At the idea of *church*, she shudders.

Suzanna moved out of Helen's flat when she was 21. She felt it was time, and didn't Helen think so too? Helen nodded then and kissed her, and turned away from her so she couldn't see she was crying. But Suzanna knew she was. She was crying too.

Suzanna now teaches piano to the little children in the Porphyrian orphanage, all sorts of little children: the empty-eyed, the brave-faced, the irretrievably lost, the driven, the desperate, all sorts – and every one of them, just by putting his or her little hands to the keys, tells their story. And such sad stories they are, even this long after the war is over.

Suzanna sits beneath a poster of a smiling, fatherly Porphyrian and doesn't say much to the little people who come, courtesy of their benefactor, to learn to play – what can she say, she's only the piano teacher, but if she gets them to hold their backs straight and their fingers alert on the keys, that's something, even that.

Sometimes, though, what their faces betray is almost more than she can bear. Those two four-year-old twin girls with brown curly hair and bottomless eyes who try so hard to please; she wants to take them in her arms and tell them it's okay, really, it's okay, I'm sure your mother loved you. But she doesn't say that. She remembers she is only the piano teacher and hopes the piano will bring them a message they can hear.

Most evenings she plays in a bar. Background music, nothing too distracting; it's that kind of bar. She feeds her languid improvisation into the rattle and chatter, as if she's behind a wall and her notes drifting over it and mingling inconsequentially with what's beyond, like dust or birdsong. That's what she's there for, that's what she provides: background.

But everyone needs an audience, even if it's only seated in the front row of his frontal lobe. Suzanna plays for the men in her life: her father (dead), her son (dead). She places pictures of them on the piano-top of her mind and shares her music with them. Sometimes she feels their spirits mingling, all three of them, or sometimes they stroke her and say, yes Suzanna, yes Mummy, that wasn't bad, play that one again. And she does. Sometimes she plays the same piece three or four times, one after the other. The punters don't notice, or if they do it doesn't bother them.

Strange that it isn't Helen she plays for, or Rokas. Drawn to the dead, she thinks, but then why not, what's wrong with that? She can reach out to the living when she wants to. They don't need to be conjured up.

Rokas left Helen's when she did, but they didn't become lovers for all those years. Brother and sister they had been, really, living together under the same roof. Rokas didn't think they should because he said they knew each other too well, all the things that brothers and sisters know about each other, the good and the bad, and that they were too full of what each other was deep inside to want anything more.

Still, they are lovers now. It happened. That first time, he carried her onto her bed and laid her down. He didn't say a word. He started to undress her and when he came to a fastening his big fingers couldn't work, she worked it for him. When he came to her birthmarks, he cried.

She asked him why he was crying. Is it such a terrible sight? He didn't answer, just kept on crying. He put his finger on the one which looked like a burn scar and asked does it hurt? When she didn't flinch, he kissed it as if the touch of his lips would be more than she could bear.

He knew about the baby she'd lost, she'd told him about that. It wasn't him he was crying for – he said it wasn't anyway – it was something else. He said he felt that somehow he'd done this to her, that it was his fault. She told him they were birthmarks, just a natural disfigurement – but it wasn't the facts that made him cry, they both knew that. What it was, what it must have been, was something in him, something too deep to get at.

A great big man like him crying; who would have imagined it? He's got his secrets, like everybody else, he must have. Brother! Lover! And those bits of paper he keeps locked up in a biscuit tin! Secrets there all right. Helen told her he came to her with those clutched in his little hands and wouldn't let go of them. They'd both laughed about it, though now she doesn't think it's funny, any more than she thinks her piano is something to laugh at; just the dear things that make them who they are.

The bar where Suzanna plays is where she first met Stephen. He sat on a stool watching her and, when she'd finished her set, she went over for a break. That's what she usually did between sets. He said to her the strangest thing then: he said she shouldn't sew in the dark, she'd go blind. She looked at him closely. There was something wild about him, wild eyes, like a trapped animal. She was drawn to him. She wanted to spring him from his cage, let him free. She asked him what he meant and he said, 'Didn't you sew that orange fringe on yourself? I can see you now hunched over by a guttering candle.' Well, she had a black dress on and, yes, there were orange fringes on the bottom of it and, yes, she had sewn them on herself, though not in the dark. She said, 'Is my sewing that bad?' He stared down at her legs and said, 'Not bad at all.' Then he looked her in the eyes and said, 'In fact, very good.' She laughed of course. That's how they became friends.

He came to the bar quite often after that and, naturally, he bumped into Rokas. She understood then that not only did they work together, they were old friends. She wondered why Rokas

had never mentioned her to Stephen. Or perhaps he had, and Stephen just pretended that their meeting was an accident.

Stephen: at the factory

Stephen passes along the factory floor as if processing down the aisle of a church. He imagines himself dressed in robes of deepest crimson and in his hand a smoking ash pot. He looks to left and right, smiling benignly at the employees bending reverentially over their machines. Shaking the smoking ash pot of his imagination, and safely hidden beneath the dark stubble of three days, Stephen feels on the skin of his cheeks a rising flush of pleasure. He feels like a hustler; he likes the act.

No one working the machines is precisely sure what Stephen does. This makes them doubly reverential. Stephen isn't precisely sure either, since his job defies precise definition. He is happy about this, happy to be passing along the factory floor hearing the hum of the hive, feeling the buzz of its bees, touching with the tips of his fingers its fecund turbidity – and being prepared to report if anything is awry. Stephen enjoys the open-endedness of all this. It suits his spirit, which also he regards as open-ended. 'Could be worse,' he tells himself.

This is not to say that Stephen's job is make-work. He provides a service and he does it well. He can hear, he can sense, he knows which way the balls are rolling. There is something of the Porphyrian about him and this has not gone unrecognised by the leader himself.

All across the floor of that great cavernous factory, line after line of machines is turning out the latest advance in self-protection for women: the Porphyrian Pistolette, a totem for the age, the hook on which the great enterprise hangs its hat.

The Pistolette looks like a tube of lipstick and comes in all shades. It is voice-activated and deadly when aimed point blank. It is single use: the thinking being that if the first slug hasn't done the trick, the lady isn't serious.

Stephen picks one up as it drops from the production line,

rolls it between his fingers and laughs. He moves across to testing and watches technicians putting the Pistolette through its paces. The wad that emerges from the case end expands on impact: any organ within two metres becomes mush. Just what ladies want in their make-up bag.

He opens a door into a large room. From a glass ceiling, light falls like the petals of a firework and lands soft as ephemera on the heads of the 115 men toiling beneath. At one corner is Rokas, standing on a raised dais at an acreage of table. Visible from afar is his croupier's visor, two immense shoulders and the rising steam of his concentration. Above him, like a giant lampshade, is a curved white board on the outside of which, jotted haphazardly, are sundry epigrams.

Rats know more than you think.

To whom out there it may concern.

Ooch. Ooch, Oooch.

Thought speed gets you there and back.

It's a thankless task.

Time is tricky.

Be kind to bears.

Stephen walks between the tables of the 115 toiling men. The men do not look up or greet him. When he reaches Rokas, he puts an arm around his waist.

Rokas, seeing it is him, smiles. Stephen is warmed by the smile and smiles back. He leaves his arm where it is for a moment and then lets it drop.

'Some weapon that Pistolette,' he says. 'Will we ever be safe again?'

'Depends what you get up to.'

'I hear there's a problem.'

'It goes off when it's not supposed to. It's not only the lady's voice-pass which triggers it.'

Stephen considers this. 'Casualties?'

'Deaths.' Rokas holds up the fingers of both hands like two

fans made of tree trunks. 'Approximately. And casualties.'

'Oh.'

'Yes, oh.'

'Solutions?'

'We're trying to identify the rogue trigger words – to see if patterns recur.'

'And do they?'

Rokas takes Stephen to one side, turning his face away from the men. 'Curiously, and perhaps significantly, the first rogue word we found which activated the mechanism was *Porphyrian*.'

'So it's sabotage, the enemy within?'

'Within maybe. Without probably – desensitising the voice signature, reconfiguring; it's sophisticated, but it can be done.'

'So the Pistolette might go off randomly, at any time, at no particular target. Quite a metaphor. Anyone claim responsibility? Any demands?'

'No.'

'And Porphyrian?'

'Not happy. I hear he's going to pay us a visit. See for himself.'

'Yes, I heard that too.'

Stephen moves away. So Porphyrian is coming. It must be serious. Terminal? He plays down the pathways in his mind, takes the one where the empire slips on its own lipstick. And if Porphyrian's empire falls, will things then be better or worse? Were the Goths an improvement on the Romans? Stephen considers his own question. Probably not, but maybe, who knows?

… And if Suzanna falls to me?

'Steady on, Joe,' he says to a man coming round the corner, almost on top of him before he notices.

'Oh, hello, Stephen, sorry, I hope I didn't… I was thinking about a horse in the 3.30.'

'Did you have much on her?'

'10 eurars! 20 to 1. Yes, I know, but I just woke up this

morning and had a name in my head: *Thought-Speed*. When I saw she was running, I decided well, why not. So I stuck 10 eurars on her.'

'It's a good name. I hope she goes where the rider tells her.'

'Yes, let's hope.' He laughs.

Three more managers come along. Red jackets, blue trousers. Stephen, who has never worn uniform since he was too young to know better, feels surrounded. The managers acknowledge him with deference – better safe than sorry, who knows what he does, really. After silence, one of them says, 'Well, Joe, looks like the drinks are on you.'

'They are? No kidding? '

'By five lengths, looking backwards!'

Joe clutches his heart. '200 eurars!' The others gather around, their faces lit up and laughing as if they've all won something this day.

Stephen, forgotten now, watches. Suddenly he feels his stomach moan and rumble. Is it something he's eaten? What has he eaten? Egg sandwich. Yes, must be that. He had a feeling about those eggs. The men are still beaconed up over Joe's win. 'Sorry, fellas,' he says to all of them and none, 'got to go.' He pulls a face and runs straight-legged towards the men's toilets, good-humoured laughter following behind at a distance. He turns to look at the men to see if they're looking at him. They aren't. Stephen, still turned, walks into a wall. He hits his head on plaster, falls to the ground and, for a moment, dreams he is lying half-dead in Suzanna's arms, dreams of the touch and smell of her, of delights improbable or yet to be.

When he comes to, he feels again the gripe of his stomach and gets himself to the gents. He sits with his head resting on his hands and groans. He groans at his guts. He groans at the demands of his desire and at the running feet of his destiny, now running faster.

Stephen leaves the building. He can't work. He doesn't feel

like working. He'll go to the polotti hall and hustle some poor nobody out of his savings. 'I must ask Rokas along – it's time I showed him what I can do.'

The cabin

They take the tram to the end of the line. Then they walk through trees. After a couple of hours, they leave the path they've been following and Stephen leads them in single file along such animal tracks as he finds. They head south for four or five hours, look through trees to a frozen lake that accompanies them below, the sun glinting on its snow crystals, star-time altogether. Presently, they ascend an incline on the forest floor and come to a cabin: wooden walls, a roof and a rusted iron stove. Not much but enough. The tins Stephen left last time are still there.

'Perfect,' says Suzanna, looking around. Rokas grasps Stephen around his waist, lifts him up, lets him go and rumbles around the room in a shambling sort of dance. 'Wonderful, wonderful,' he says, 'I feel so... so... back home, thank you.'

Rokas carries the stove outside while Stephen and Suzanna forage for dry bark and twigs to start the fire. When it catches, they build it up, shut the stove door and let the heat get into the metal. Before long, they have their supper. Stephen produces a bottle. Rokas says, stretching out, 'Oh, my feet. I wasn't built for walking.'

'Did you hear about Joe's winnings? A horse called *Thought-Speed*, 20 to one.'

'Nothing travels faster than thought-speed.'

They talk for a while about not much, the men mainly, Suzanna listening. Factory talk, a lot of it, snippets which she doesn't try to understand. And finally they come – because they can't not come – to the polotti, the mugging and the muggers, the sadness and the hopelessness of it all. Stephen says, 'Somebody points a knife at me, I can't just let it go... ' He looks around for recognition, support. Suzanna says, 'He got what was coming to him, I suppose, poor man.' Inside Rokas' head, there is chanting: *ooch, ooch, ooooch*[5].

They fall into silence. Their silence stretches as far as the fire glow and the snow-light around it. Beyond that is a deeper, blacker silence. This they cannot penetrate, do not want to. Yet every now and again the silence speaks. *Pff, kaa, whoo, paaa.* The silence breathes. The lake? But the lake is frozen. A fall of snow from a branch then? Must be that. Or an animal on the move. Black, silent eyes, watching eyes. Tigers' eyes, thinks Rokas.

The three friends are afraid of nothing. They stare out and they stare in, each in their own thoughts. Suzanna and Rokas are the first to return to the cabin. They roll out their sleeping blankets. They lie close. Their hands touch.

Stephen stays outside. Below him, he makes out the white arms of a willow, like the skeleton of a broken woman, hung down. He hears a plover whistling in that wilderness so plaintively that Stephen feels an equal loneliness, an equal sleeplessness. When he returns to the cabin, he unrolls his mattress at the farther side, away from the two lovers. There he waits for morning.

He wakes to sun streaming in and the smell of ersatz sausages frying. Suzanna is about and bustling. She is singing softly. Stephen comes out, his eyes half open, his hair tousled. 'Breakfast?' she asks. Stephen nods, sits down half-asleep and eats. He takes a bucket to the stream, holds on to an overhanging branch and slides down the small incline to the water. He breaks the ice with his boot. When he's made a large enough opening, he bends down and washes his face with the ice water. Then he fills up his bucket.

Suzanna is behind him. He says, 'I'll help you.' He holds her arm as she comes down slipping cautiously, and the two are suddenly together. They are between the bank and stream on a piece of frozen mud wide enough for a single foot and she is in his arms, laughing. 'Oh, Stephen,' she says, her face all creased, 'and all I came for was a drink.' He laughs, too, and because he's laughing he can kiss her, kiss her under cover of laughter, on the lips.

'Here,' he says, and bends down to the water, wets his hand and places it on her eyes. Water drips down her cheeks.

'Let me,' she says. She slides past him and stoops to the running stream beneath the ice and lets her hair fall over it and her face look down not an inch above at its own reflection. She splashes the water up, first a little, then in big handfuls so that, when she stands, it's as if she's had a shower. She allows the water to settle on her, so she can take it in through her skin and taste it on her lips. 'Wonderful,' she says savouring it, and she runs past Stephen up the bank, with him behind her.

Rokas is just coming out. She calls to him. 'There's a stream. Go and taste the water. You've never tasted anything like it.'

The two of them watch him lumber out of sight. Presently, they hear loud grunts, *ka ka ka*, and hear tramping, cracking sounds and a splash. They run over to the stream and find Rokas lying in the running water, his legs stretched out in front of him, his hands on his chest and not a stitch on but the thick hairs of his body waving in the water. They look down at him and he says, pertly, with a smile on his big lips, 'I'm having a bath, do you mind?'

They have to laugh and they do. Stephen says, 'I'll go and build up the stove.'

They sit around it with its door half open, drinking tea. Stephen is whittling on a dry pear branch he's found. In his hand is a Porphyrian all-purpose survival knife and he's making his first cut: the top of a soldier's head. Rokas is restless. 'Come on, let's move,' he says. What a day this is: too beautiful to sit around.'

The others get themselves together but Rokas can't wait. He charges off into the trees and they hear the sound of branches snapping and undergrowth trampled.

Suzanna and Stephen walk. Like all walks in rough country, this starts in chatter and ends in silence as each picks his way from stone to stone or over the easier crossings between this obstacle and that. When they come to a flat snowfield, she puts her arm in his, the two of them together, the two of them alone. Different now, different chemistry, this togetherness, this aloneness. She feels the wildness of his body against hers, feels it in the way wildness is felt, not by mass but by the energy of the something that is struggling to get free. She imagines what it would be like to hold this energy to herself, to release it, to feel his moment of calm – and, imagining, she holds him with a greater intensity; an intensity hardly discernible by the man whose arm is in hers, but discernible within her as a deeper pulse in the blood and its corpuscles, as punctuation in the subtle vibrations on her skin.

'You didn't want to bring Angie?'

'She's left me. She says I don't love her.'

'Don't you?'

'No. Not like you love Rokas.'

'I do love him, it's true, but I can't stay with him. I'm 30, I want a child. Rokas doesn't... won't. I don't think I can forgive him his cruelty.'

'Yes, it is cruelty,' Stephen replies.

'Oh,' she says, surprised at hearing what she's said come back to her endorsed, surprised at him for saying it.

They walk on, she following the pace he sets along an old animal track beside which the first snowdrops are beginning to show. The winter sun has some heat in it now and she turns her face to it gladly. She wants to bend and see the snowdrops and let the sun warm her, but he's in a faster rhythm and won't slow to let her bask. He pulls her along with him, a gentle enough drawing along, but insistent and steady. And after they've walked like this for a while, she feels something else: not that it's just him being careless of her or too immersed in himself to see, but that there's will behind it, some need in him to bind her to him, perhaps even to subdue her as if she is his to subdue. She

79

pulls her arm from his. She will not be subdued. She is not for that, though other women seeing him in all his wildness might be.

She stoops to the snowdrops and presently he comes back to her. 'See,' she tells him, 'life… and the beginning of the end of winter.'

From high up and a way off, they hear a call. 'Suzanna… Stephen… ' They look about them and there is Rokas, hanging by one arm from the top of a tall pine and the weight of him making it bend. He is waving and laughing, and when he's not waving he's pointing at the sun and the beauty of the day and exclaiming to them and to the world in the craziness of his mime, 'Look, see, there must, after all, be something *other*, don't you think?'

'Come down,' shouts Suzanna. 'The tree will break, you'll fall, you'll kill yourself. Come down for God's sake.'

Rokas beats his chest and lets out a deep rumble, *aaawm*, that causes an eagle to fly a little closer and then veer away as if it's seen all it needs to see for one day.

The wind picks up and blows strong under the sun. The trunk of the pine bends now in circles, down because of him and round because of the breath of God. It is a sight of recurring madness or genius, or light or dark, or anyway, above all that, a sort of inspired and alien phantasm. 'Let's go back,' says Suzanna. 'I can't bear to watch.'

The fire is lit and they are drinking tea. Rokas is quiet as if he's returned from somewhere and knows he's seen something whose precise nature he can't quite recall.

Stephen says, 'You bathe in icy streams, you swing from trees, you're twice the size of anyone else – perhaps you are part bear after all?'

'Finally,' says Rokas.

Stephen turns to Suzanna and shakes his head sadly. 'Can't imagine why he wasn't squashed by the other cubs and served up for lunch.'

Rokas barks bear-like. 'Life is full of mysteries.'

'Do you buy any of this?'

'Don't look at me,' Suzanna replies. 'I didn't know him until he was 16.'

The cabin (continued)

Stephen is whittling. He has finished the head of his first soldier and sees, suddenly, how his carving, in more skilful hands, might look. He imagines, across his soldier's head, a column of such soldiers criss-crossing a city, each soldier different, different in wonder, in incredulity, some bleeding, some lapping up blood but, on the face of each, desire.

Rokas takes a tube of lipstick from his trousers. He surveys it, top and bottom, and then loops it, follows it in flight. It hits Stephen on the arm and he turns sharply. 'We did too good a job,' says Rokas. 'How many women could tell theirs from this?'

Aroused from his artful dream, Stephen chokes back resentment… the careless throwing… belittling somehow… was it intended? Perhaps. He picks up the look-alike and rolls it over in his hand. 'You and I and a few others. That's about it.'

'So we'll never get the Pistolette out of circulation. They're lost now, indistinguishable, randoms in the gene pool.'

'How many are out there?'

'Hundreds of thousands. Women have been lapping them up.'

'But only a tiny number have been sabotaged.'

'It doesn't matter. Even if it's only 100, even if it's only 10, someone says the wrong word… '

'… and Porphyrian is coming.'

Stephen holds his hand to his mouth, mock aghast. Wide-eyed, the two men look at each other and laugh. 'Yes. He's coming.'

'What do you think he'll do?'

Rokas shrugs. 'What can he do? Stop production, recall them, give refunds?'

'You don't know Porphyrian – someone will have to pay, some poor staked-out sacrificial goat. Otherwise the Pistolette is his fault and we all know Porphyrian doesn't make mistakes.'

'Poor goat.'

'Yes, poor goat,' echoes Stephen.

'What are you talking about?' asks Suzanna.

Rokas tells her about the problems of the Pistolette. 'Why did you make it?' she asks.

'We thought it would keep women safe, safer. Women thought so too, that's why they've been buying them.'

'And now they're dying.' Suzanna doesn't know what to say, where to look, who to blame. She asks the question whose answer she doesn't want to hear. 'And you, Rokas, what was your part in this?'

'I designed it.'

'And you, Stephen?'

'I made sure it was manufactured efficiently.'

'So you both have blood on your hands.'

Rokas looks down, reflecting on blood and the ways it comes to be spilled. He says, 'Anything can be sabotaged. A bomb can fall into the hands of terrorists. A bus can be driven into a crowd. A pram can run down a hill and kill the baby inside it.'

Suzanna hates him for what he says, for the truth of it and for its apparent disinterest. Her eyes mist over and the points of light within are fractured. She says, 'Women make life and men take it. Will it ever stop?'

Stephen turns from her. He places his knife and his carving on the ground. He wants to take himself off, away from this sanctimonious prattle. He makes guns, he gets paid for it, so what? Is he supposed to make violins and starve? And, if he didn't make them, someone else would. Guns are hot. The latest oldest fashion. Don't pretend we can do without them. Or want to. Not in this life.

He walks to the edge of the clearing, his mouth sour and his mind etched with reproaches, with charges laid against him in years past suddenly resurfacing: all of them false or petty or complaining. He stares out into the trees, seeing only the nagging images that come from within. And when the world outside appears again, it appears as dapples of light between leaves, formless, unspecific. Slowly, the dappling takes shape. A young woman is there, he thinks. Yes – he concentrates – a young woman. There. How strange. I have never seen a Tribal before.

She is standing, almost invisible, beneath a blackthorn still bearing its berries, iced and dried out. She steps forward. She is wearing animal skins and has black hair that falls to her shoulders in clusters.

Stephen moves towards her. Suzanna and Rokas, now seeing what he sees, follow. When they are within a few yards of her, she steps away. They follow and she retreats but not so quickly that they think she is trying to escape. Stephen is sure that if she wished to disappear she could do so in an instant.

She leads them for some time, moving between dense trees. As the trees thin into open ground, they come to the top of a valley folded like a pocket between the undulations of the subtle landscape. In all his wanderings, Stephen has never noticed this valley before. She beckons them down.

The country within is older, the trees ancient, their barks misted by lichens and so tall that they rise from the valley floor to the height of those growing above. Vast, cracked boulders line the valley sides. Ferns root in their fissures. Mossy boluses, like round tombstones in a graveyard of elephants, poke out. When Stephen presses his hand into one, expecting to touch the rock within, he finds only moss layered on moss. He hears the static crescendo of a waterfall: enduring, primitive noise. They move closer, watch it plunge, a cascade of silver, white flecked.

At the bottom of the valley, everything is green. Even the dead branches of trees with their desiccated, twisted leaves, have hanging from them the palest of green hair, like the maidenhair of lost love. Even the bluebells when they come with their mournful arches will only punctuate the green that is all around.

In front of them stands the woman. With her is a man, perhaps her husband, and their child. Others are gathered behind. They point towards a pile of living bones, whose legs are tucked around him. The bones hold a carving and they lift it up for Stephen to take.

Stephen cradles the carving in his two hands. It is of a deer and its rider. The ears of the deer are pricked and its eyes are twisting back, awaiting the word of command. Its legs are poised as if it will at that very moment gallop off. The rider's feet are welded into the animal's side, man and beast one flesh. Stephen bows his head to the old man. The old man also bows.

The man, the husband, comes up to Rokas and puts his arms around him, laughing joyously and making grunting noises. Rokas grunts in reply and the two dance slowly round, their backs bent and their heads on the other's shoulders. Others form a circle around them; they stamp and chant. Suzanna finds herself amongst them, stamping and chanting.

Stephen stands apart, watching. Presently, the woman approaches him and lays her palm on his chest where his heart is. She engages him in so gentle a way he is overcome. Her eyes suck him in and he travels joyfully, beyond the calluses and burn-marks of her face, into her abundant youth. A wailing noise like that of a plover's call comes from her. She gently removes his gloves, takes his hand in hers and places it beneath her furs on her naked breast. She shakes her head from side to side as if in sadness, as if aware of things to come.

The softness of this woman's breast overwhelms Stephen. He feels as if he is sinking in this softness, as if he would sink to the bottom of it and drown. He can't look at her. He doesn't know what he should do. He doesn't know what he can do. Her husband is there, her family are all about. He wants to let his hand wander over her body, but he cannot. He feels trapped, as if frozen in ice.

Presently, she moves away and another leads them back to the cabin. The wind rises and branches come down about them.

Jazz Club

The jazz club has tables gathered on three sides around a floor set aside for dancing. Corny Kelleher will be playing later. Now, as filler, there is easy music – muted sax, double bass, drums – to which couples embrace and sway.

The club has seen better days, and worse. Its floor is of dark and pockmarked hardwood. Its walls are covered in cream and yellowing wallpaper on which are pinned reproductions of paintings from an earlier century: boats, lakes, elegantly dressed men and women picnicking beside a pond under the falling leaves of a chestnut tree. Between two art-nouveau lamp holders is a visionary picture of Porphyrian as he was in his pomp, silently reminding the diners and the dancers and all who pass beneath who owns the joint.

Suzanna turns to Stephen. In her head is an image of his hand beneath the furs of the tribal girl and she asks, 'What is the longest you've stayed up in the forest?'

Stephen pauses, playing back his forest time. 'Two months, maybe three. I was 12. That was before I came to this town. My mother was just dead and I thought if I stayed out there I might find something to make me feel good about myself.'

'And did you?'

'I found something. Survival: that's something. The meaning of black. That's something, too. No moon, no nose in front of your face, no mummy to take you in her arms. A twig snaps. Does the forest have wolves? I didn't know; how could I? But I stuck it out.'

'Why?'

'What was there to go back for? No mother, no home and there was still shooting. You know what it was like.'

'But you did come back… '

'I did. I don't know why. Change of scene probably.

Porphyrian's *Academies* were looking for lads like me, so that's where I went. Home. They've had a bad press, but the *Academies* were okay. Gave the lost boys something to belong to. Taught me how to look after myself. Even gave me enough of an education to get me started.'

Rokas asks, 'Did Porphyrian know what his *Pups* were doing?'

'I think he did. He visited us every now and again, inspected us in our uniforms, very military and proper, gave us his speeches about how we were the future, all that stuff. We lapped it up. We were very young remember and, well, he was Porphyrian wasn't he?'

'Were there punishments? How did he keep you all in line?'

'What else did any of us have but him? We weren't going anywhere, not then.'

'So you all did as you were told?'

'If we had any sense. Those that didn't, didn't last long. We'd wake up and find their bunks empty.'

'Where did they go?'

'Who knows. We used to say Porphyrian ate them, but that was just boys talking.'

The waitress comes across. She's all in black: short black skirt, black blouse worn loose and a croupier's visor underlining an aura of spiked black hair, like the sun's rays at midnight. 'What sort of meat is it?' Suzanna asks.

The waitress shrugs. 'It's served in a stew with beans and carrots. Spicy, if you like that sort of thing.'

'I'll have it,' says Suzanna. 'I don't mind which animal it comes from, as long as it's fresh.'

'Oh, it's very fresh,' says the waitress. 'It was only unfrozen this morning.'

When the food comes, the men watch Suzanna. She cuts the meat, forks a cube of it and turns it once before their eyes. As they stare wondering, she dances it in time to the music into her mouth. Her lips close around it, the fork retreats, she chews cautiously and swallows. The men follow it down, their own mouths dropping open.

'Well?' asks Stephen.

'Hmm.'

The men attend on her pronouncement but she just smiles. If they want to find out they'll have to try it for themselves.

They finish their meal, sit back, drink beer and wait for Corny. Something has delayed him. Perhaps he isn't coming.

'Well then,' declares Suzanna. She steps onto the dance floor. She puts out her hand and beckons Rokas. He comes towards her and takes her hand, holds it… while Stephen sits watching with blank hurting eyes, feels the dismissal, the loss in his guts, wonders how he can watch at all. 'Come.' He hears the word from somewhere off. 'Come, Stephen.' And this time he lets the words enter and looks to see Suzanna with her other arm outstretched and a quiet invitation on her face. 'Come,' she repeats, and now he is on the dance-floor, the three of them in time to the intimate rhythm of music from days long gone, one-two-three, one-two-three. And though Stephen is not holding her by more than her forearm, he imagines her in his arms, one-two-three, he crooks his right elbow as if holding her tightly at her back but softly so as not to break what he holds, and he turns a circle and another and again and spins her once more, tracing orbits he knows they have traced a hundred times before.

And then Rokas is alone at the table watching and smiling and she moving with Stephen lightly and letting him take her where he will to this corner and to that and ever further from the man who sits and watches and, sometimes, so it seems, even smiles a blessing upon them both, like a man of the cloth upon his children before their wedding night.

Rokas' second short story: Escape

I opened the gate, stood behind it and tried not to imagine those great heads twisting from side to side as they tugged my flesh from the bone. I concentrated instead on a question which I had idly considered many times from a safe distance: freedom or food – which means more to a pair of Siberian tigers? My life seemed to depend on the answer.

Both of them were no more than twenty yards from the open gate, and from me, when their attention was drawn to the laughter and derisive shouts of the guards. The tigers paused, they waited... so that when my pursuers came into view what greeted them was power in a half crouch, the quizzical stare of the never-afraid, a hint of fang emerging from vast jaws, the curious maw of death.

I suppose the guards must, for an instant, have thought of shooting them. But to shoot the Commander's tigers was unthinkable: they'd have done better to shoot themselves and be done with it. Those tigers were the Commander's greatest joy.

The Commander did not come to the camp often but, when he did, he waved away the salutes and went straight to their enclosure. He liked to stand, sometimes for many hours, peering through the trees for a flash of power among the leaves, listening for that roar which froze the marrow of the rest of us. Then the squeal, the grunt, the bay, the bleat, the wail or the silent surrender – it didn't matter whether we heard or not, our imaginations were enough. We saw it clearly as if we were both victim and victor of those games: the leap, the jaws taking hold of whatever offering the Commander had brought – a goat, a deer, even a dog – the first suck of blood.

The Commander found the process calming. It was passed down to us that only these tigers made his stay in this part of the world, abandoned as it was by men and civilised gods, bearable. We were left in no doubt where we stood. We were encouraged to believe, and did so without difficulty, that those who disappeared had not been pardoned or moved to other camps, as was stated officially, but had been eaten.

Within the compound, the guards left us to ourselves. We lived in wooden huts. We slept on wooden slats arranged in bunks. The violent prisoners, or those with powerful friends, ate more than the others, did less work, lived longer.

I was the largest man in the camp. They could have brought me down if enough of them had wanted to, but I gave no-one trouble. They found it convenient to leave me alone.

By day, most of us went out in groups to the forest to fell trees. We were closely watched. One guard for every three, so a work detail of twelve had four guards in attendance, each of them armed and not in the least hesitant about firing at the first sign of trouble. Better to bring back prisoner-meat than nothing at all.

Prisoners who slipped away among the trees never got far. The weather was against them. In winter, it was sometimes so cold that spit froze in mid-air. If the climate didn't get them, the helicopters did. It took them less than three hours to arrive from headquarters and what good were three hours in that wilderness.

Our camp was in the shape of a swan, with a wide base and a long thin neck. The enclosure for the tigers covered the entire south end (the swan's body) and included in its fenced area a large tract of the surrounding forest. The tigers roamed over this and hunted down whatever came through the gate.

The prisoners were confined to the 'neck' portion and even this was divided into two halves, men on one side, women on the other. The segregation was strict. In our camp, where life was so little valued, it was strange that anyone should pay attention to the sexual proprieties: but so it was. Perhaps the Commander had daughters and saw, in the protection of these women, some universal law which would therefore apply to his own.

We had precisely marked tracks on which we were allowed to walk. At one point, as if to make us aware of the temptation we were obliged to resist, the men's pathway and the women's came close together. This was always patrolled. If a man and a woman exchanged a word or two as they passed, the guards used their boots or rifle butts on them. The female guards were as bad as the male.

There were two kinds of walkers among the men, and among the women, too, I couldn't help noticing. There were the brisk ones who tramped up and down as if on their way to some important meeting. Perhaps, for these people, walking was a reminder that once they had been doctors or engineers, people to whom others showed respect. And there were the strollers, for whom this moment when they were not working or being threatened or being hit was precious, and they would savour it. I was a stroller, even though before I came here I had been somebody. So was Katerina, a stroller and also a person in the life before, an anthropologist at the University. We had known each other then and had shared what we had: time, ideas, intuitions, a bed.

Where the two paths came together, the men's path and the women's, we walked more slowly than usual. I knew she had something to tell me. I also knew what it was, had already seen in my mind the whole proposition. We sauntered along and when we passed shoulder to shoulder, she whispered, 'Now.'

I stopped. I said, 'Are you sure?'

'Yes, now, why not?' She stopped too and then it was that the guard came running. 'Hey you,' she shouted, readying her rifle as she did so. 'You! Stay where you are!'

I didn't stay. I ran, zigzagging as I did so, in case she took it into her head to shoot. Her shout was joined by a male guard and then another. 'Come back,' one of them laughed through his panting, 'You can't go anywhere. There's nowhere to go. You're dead meat whatever you do. So stop, save your energy, don't be stupid.'

I didn't stop. I ran on until I reached the tigers' enclosure. I pulled back the bolts which secured the gate and stood behind it.

These tigers never hurried. Out of boredom, perhaps, or some other effect of captivity, they chose to defer the pleasure of the kill. They allowed their victim to see them and to smell them. They watched as it was rendered senseless by fear. They watched as it urinated and trembled. They did not move. They allowed it to look around, to step hesitantly away from them as if expecting to be pulled down at any moment, even to make a dash for the apparent safety of the forest. The tigers never minded waiting. Sometimes, if they weren't hungry, they waited for hours. Then, with that deep and dreadful aaaong, the game in which only one outcome was possible began.

From behind the open gate, I heard the guards laughing and taunting. Then I heard their boots scrabbling on the hard ground as they turned for their lives.

The tigers loped slowly after and into the camp.

Those who saw first and understood, ran. The rest followed. Some, even though they lived daily with death, screamed. Some prayed. Terror spread across the camp and found its voice in the panicked scuffle of men and women searching for somewhere to hide, in the banging of doors, in the assembly of hopeless barricades. Then silence. Everyone, guards and prisoners alike, had taken cover, scarcely daring to breathe. Most were in the huts. Some were on the roofs as if believing that tigers couldn't climb.

I ran to the women's quarters and met Katerina coming towards me. We went to the gatekeeper's lodge. She crashed her palms against the door. 'Help,' she cried, 'for the love of God, let me in.' The gatekeeper, who was a decent sort, opened it. I stepped through and knocked him unconscious with a single blow. I took the keys.

It was then that I remembered Stumpy. I have done bad things in my time, but the thought of Stumpy being eaten by a tiger, well, I didn't want that on my conscience. Stumpy had no legs, that's why we called him Stumpy. His real name was Stiva. He could walk well enough considering he had two metal poles with rubber disks at the bottom, but that didn't mean he could outrun a tiger.

'I'll have to go back for him,' I said.

Katerina nodded. 'I'll wait for you here.'

Everybody liked Stumpy. We didn't have enough to eat ourselves, but we each gave him a bit of crust or a mouthful of our soup-water. The guards must have fed him, too, and clothed him because, instead of the threadbare woollen coats and felt trousers that the rest of us had, he was always well padded. We didn't mind. He was like a mascot or the regimental flag. If he was fine, the rest of us could get along.

The guards let Stumpy have the run of the place. They even let him visit the women. When he was going courting, as he called it, he put on his legs with the artificial knees. This lifted him from his usual four foot six to about five foot eight and what with his smart clothes and the sheen on his skin that came from all the food he was getting, he looked quite the man about town.

His knees were his pride and joy. He never let them out of his sight except in the women's area where, so he liked to proclaim, he had other things to entertain him. This led to a standing joke among us. 'On or off, Stumpy?' we'd ask as he returned. We didn't begrudge him his fantasies, or he ours.

I found him under a lean-to among some axe handles. 'Come with me,' I said. I picked him up and carried him to the gate. Katerina unlocked it. No-one was there to stop us. All the guards were hiding. We ran across the open space towards the forest, and it was only then that I remembered there was a second line of fencing that marked the camp's outer boundary.

I knew that, from the outside, the gate through this fencing opened easily enough. I'd opened it myself many times when returning with a logging party. It was just a wheel that rotated. But from the inside, as I now observed and berated myself for forgetting, the bolt was turned by a key.

I didn't know how we'd get over. The fence was 10 feet high and of barbed wire. We couldn't climb it. Katerina and I sat on the ground. This was the end. As soon as the tigers were captured, we'd be their next meal. I didn't fear death, but that didn't mean I wanted to die, not today, not one mouthful at a time. I put my arm around Katerina and we touched our lips together – our first kiss since coming to the camp and our last.

Stumpy watched us. Then he said, 'Do you think you can throw me over?'

I stood up. I am seven feet tall. With my arms fully outstretched I could almost touch the top of the barbed wire. 'Yes. Will you survive the *fall?'*

'*Just throw me.' He took off his poles. 'Throw me head first.'*

I did. He went over like a diver and when he reached the ground, his little torso contracted into a ball and he rolled forward head over stumps. I threw his poles over and then his knees. I knew he wouldn't go anywhere without those. He went to the gate and turned the wheel which unlocked it.

'*Stumpy,' I said, 'you're a good man.'*

I picked him up and carried him into the forest. There we stopped, breathing in the beauty of all about us, a beauty made more precise, more perfect, by our first moments of freedom – the grass damp in the dappled rods of spring sunlight, the larches holding us silent in their tranquil arms, the sweet briar still carrying its winter berries wrinkled like the indulgent faces of old women.

Katerina stood in a clearing and, raising her arms above her head, called as she'd been taught to do, a haunting sad call that might have been a bird mourning its loneliness. Phee-oo, phee-oo, once, twice, three times. From the trees came an answer, bew ip, bew ip, and then faces appeared, and then the bodies of men clad in animal skins.

'*These men will keep us safe. Come,' she said to Stumpy and to me.*

We followed her and soon arrived at a clearing in which a man held two stags. He indicated to me that I should mount the largest, a huge beast with a great head of horns. Katerina mounted the other with Stumpy behind her holding her waist. We were given dried meat to chew and a guide to lead us. So we went, south, south, away from the camp, the tigers and the brutality of men. We heard no helicopters. Perhaps we had passed beyond the range they anticipated.

After two days, our guide left us. Katerina spoke to him in his own language, bidding him an extended and elaborate farewell. This, she told us, was customary among the Tribals. We carried on in the direction indicated, both of us now accomplished deer-riders. Stumpy, having no legs, had to hold tight to Katerina just to stay on. He didn't complain. He travelled with his head resting on Katerina's back and his arms around her waist. From time to time, his hands came to rest high up on her thighs. I assumed then he had dozed off and kept well behind in case he should fall.

We slept that night in a sheltered glade in the forest, covered by the animal skins that our guide had given us. I thanked God for that man and his people who, in helping us, had risked everything. Katerina rested in my embrace. Stumpy, fearing it might rain, pitched his camp some distance away in a small cave he'd found.

I had never slept better since coming to the camp. Even after our escape, I still felt that our freedom was an illusion and that at any moment we would be captured and dragged back as living food for the tigers. Now I knew that our freedom was real and for the first time could enjoy, without distraction, its sweet smells, its clean air, its nature untainted by man's defilements. Katerina was in my arms and so blissful was I, that I believed that even if they came for me, I wouldn't care.

When I woke from my reverie, I saw Stumpy watching us. He was leaning against a log with the circular disks at the end of his poles digging into the ground. He was as casual as if he was in some smart café having a smoke. In his right hand was a pistol.

'We're going back,' he announced.

'Back?'

He pulled a device from his knees. 'I called them. The helicopter will be here any minute.'

Senseless though his words seemed, I tried to understand them. I reflected on what skein of miserable calculations had driven Stumpy to this. I watched as his eyes flicked between me and Katerina. I saw desire in those eyes and scratches of blood deep within. I listened for the whirr of rotor blades but heard nothing.

'What if the helicopter doesn't come?' I asked. 'What then?'

'It'll come.'

All I could hear about me were the sounds of life, of small flowers pushing through the green carpet at my feet, of birds whispering to their mates, of life even in this wilderness, of life in all its irrepressible possibility.

Among the Cathars, Languedoc, Mid-13th Century[6]

✝

'So, Stefan, here you are at last. Good. Perhaps you will now enlighten the court as to why you have given us so much trouble finding you.'

'I didn't know you were looking for me. I was in the hills, with our sheep.'

'But when we found you, you had no sheep.'

'I had sold them by then.'

'You had no money either.'

'I gave it all away.'

'I see,' says the First Inquisitor. 'You gave away all the money you received when you sold your sheep?'

'I did sir, yes.'

'And the sheep belonged to your family, did they not?'

'They did.'

'Well, Stefan, I don't know what to say. You surprise me: a shepherd giving away everything he has!' The First Inquisitor chuckles at the sheer gall of it. His fat face creases in pleasure. 'You know,' he says still chuckling, 'I can't wait to hear how all this came about. I imagine your account will be most instructive. Please, go ahead, tell us.'

Stefan smiles. He likes to tell stories. 'The life of a shepherd is a lonely life,' he begins, fingering pensively the dark stubble of his cheek. 'Of course, we meet other shepherds in the cabins that are scattered over the hills to the west, but mostly we spend our hours alone with our sheep, just walking or whittling on a stick or lying on our backs in the sun. We have plenty of time for reflection. So although we are only shepherds, we are also thinkers. We think about St Peter, St Paul and the other apostles. We try not to lie. We try to do to others what we would have done to us.'

'Very commendable. I am pleased to hear you say so,' says the

First Inquisitor.

The Second Inquisitor meanwhile is fidgeting on his chair. He has not yet learnt the fine art of dissembling. His fidgeting betrays his feelings and his feelings are those of someone unsure of the ground on which he stands. 'Am I prosecutor of this Stefan?' he asks himself, 'or defender, as I am of Suzanne? Why don't they tell me? How can I do what they expect if I don't understand what that is? Perhaps it amuses them to keep me in the dark, not knowing whether I should turn this way or that?'

From the perhaps of this question repeated over and over, R moves towards the certainty of an answer. 'It does amuse them, no doubt about it, I'm a sideshow, a joke, well, we'll see about that, they may be laughing now… ' Through the top of his head, in fact on the top of his head, growing into it like pustules, he imagines the beaming faces of *them*, the lord and bishop and all the rest in their unassailable places on high. His fingers go to his scalp and he scratches. With each scratch, the last one deeper than the one before, his resentment grows. He will not be a figure of fun, no, not him, not for anyone.

Behind closed eyes he reaches for a sentence that he has been rehearsing for some time but which he has, so far, been unable to deliver with conviction. 'The time will come,' the sentence goes and he accompanies it with a grinding of teeth, 'when it will not be them looking down, oh no, it will be me.' He tries it again. He grinds harder. 'Yes,' he says to himself, 'it will be me. Me!' He opens his eyes. The light floods in and, with it, as always, as ever, the doubts, the damned doubts. 'But how? They are there. I am here. How?'

Then, he takes a decision. It is a simple, practical decision and therefore achievable. It is a decision which, though small, will change the course of his life, will indeed, like all deviations, change the course of history. Here, in all its microscopic unimportance, it is: 'I will defend this Stefan. I will defend Suzanne. I will take on the task to the best of my ability. It is my only path and it will lead me where it may.' He lifts his head and regards Stefan as if for the first time. He doesn't like him. Even so.

'Well,' says Stefan who has been continuing throughout R's meanderings, 'I was at this time with my sheep in the hills when I saw a man coming towards me riding a mule. When he was close I realised I had not seen him before. I thought this strange. Most of the people who travel the hills are familiar to us shepherds, but not this man. He carried himself erect on his mule and greeted me. He was thin. I thought he looked hungry so I reached into my bag and brought out some bacon. I would have offered him this even if he hadn't looked hungry. It would be just common courtesy.'

'Excuse me,' says the First Inquisitor. 'Tell me please, was this your bacon? Where did it come from?'

'From my home. I had just been there, you see, and Suzanne had sent me back to the hills with it.'

'Do you often go home?' asks the First Inquisitor.

'Oh, yes, quite often. I like to see my family and my sisters. To check they are well.'

'And were they?'

'They were.'

'All of them? Your uncle the priest also?'

'Yes.'

The First Inquisitor weighs up the silence which follows, listens to its vibrations. 'Do you like your uncle?' he asks.

'I do not,' says Stefan.

'I see. And why not?'

'I can't say.'

'Does your uncle, the priest, like you?'

'He might. He might not.'

'Well, maybe you can answer this; does he like your sisters, his nieces?'

'I believe so.'

The First Inquisitor waits. Again there is silence. Again he sniffs the air for nuances unspoken. 'Does he like Suzanne in particular, do you think?'

'He might.'

'Does he like her too much?'

R jumps to his feet. The jump follows from his decision to defend the brother and is therefore to be applauded. It is also, and less helpfully, set in motion by an impulse which he finds rising uncontrollably from his own murky depths and which he has neither the understanding nor the tools to explore. It just comes up and fills him with an overwhelming desire to put a stop to the First Inquisitor's questions. He wants to swat them away as he would swat a bee buzzing around his head. He even raises an arm. 'But, sir,' he says, and then he stumbles, the thought that he had as he rose to his feet somehow disappearing in the act of standing. His arm collapses to his side. How he hates himself. How he feels back yet again in that old place of humiliation. He wishes he had never got up. 'How can the accused answer?' he manages to ask. 'When it comes to liking, how much is too much?' He sits down abruptly.

There is again a titter around the court and pleasant laughter as if a familiar and much loved jester has run in from the wings, tripped over, turned two somersaults and landed in a pail of water. 'That, my dear colleague,' says the First Inquisitor beaming, 'is indeed the question. Thank you for putting it so well.'

'Continue if you wouldn't mind,' says the First Inquisitor to Stefan. 'I have interrupted. You met this stranger and you offered him bacon.'

Stefan is still looking at R. He looks in amazement. It is the first time he has noticed him, but now he wonders how he could not have noticed him before. 'What sort of man is this?' he says to himself. 'What is his game? Is he for me or against me?'

'The bacon, Stefan, the bacon,' encourages the First Inquisitor. 'You offered the stranger bacon.'

Stefan emerges from his reverie. 'I did. But he didn't accept it. He said, "Take away this horrid wild meat." Then he spoke to me of the Apostles and said that I, like them, should not eat flesh, none at all except for fish. Fish was the only flesh that was not corrupt.'

'And how did you reply?'

'I replied that that was not the teaching of the Church.'

'What did he say to that?'

'He spoke to me at length about the evils of the Church – excuse me for saying this, sir – about how the priests grow fat on the tithes of the poor and how no-one needs the intercession of the Church to go to Heaven.'

'I see,' said the First Inquisitor gently. 'Do go on.'

'Well, then he talked to me some more and in the end he said, "All these sheep that you have, you should sell them and give what you receive to the Perfect Men. They have nothing. They live simple lives, as did the Apostles before them. They will use this money for the benefit of the poor and will pray for you as for all their benefactors." All the while he was telling me this, he remained seated on his mule and did not get down.'

'And what did you say when he had finished?'

'Well, sir, I went to the nearest town with a market and he came with me, preaching all the while. I sold all my sheep as he instructed and gave him everything. Afterwards I realised I shouldn't have done this, but he was very persuasive and I am just a simple shepherd.'

'Hmm,' says the First Inquisitor. 'Perhaps you are what you say, and perhaps you did what you said you did, but perhaps you did not.'

'Every word is true, sir, I swear it,' says Stefan, making the sign of the cross on his chest.

✝

Stefan stands in the courtroom preparing himself for whatever is to come. He feels that so far he has answered well. With one side of his mind, the side that loves to be out in the hills, leaning on his shepherd's crook or whittling on a piece of wood, the whole world stretched before him, he begins to believe that he might again be free. With the other side of his mind, he closes the door on hope. He steels himself for the traps that he has no doubt lie all around him, sharp-toothed traps, word traps. He hears a tune being hummed softly and tunelessly. He looks across, sees that it is R who is humming and understands – he is a shepherd and therefore a man of instinct – what lies beneath, what will be found when all the disguises have been stripped away. He knows, as shepherds do, that a wolf is about.

The First Inquisitor enters, smiles in a fatherly way at the prisoner and regards the gallery above. It is full and expectant. He nods to one of the guards, adjusts the cushion on his chair and sits carefully down. A few minutes later, Suzanne is led in. The guard takes her across the room to where Stefan is standing. The two of them look at each other and what passes between them is a communication. The First Inquisitor watches with attention.

'It must be pleasant for you two to see each other again,' he begins. 'How long has it been?'

The accused do not answer.

'Well, it's been a while anyway,' continues the First Inquisitor. He pauses, begins again, 'I was sorry to hear about your mother.'

Suzanne looks at Stefan. 'My mother? What… ?'

'Oh, you didn't know. My apologies. I had no idea.'

Suzanne is frightened now. 'What's happened to my mother? What have you done to her?'

'We have done nothing, the Church has done nothing. Your

brother had better tell you. He was there.'

She turns to Stefan and says softly, 'Please.'

'We were in a cave. It was dark. She slipped on a ledge and fell. The fall must have killed her.'

The First Inquisitor intervenes. 'I know this must be difficult for you, Stefan, but I believe your sister deserves something more. Why don't you begin with how you both found yourselves in the cave.'

Suzanne, raising her hand to warn him, says, 'There's no need, Stefan. You don't have to explain.'

'Ah, but he does, don't you see? To put it bluntly, as I feel I must, your brother ran away, ran out on you I might say. And why? To save his precious skin, that's why. He abandoned you to battle the forces of heresy alone. He caused your mother to come after him, with what fatal consequences you need not be further reminded. Your brother's actions had her death at the end of them as inevitably as if he'd killed her himself. So, Stefan, tell your sister of your mother's last hours. She has a right to know.'

Stefan is silent, cast down. 'We were in a cave. She fell. It would have been better if she had stayed at home.'

'It would certainly,' says the First Inquisitor. 'She would be alive today.'

'It happened as it did, Stefan,' says Suzanne gently. 'Perhaps it's better this way.'

'Better to be dead than alive?' asks the First Inquisitor.

'Better to die quickly than to die slowly at your hands,' replies Suzanne.

'Those who die at our hands are those who deserve to die. Did she deserve to die, Suzanne?'

'Aren't we all sinners? Isn't that what the Church teaches?'

'We are all sinners, it is true. But not all of us compound our sins with heresy. Was your mother a heretic?'

R stands up, but this time, slowly. He feels on safer ground, surer about what he is about to do. Where this certainty comes

from he can't say. Perhaps, finally, his destiny has caught up with him. Or perhaps one possible destiny opens in front of him and the urge to explore it conquers all his other trepidations. Perhaps it is neither, no more than a change of heart, or a coming of age. Many labels might be applied. Which one is chosen matters little – the upshot is the same; R speaks. 'Her mother is dead,' he says. 'Her beliefs go with her. What can one person know of the beliefs of another?'

The First Inquisitor notices the change in R. He reassesses. He sighs. 'But surely, we can judge a person by what he, or in this case she, does, can we not? If her mother committed acts of heresy or uttered heretical beliefs, we may assume, safely I believe, that she was a heretic. Do you disagree?'

'No sir, not at all. You are right in every respect,' says R, bowing slightly as to a superior, 'but is there evidence of such acts or such utterances? I have not seen any.'

'Her house was known to harbour heretics. You know that.'

'That has been alleged, but where, sir, is the evidence? There has been gossip but there is always gossip. And who can tell what might be behind such words? The family was well enough off, better than some, and this can lead to jealousy and jealousy to wagging tongues. Truth cannot easily be discovered in such gossip. And, furthermore, even if the mother was a heretic, she has paid the price. The sins of the mother cannot be laid at the door of the daughter.'

The First Inquisitor beams, the fat under his chin wobbling in delight. 'This is good, my dear R, good. I can see that when I appointed you as defender, I did not err in my judgement.' He looks up at the gallery and catching the eye of the bishop, declares, 'We have a defender! With this man, the Church breaks new ground. Never again can it be said that the ways of this court do not accord with the strictest ideas of justice. Thank you, my dear R. I will henceforth confine myself to the sins of the accused. The dead may be left to answer for their conduct in a higher court.'

R smiles awkwardly and the R of old can be glimpsed in the way he re-takes his seat. Glimpsed but no more than that. No one in the gallery laughs. A slight smile, perhaps, at most. R has taken a step forward: of that there is no doubt. If it is followed by half a step back, still the journey has begun.

The change in him has been noticed also by the defendants. Suzanne looks on him with gratitude. She begins to trust him. And her brother catches the look and keeps whatever he thinks to himself. Now he expects death. There is a finality to death that postpones all other questions.

The riders are still a few miles away. They are travelling slowly, carefully, as if about ordinary business. Tip-offs, such as the one they have received, are not always reliable and they understand that they may go home empty-handed. Still, this particular source has been reliable in the past and the risk seems worth taking; those who don't seek, don't find.

Night is approaching. In the church a priest bends over the body of a girl. She is looking up at him in the candlelight.

'Isn't it a sin?' she asks and hears the echo, *sin*, thrown back from the stone walls of the old religion.

'My child, how little you know.' The priest smiles his handsome smile, a smile that has served him unfailingly through the years. 'This world is full of sin. Are we not, all of us, you, even I, your priest, the Devil's creation?'

'We are not God's creatures then?'

'Some priests will tell you that we are but others, who know better, don't agree.' The priest bends lower and places a hand between the folds of the girl's dress. Holding her breast, he caresses the soft skin and says, 'We were once God's creatures, it

is true, but after the Devil enticed the human spirits out of Heaven, he captured them in bodies of flesh devised by himself for the purpose. And now each spirit passes from body to body until it can cast aside its devilish tunic and return to God's Kingdom.'

'How does it do that?' asks the girl, her eyes agape in wonder.

'Through love and love alone, my child. In this Devil's world, the only innocent act is one that comes from a loving heart.'

'And do you have a loving heart?'

'My heart is aflame with love. When you mingle your body with mine, my heart will save you from sin.'

'Will it? Are you sure?'

'Love was planted by God in our spirits before we left Him, and it is only through love that we may find our way back to His bosom.'

'But, Father, this is a church. We are beneath the statue of St Peter! How can we do such a thing?'

'Ah, St Peter. Do you think he'll mind? He is only made of wood, you know. Why, I shouldn't wonder if your own relatives in days gone by weren't the ones who took the axe to the very tree from which he's carved.'

The girl thinks. She says, 'Yes, I suppose they may have, but ...'

'Ssh, enough,' whispers the priest. 'Here, come, grasp your love' – he takes the girl's hand and guides it – 'do you not hear its urgings? Do you not yearn to surrender to its bliss?'

'I'm afraid, Father, what if I become with child? What will happen to me then?'

The priest's smile turns indulgent. He pulls out a herb, an inch long and attached to a cord. He puts it round her neck and the herb hangs down between her breasts and rests between her legs.

'What is this?' says the girl.

'It will keep you safe.'

'Will it? Are you sure?'

'It will, it will.' He looks up suddenly so that his face catches the candlelight and makes his eyes twinkle. 'Wait. What is that? Can't you hear?'

'Hear what?'

He cups a hand to his ear. 'That knocking.'

'No, I can't hear anything. Who is knocking?'

'Don't you recognise that sound? Why it is love that is knocking of course. Love is at your door and he's getting impatient. Are you sure you hear nothing?'

The girl laughs. 'Well perhaps I am aware of something, now you point it out to me.'

'Should we let him in, do you think, this impatient fellow?'

'Maybe, if you think it best.'

'I do my child, I do.'

Moments pass, ah such moments, thinks the priest, lost in the bliss of creation... and yet, even as he enters and re-enters his dulcet kingdom of love, the riders have reached the village, penetrated the inner sanctum of his house, found it empty and now stand outside his church, that holy of holies. The one in charge spits into the dust. 'If he's not here, I'll flay the man myself who gave us this worthless information.' They throw open the door, see in the shadow thrown by a candle a devilish figure with three-legs crouched over a body. They draw their knives, rush him, and then, realising what it is they have in their hands, give themselves up to the gentler pleasures of ribald commentary and good fellowship.

✝

Into the courtroom comes the priest. How long he has been under lock and key is unclear. He may have been held for some time or he may be fresh from his arrest. Those whom Justice wishes to

age do not weather well, however short the interval.

Now that he has reached the court, he wants his trial to begin. He is restless, his fate uncertain. To while away the time, and to sweeten it, he muses on all that he has lost. His musing takes the form of lips, of a breast he once admired, of smooth undulations disappearing into the dark, and when these depart he comforts himself with words. 'Such sweetness was mine,' he thinks, 'and for this now to be taken away… For what? Against whom have I sinned? Were not the pleasures of the flesh given to all so that the cares of this world might be, for a few fleeting moments, forgotten? Ah, for bliss once more, one last time,' and his imagination returns to an old love and a moment in a byre when he took her from behind and she murmuring in whispers of encouragement for him to stop.

So he beguiles himself as the preliminaries begin, for preliminaries there are; the theatre has its conventions.

The First Inquisitor is a man who likes his audience to understand that God's pleasure can be their own, that Justice is not only divine but also a spectacle. So he acknowledges with a bow those who have travelled far to watch. (R has also learnt to bow – his flourish deepening as the weeks progress – but never so deep as his master.) So the First Inquisitor now drops, by means of no more than a raised eyebrow, the subtlest of hints that the gallery and its notables may today expect a treat. Then he clears his throat.

'You are an educated man, are you not?' he asks.

'I am a priest.'

'So you read, of course. You know the Scriptures. You know Latin and Greek.'

'My Latin is better than my Greek.'

'Of course. Mine too.' There is jollity in the gallery. They look forward to the sparring of educated men. 'We are used then, both of us, to interpreting texts are we not? When we read in a foreign language, what else can we do but interpret?'

'This is so.'

'And the Scriptures are particularly difficult, are they not?'

'They are, but it is fortunate that we have the Church to interpret for us.'

'Indeed it is. But, as I am sure you are aware, not everybody trusts the interpretation of the Church. In these dark days and in this place, heresy abounds.'

'It is a constant battle, sire, this fight for the truth.'

'You have no doubts that the Church is the guardian of the truth?'

'None.'

'None?'

'I have difficulties on occasion, it is true, but no doubts.'

'Well, we all have difficulties. But let me ask you this. What does the teaching of the Church in which you believe, and which I assume you preach, have to say about incest.'

'Incest? The coupling of brother and sister? The Church does not condone it.'

'Indeed it does not. And between father and daughter, or mother and son? Or indeed between uncle and niece. Does not the Church regard these as a sin?'

The priest pauses. 'It does, and with good cause,' he says.

'Yet there are some in this country who believe that if a sinner is consoled by one of the Perfect Men before he dies, all his sins will be forgiven. So, they say, incest is acceptable.'

'I have heard that said and I preach against it.'

'From whom have you heard it?'

'A priest hears many things.'

'You have heard many things, I have no doubt, but you have reported nothing.'

'I would not violate the sanctity of the confessional.'

'No, indeed, but a word perhaps to another priest, no names, to alert the Church to the dangers it faces… ?'

'Perhaps in honouring the sacred nature of the confession I

have been in error.'

'Perhaps so. But let us move on. I take it from what you have told us that you regard the practice and condoning of incest as heretical.'

'I do, sire.'

'You have a niece, I believe.'

'I do. I have several.'

'And one is called Suzanne, is she not?'

'She is.'

'She is 19 years old and unmarried.'

'She is.'

'It is surprising that a beautiful young woman like her is not married, is it not?'

'Perhaps.'

'There has been talk that she has had a child.'

'Has there? I know nothing of that.'

'There has. The child is dead, of course. What is not clear is who is the father.'

'I have no knowledge of child or father,' says the priest.

'Really. You who know so much, who hears in the confessional all the secrets of the village, have heard nothing?'

'Nothing. Perhaps there was nothing to hear.'

'Perhaps there wasn't. But then again it has been whispered, no doubt without foundation, that the father is none other than the priest.'

'If it has been whispered, it is indeed without foundation.'

'The whispering of jealous tongues, I suppose.'

'Perhaps.'

'The whispers have come from other young women in the village. This in itself is not surprising. Young women are prone to whispering. But I can't help but wonder why they might be jealous? Of what?'

'I cannot answer, sire.'

'Oh, come, come, we all know that you grant your favours, let us say, liberally. You are almost a byword. "The priest of Tarasac" they say, "a handsome man, the father of his village." '

'In my work, I do have to visit young women or have them visit me. The situations may sometimes appear compromising. I can understand how misunderstandings may occur, but I am not compromised.'

'What never? Not once?'

'Never.'

The First Inquisitor laughs. 'Well, my dear priest, what an example you set. The Church is in need of priests like you!'

'Thank you, sire.'

'Not at all, not at all,' he says, still laughing. 'But let us return to your niece and her poor dead baby. We have a missing father.'

'Why don't you ask Suzanne?'

'We have and she denies the existence of a baby. However, I am sure with a little persuasion, she will agree to own it once more.'

'You are sure?'

'I am sure.'

'And does that mean that persuasion has already been applied and she has admitted to its existence?'

'It does.'

'And who then does she say is the father?'

'So far, she has been silent on this point, but you do see, my dear priest, that having been persuaded to acknowledge the existence of the child, the name of the father cannot be long in coming. If there is a child, there has to be a father. The one always seems to go hand in hand with the other, or so I am led to believe.'

The lord and bishop guffaw. The rest follow.

The priest is aware that the space he now inhabits is not one in which truth holds sway. He knows that truth is a phantasm in thrall to the greater god of perception. What is seen to be the case becomes the case. Or perhaps it is not even perception which rules but policy. The truth is what serves the interest of the higher power and so becomes pliable in skilled hands, capable of being twisted one way or another, whichever suits the purpose of the moment. And the purpose of the moment is his demise. The priest wonders why this should be so. What danger is he thought to present? What harm has he done to the Church? Yes, he has preferred other doctrines and has even advocated them when in private. But never from the pulpit. There he has always been the Pope's man. Faithful is how he would describe himself. So why is it, he asks himself once again, that they seek to condemn me?

The priest stands quietly in court. He considers his situation once more and begins to think that he might have jumped to conclusions too quickly. Perhaps, he says to himself, all that they want of me is that I toss them a name, someone they can burn so as to encourage others into fidelity. There can hardly be advantage in burning their own priest. What message would that send?

'If there is a father,' the priest says, 'and may I repeat that I have no knowledge that there has been a baby, but if there is a father, I could hazard a guess as to who that father might be.'

The First Inquisitor chuckles to himself. He loves these moments when the dam breaks, when resistance crumbles and all that has been blocked up comes swimming out in a great flood, all the fish and the things alive and dead, all the rumours and the hates and the feuds and the jealousies of the one for the other. In these moments, he sees life as it is. He even finds within himself a certain sympathy for the heretic. If this isn't the Devil's world, he thinks to himself, I can't imagine what else it could be.

'Please,' he says aloud, 'enlighten us if you wouldn't mind. Who then is the father?'

'If there is a father, and again I say that I have no knowledge of this, but if there is one, then he resides close by the mother.'

'Resides close by the mother; what can you mean? Let me see now. Perhaps in the same house. But you live in that very house, my dear priest. Are you admitting that you are the father?'

'I am not.'

'Then who? Who else resides close by the mother? Ah, I see, you mean the brother, the shepherd, yes, we have wondered.'

✟

The crack of joints heard in the head is more terrifying than the rack itself. Why? Because imagination is not limited to time and place. It doesn't negotiate.

This is true for the unenlightened. For the enlightened who can watch their thoughts without attachment, such fears are manageable. But enlightenment is rare, and Suzanne and Stefan sitting huddled together bound by loose chains are not able to let enlightenment come to them. They look around at the wheel with its devices for securing hands and feet and they wonder. They look at the thumbscrew and they hold each other, each in his own thoughts. The pyre will be a relief. Better that than these. They hear footsteps on the stone steps, a key in the lock, a brief conversation and then they see a man, bent almost double in the attempt, come through the door. He looks behind him to check he has not been followed and straightens. Up and up he goes, his head almost to the ceiling of this dank vault.

'You know me, I think,' he says.

'I do,' replies Suzanne. 'What have you come to do to us?'

'I have come to save you.'

At this Stefan laughs. 'Save our souls, you mean.'

'Save your bodies and trust your souls to God.'

'You don't intend to torture us?'

'I have come to make you an offer. You will only be tortured if you refuse.'

Stefan looks at him with disdain. He believes nothing. He trusts nothing. It is Suzanne who says, 'What is this offer?'

'Your lives for a piece of information.'

'What information?'

'The name of the father of your baby.'

'What baby?' says Suzanne.

R tugs at his hair as if her intransigence pains him. 'If you persist, you will be tortured and then burnt. We know you have had a child. Accounts have come from several in your village and are consistent. The child died or was disposed of. It doesn't matter. What concerns us is the father.' He looks at Stefan. 'Is it you?'

'It is not.'

'Then who? You have been accused. If the accusation stands, you will be tortured and burnt, you and your sister.'

'Who has accused us?'

'Someone who knows you well.'

'Who?'

R walks over to a rope suspended from a hook on the ceiling. He plays with it, pulling it up and down. 'Do you know how this works? It's simple enough. Here, see. Your hands are tied... ' Suddenly he grabs Stefan's hands and locks them behind his back. Stefan feels the strength of the man and, beyond that, he feels the raw desire that congeals in the pain R chooses to inflict. 'Then,' says R, his voice gentle, innocent, matter-of-fact, 'you are raised. It is painful, particularly after the bones in the shoulder have broken, but we have found this method effective. Truth seems to follow quickly after pain.'

'Were you not appointed as our defender?' asks Suzanne.

'I was,' replies R, 'which is why I am here. To save your lives. But if I am to do this, you must tell me the truth.'

'We have,' they say.

'Well, then, tell me another kind of truth. Tell me about your uncle.'

'He is a priest.'

'Yes, he is a priest of sorts, but also a fornicator. Well, plenty of priests are fornicators. It is, I'm told, almost a benefit of the position, but the Church draws the line when the priest loves his own family too well.'

'Was it he who accused us?'

'Perhaps. But now I am asking you for your account.'

'If I tell you, will we go free? Without torture? Do you give your word?'

'I do.'

'Are you telling us that my sister will go free,' asks Stefan, 'even though by accusing our uncle she accuses herself?'

'It has been arranged.'

'But why?'

'Why? For speed. For convenience. The life of your sister is of no account one way or another. Whether she lives or dies is of no interest to the Church. But your uncle, well, he is a different case altogether. He is the snake within the Garden. The Church has no fear of heretics without. It knows how to deal with them. It has always known that. But the heretic within is a different matter; he not only deserts the Church but betrays it, and that is a thing that causes even the Holy Father in Rome to shake his head in wonder. So, Suzanne, you have it in your power to help the Church, to save a life and to save your own. Tell me then, who was it? Your uncle or your brother?'

Suzanne is silent. She is now judge and jury, truth for her to decide. She conjures the face of her brother as he was when he was young. She feels his skin on hers, the softness of it in her hand and his weight upon her and then, from love to agony, she is drawn, she is quartered by the advancing flames, the blistering of skin, the heedless lick of the caustic tongue. It devours her, body and mind, and she must put an end to it. She hurls herself to the ground. She groans. She implores Christ himself to show her mercy. She crawls towards the feet of the Second Inquisitor believing for a moment that he is her Saviour. She begs him to spare her this. The Second Inquisitor pushes her away with his toe.

Suzanne falls backwards. She is in the wood, the three of them, and her brother raking the leaves, building the fire, his tears and hers, and his smell, such a tiny scrap, hardly born, hardly alive, her own body going in smoke and she with her hands up, clasping at it, drawing it back to her legs as if she could shut the box and return to it its content and keep it within, bound in tight, from where it would never again escape.

'It was my uncle,' she gasps. She is drenched, drained, nothing.

'Ah, him, as we thought. Good. That is good.' R breathes in deeply savouring his success. 'How did it happen, tell me that, they will want to know,' he says, and then adds for her benefit, 'I imagine you were young, too young to resist. Nobody could hold you responsible for this crime.'

Suzanne gathers herself for what must be done. 'I was young, in my first blood. I was feeding the beasts when he came behind me and took me.'

'Did you resist?'

'I did. I shouted to him to stop, but he only laughed and told me that I was of an age and his to do with as he pleased.'

'Where was your father?'

'Away. I don't know. I don't remember.'

'Did you tell your father?'

'No.'

'Why not?'

'I was ashamed.'

'I see. And did your uncle use you more than once?'

'He did. Many times.'

'That is enough,' says R. 'That is a good story, told with conviction. It is believable even though for some reason I can't explain, I don't believe it. Not that that matters.' He looks at Stefan. 'You are a lucky man, but I daresay your time will come. For your sort it always does.'

'For us all, and you also,' says Stefan.

The smell of burning, of human flesh being first toasted, then barbequed and afterwards fried, is sweet. And pervasive. It is as if the slightest trace lingering in the air reduces the usual aromas of daytime – the grass, the trees, the animals and their excrement, the passage of humans – to nothing more than accompaniment, a light salad in attendance on the main course. For those who catch the whiff, in whatever minute concentration it may appear, even one part in a million, it is a reminder of their own mortality. It is a reminder for all, for those who pass sentence and for those who thank God's grace that it is not them: both.

The priest draws a good crowd, though mainly women, to breathe him in on his last day. He has had time to prepare his parting words and does not intend to disappoint. He will approach death like an old friend, with a wave and a handsome smile. The future is still romantic and too far off for him yet to imagine the flames at his heels. When that moment comes, who knows how romantic he will feel.

He is brought out, his hands bound behind his back. A guard encourages him with the point of his spear to move forward. As he passes through the people, he stops to address them. Again he is poked. 'No speechifying,' he is told. He sees a stake rising above a bonfire and feels his own warm water down his leg. The coarser women in the crowd point this out to their friends and jeer. Others, thinking of the priest in happier times and the intimacies they have shared, say nothing.

The priest is bound to the stake. The securing of the ropes is a lengthy process in which the priest co-operates. It takes his mind off what is to come. He looks at the expectant faces of the women about him and smiles. If his hands were free, he would bless them. He sees the executioner approach. He wonders why he doesn't carry a torch with which to light the fire. Perhaps, he has come to release him. Perhaps the bishop has granted him pardon.

The executioner clambers up the pyre. He is to be freed! He hardly dares to believe. The man is close now. The priest thanks God and waits for the word. With a flourish, his executioner lifts the priest's robes exposing what is beneath for all to see. He holds up the bundle of cloth in one hand and takes a knife from his belt with the other. He waves it so that the crowd might speculate as to its purpose. Such are the perversities of man, so contrarian are they, that the priest's member rises. It is against all logic. It is against the desire of its owner. The executioner smiles. The crowd roars. So fine an end, they think, what a man this priest is. In a flash, it is done, member and testicles separated, all three laid by his side on a flat piece of wood put there for the purpose, a plate for the offering.

The pyre is lit. The flames blossom and bloom.

The smell of burning is pervasive; enough to reach even to the cell where sister and brother are standing up, tied by ropes to a wall; enough to agitate their brains into imaginings that do not lead to happiness.

Stefan's imaginings are those of revenge, of his knife moving silently as a thief into the gut of the man who made them promises yet put them in this cell. He feels the blade in the meat. He twists it against the stomach wall, hard work this. The muscles resist, shout out, scream, but he twists some more and this time the blade turns. He thrusts deeper and turns it again, and then again, only at the end looking up into the face of the man whose life flits like a shadow across the stone and is gone. As Stefan dreams, he sweats into the fetid air.

Suzanne's dreams are of a different kind of death. She sees the bare, black flesh of her uncle, seared just enough to keep enchained the spirit within, and her wishes are merciful. 'Die,' she begs, 'please die.' Her prayer is addressed upwards to that very God who gave the spirits of his children into captivity.

Towards herself, she is unable to extend the same charity.

'Why did I throw him to the wolves? Just to save my own skin. Look where it has got me, a lifetime in this cell, a lifetime of torture. Why did I trust that man? We will go free, ha! The promises of the Church. Well, I have what I deserve,' and thinking this, she thinks also of the others she will betray before they finish with her. Now, for herself also, she wishes only for one thing: Death, Queen of mercy, sweet releaser, just Death, to have it over with and done, until the next time.

She falls into sleep which is as close as she can get to what she craves and is woken by keys rattling in the lock and heavy boots. She looks up. R is standing above her. He is wearing a cape that covers his face – as ludicrous a disguise as can be imagined. In spite of everything, she laughs. Stefan laughs, too. They look across, the one to the other, and suddenly love is in the room with all its energy, heat rising, shimmers visible above the stone.

R doesn't notice. He says, 'Be quick, I've come to save you.'

'You? Why?' says Suzanne.

'I gave you my word you would go free.'

'And you broke it.'

'Not I. Them. The Church.'

'Why should we trust you?' says Stefan and he reaches for the knife he doesn't have.

'You should not. I have not come to save you. But I was appointed Suzanne's defender and I will try to keep her from this.'

He undoes the rope that binds her. 'Follow me. Be quick. The guards will return soon.'

'I won't go without Stefan.'

'Come. I will not take him.'

'Then I won't go.'

R tries to drag her. She says calmly, 'If you touch me again, I will scream.'

R moves over to Stefan and unties him. 'Quick.'

There is a small gate leading out of the dungeon known as

Torturers' Gate for the reason that torturers like to slip through it unannounced. The spontaneous visit, they have found, oils the wheels of persuasion. R takes his key and opens it. It is now dark.

Crowds still gather around the embers, watching as the priest does not die. A guard throws on enough wood to perk up the flames just a little. The priest groans, his groans growing weaker but still sufficient to keep the people interested. Some are taking bets on when he will finally give up his ghost. 'Not before the moon rises,' says one. 'Not before my husband gets hungry,' says another. 'Not before your husband gets hungry!' exclaims a third. 'Why, what kind of bet is that? Your husband is always hungry.' And the people laugh loudly, as if it is the funniest thing they have heard, nothing being better than hilarity for drowning such other noises as they dare not listen to.

The three of them mingle with the crowd, R bending as low as he is able, his cloak masking him almost completely. Beyond the crowd, a horse is tethered to a tree. R leads it out and indicates to Suzanne to mount. 'You too,' he says to Stefan. The brother is first up. He leans down to help his sister, but R has her by the waist. He looks at Stefan, holds the girl like a rag doll and smiles in the knowledge of the power he has within his hands and the uses to which it might be put. Stefan readies himself for what will come. The moment holds itself, stretches into the next and, unchanging, rolls over time without moving its pieces. When it ends, R is smiling no longer. He shrugs. Perhaps he has noticed Stefan or perhaps he no longer entertains those unworthy thoughts which caused the smile in the first place. Whatever the reason, he swings Suzanne onto the horse and walks away.

'Thank you,' she calls into the darkness.

Northern Europe, Mid-21st Century

Rokas' third short story: Release

It was one of those nights. When the wind starts to blow up here, it blows, I mean it howls, it roars, wails like a fucking banshee. Trees were coming down all over the place – well, to be precise, one tree, an ancient pear that had survived everything the last 500 years could throw at it – but even those that stayed upright lost branches. It was like some diabolic autumn, branches falling like leaves, except it wasn't autumn, it was May. The climate's gone to pot that's what it is.

I live up here alone. Down in the village they think I'm some sort of crazy woman, a witch probably, but I'm a bit young to be a witch. Can you have a 19 year old witch? Don't you have to be wrinkled before you qualify, transmogrify, metamorphose? Or perhaps witches don't become; they are born.

You'll have gathered that I haven't a clue about witchdom, wouldn't know a newt's testicle if I saw one, can't stand (being a vegetarian) entrails of any description – which ought to rule me out. As a witch I mean. I don't pass the test. Unless I'm faking it. That's probably what they say in the village. She's faking it, that one (nudge nudge), yeah her, coming out of the grocer's (stare stare.) By day, sure, butter wouldn't... but peer through her window at night...

I hope they don't. Christ, that would freak me out. Get up to put the kettle on and see this face peering in. Freako. I mean. It's one thing in a town, neighbours all around, someone to come running when you scream, but here, what're the sheep going to do? Gather into a big huddle and trample the intruder under their skinny little legs? I don't think so.

The freakiest place would be the bathroom, if I was in it of course, stark naked. Doesn't help does it, no clothes on, puts you at a disadvantage before you start. But the bathroom doesn't help either. It's just a single layer of bricks built on to the outside of the side wall. The overflow pipe goes straight out and the wind comes straight in. There are ripples on the bathwater, no kidding, so I like to fill it up and lie as much under the waves as I can.

Anyway, look, I'm 19 years old and I live up here in this stone cottage with paint peeling off the damp walls and a tidal bath stuck in a brick outhouse. The landlord is a farmer and in the old days this place used to be for one of the men. Now there's only him. He doesn't have a family either, but I don't see him much so I don't know whether he's living it up over there or leads the life of a monk. I doubt he's living it up somehow. Not the type. If you met him you'd know what I mean.

But, as I was telling you, it was one of those nights, howling wind, trees falling left right and centre, when I saw car lights playing on my window pane. I'm not on the main road. Not on any road at all to speak of. The road to and from the village turns round at the bottom of the hill and joins the by-pass they built years ago. To get to mine, you have to cross over a cattle grid and come up a grass path for a couple of miles. So car lights are not exactly run of the mill.

The lights came closer, and I'm starting to think, Christ what's this, who do I know who might be paying me a visit? I run through the list. It's not long. The farmer, Frank, though I can't imagine why he'd want to come out on a night like this. My sister, who I haven't seen for years. The baby's father, except that's all over with now, thank the Pope. Joe, who ought to have been the baby's father but didn't want to... After that I'm struggling to think of anybody. It doesn't say much for my life, I know, but that's just how things turned out. Which is not to say that my life will always be like this. I don't see why one day I shouldn't have friends like everybody else. It's not as if I'm actually a witch or anything else along similar lines. I'm perfectly normal or as normal as anybody would want to be. And, in case you're wondering, I'm not totally unattractive either. I have decent enough legs and a few have admired my slinky charms. The baby's father, not that he was a judge of anything, used to say my neck was good for seeing round corners.

The lights continued up the hill. I didn't sense it was the baby's father. I didn't feel that anger half strangling me, I didn't feel like I wished I was dead. I didn't sense it was Joe either. A visit from him would be a first. Which all went to making me a little nervous or, more *precisely, shitting myself.*

The lights came to within I don't know 20 yards and then went off. Black. Through the wind, I could just make out the sound of a car door slamming. Then another. Two of them? Then another. Christ, this is a fucking delegation, I thought. Now a second set of lights shone in my window and vanished. These came from lower down the hill. I worked out where from the angles. Over a mile away at least.

Heavy boots outside the door stamped up and down on the bit of gravel. Then a knock. I didn't know if I should open it, but I thought that if they wanted to come in badly enough they would, whether I opened it or not. I undid the catch and peered out. The wind was pretty crazy, so I didn't open the door more than a crack.

It was only Frank, the farmer, and another man about his age, wanting to know if I was all right, what with the wind and everything. I made it clear that I was fine. Then I thought I should offer them a cup of tea. 'T'? I mimed, using my fingers to make the letter. They looked at each other and nodded. Frank held the door so it didn't fly off its hinges and then slammed it behind him before half the field could blow in. They sat around the table while I boiled the kettle.

Well, I thought, since they'd bothered to come over, I should do my best to be polite at least, so I started talking, the usual small stuff, no I was fine, nice of them to come and check up on me, yes it was windy, all that sort of thing – well, they were farmers – and then a thought struck me.

'Where's the other one?'

'Other one what?' said Frank.

'Didn't three of you get out of the car?'

'Oh yes, that was Bill, he came up with us from the pub.'

'Where is he now then? Why isn't he here?' I had the crazy idea, don't know why, that he had stopped off in my bathroom and was having a soak.

'He took the car back. We told him we'd walk.'

'I didn't hear a car leave.'

I got up to have a look outside the window. No car, nothing visible

anyway. No sign of the other car either. I suddenly felt a bit nervous. Well, I was feeling nervous before. A bit more nervous.

'The wind,' said the other man. 'Can't hear yourself think in this.'

I sat back down at the table while the men drank their tea. I didn't know whether I wanted them to stay or to leave. Frank said, 'I see they've got him then. Fifteen years.'

'Got who?' *I asked.*

'The father of the baby, the one who said it'd died in its sleep.'

'What did the mother get?' *asked the other man.*

'Didn't hear. She said it had nothing to do with her. He was doing the looking after.'

'Did they believe her?'

'Must have done. The newspaper didn't say anything about her being banged up.'

'It's always the mother, whatever she may say,' *said the other man.*

'I think I've got a biscuit somewhere, if you'd like.'

'Thanks, that would be nice,' *said Frank.*

'How do you like living up here then? All on your own,' *asked the other man.*

'What's your name?' *I replied. At times I can be a bit frosty.*

'Oh, sorry,' *said Frank,* 'his name's Peter. He's my cousin. He owns the abattoir between here and...'

'Yes, I've seen it on the road.' *After that I couldn't think what to say. What is there to say about a place where they spend all day long electrocuting dumb animals, or cutting them into bits, or whatever it is they do? But I thought I should say something, so I said,* 'A lot of blood swilling about, is there? Must be, I imagine.'

The man shrugged. 'It's a living.'

I wasn't going to let him get away with that. If he was going to own a fucking slaughterhouse, the least he could do was come up with some reason better than just money. 'And if you didn't do it, someone else would, is that it?'

'It's not everyone's cup of tea, but the fact is people eat meat. Animals have to die and ours is a clean place. We give them as decent

an end as we can.'

'Hymns, flowers, comfort for the grieving relatives?'

'Not quite. Look,' said the man, 'I think we'd better be off.'

Frank nodded, put the rest of his biscuit in his mouth and stood up. Just then there was a knock at the door.

'A bit late for visitors,' he said.

I went to see who it was. If it was some friend of theirs come for a gang rape, I'd had it anyway. If it wasn't, I was glad these two big men were here with me. I held the door open against the wind with my foot and poked my head out.

A man emerged from the darkness, his hair blowing all over the place. He was a solid looking fellow, early 50s, maybe more, hard to tell in a suit. He had a hat in his hand, a soft felt thing with a bit of a brim. 'Excuse me,' he shouted over all the clatter that was going on out there, 'I hope I haven't frightened you, appearing like this at the dead of night.'

'You'd better come in,' I shouted back. He stepped inside and helped me close the door. I thought the wind might be calming down a bit, but it was still crazy.

When we'd straightened ourselves out, I said, 'This is Frank, this is Peter. And you are?'

'Martin... ' I didn't catch the rest of it but it didn't matter anyway.

'Look this is very good of you, inviting in a complete stranger. You'll want to know what I'm doing out here on a night like this. Well, the truth is I'm lost. I was on the bypass when I saw the sign to the village and I thought maybe there's a pub still open and I can get a sandwich or something. I haven't eaten all day, business, things to attend to, I just forgot. Anyway, I was on my way in when a tree came down in front of me. I swerved, came across a cattle grid and found myself in the middle of a field surrounded by sheep. I was a bit shaken, but then I saw some lights up ahead and thought I might as well follow the track towards them. It was a silly idea. Thoughtless. I don't know what I was thinking. I should go.'

'Have a biscuit at least.' I passed him a biscuit. He was a handsome man, silver-grey streaked hair now neatly in place, what you'd call

distinguished, I suppose. Also, strangely, familiar. A bit like my father would have been if he'd lived. He had a father's eyes, I thought, protective, forgiving. 'Let me get you something, since you've come this far. A couple of eggs, tomato? I'm not much of a cook, but I can fry.'

'Well, it's very kind of you, but I can't just turn up and get fed. No, thank you anyway.'

'Come on, how do you like them, sunny side up, over easy?'

'Well, if you're sure, really. Over easy would be perfect.'

'Toast, tea?'

'This is a feast,' he said. 'At least let me pay you.'

'We'll see about that.'

Frank and the other man had been about to leave when the knock on the door came. Since Martin had arrived, they'd sat down, stood up again, didn't know what to do.

Frank said, 'We should go really. Will you be all right?' This last was in a whisper. He looked across at Martin sitting at the table smoothing the hat in his lap, then back at me, his eyebrows raised in a question.

'I'll be fine, thank you,' I told him. I don't suppose I should have said that, not knowing the first thing about this stranger, but that was what I felt.

'Friends of yours?' Martin asked, when they'd gone.

'No. One's my landlord. The other's his cousin. I've never met him before. They just dropped by.'

'An odd time to come visiting.'

'You can talk,' I replied.

'Indeed,' he said laughing.

'They were checking to see I was okay.'

'Nice of them.'

'Yes, maybe.' I don't know why but I shuddered.

'Are you okay? Did they frighten you?'

'A little. Serves me right for living up here all on my own. Now... your eggs.'

I turned on the gas.

'Why do you?'

'I don't know really, or at least I do, but I'm not going to blurt it out in front of a complete stranger.'

'No, you're right. I've no business asking.'

I made him his food and put it in front of him. He was silent for a while as if saying some sort of prayer and then picked up his knife and fork. He ate slowly, carefully.

'Sometimes only silence will do. I imagine that's why you've come here.'

'Perhaps.'

'Sometimes you have to be so alone that nothing, no distractions, no comments, no judgements, can come between you and the thing in question.'

'What thing is that?'

'That's something which it wouldn't be proper for me to ask about.'

I busied myself with adjusting the chairs. I knew that if he pressed me only a little more it would all come blurting out, all my secrets. I began to cry. He stood up. I was close to him, close enough to rest my head on his chest. He held me with one hand and with the other undid the clasp in my hair. It tumbled down and he stroked it.

We stayed like that for a while until I looked up at him and such was the need in me that I suppose he had no choice but to bend and put his lips to mine. He had the kiss of a baby, his lips touching mine with such exquisite softness that I had to take his head in my hand and lead it down to my breast. He knelt down, opened my blouse and released me. When my nipple was free before him, I let him take it in his mouth and draw me to him with his soft lips. He sucked me out then, all that I had to give, all that had remained for so long ungiven.

Suzanna: loves

Back at her flat, she is in a frenzy for him; she can't wait to get his clothes off him and get into bed with him and feel him all over. She thought those days of passion had gone for her, but now she has this picture of what she is going to do to him and what he is going to do to her, and the heat is something she hasn't felt forever, has never felt with Rokas.

So they get into bed, or she drags him in, and she holds him and he wants it all right and she waits for him to come on top of her, or behind her or however he wants to do it, when he smells something on the sheet and he goes all limp in her hand and he says, Was Rokas here, in this bed? Of course he was here, she replies. We were lovers, you know that. We have to change the sheets, he says. I can't fuck you while I'm breathing him in, he's my friend, it wouldn't be right, it'd be like I was fucking him. She looks at him like he's gone mad and he says, I just can't that's all.

So she gets out of bed while he stares at the ceiling thinking god knows what and she finds fresh sheets and he gets out and watches her as she makes the bed, all naked herself. Doesn't help or anything, just watches.

Right, she says, clean sheets. They get back in and they hold each other but he isn't with her any more. He is away somewhere. She tries everything, hand, mouth, she strokes him all over, soothes him, tells him it is all okay it doesn't matter not at all, and this seems to perk him up and he gets over her and she thinks, yes, at last, once we start... but they don't start, he lies back down and says, He's here, I can see him, he's watching us, I see him in your eyes, he's staring at me. It's me staring, she says as gently as she can, not Rokas and even if he was watching, he wouldn't mind, he isn't jealous, that's not him at all.

It does no good. I'm sorry Suzanna, he says, I just can't. Not tonight. Maybe tomorrow. Let's sleep now and see how it goes.

She eyes him sort of sideways and says, That's okay, lover boy, and she shouldn't have said that she knows, but it just comes out and he gets up from the bed and gets himself dressed and goes.

She doesn't know whether to laugh or cry, but she feels his pain right enough so she supposes she wants to cry for him and also for herself, because she had such desire for him and look where it has got her, to nothing, to an empty bed. Nothing. Always nothing. Always emptiness.

Come next morning, and she knows she can't stop there because it is like they are on a bridge crossing a river and the bridge has broken in front of them and behind and the only way forward or back is to rebuild it. They can't just leave it sawn off in mid-air.

She goes round to his place. She thinks of bringing him something, a book perhaps, or a flower, but she doesn't know how he'll take it, if he might think she's insulting him. So she brings him nothing, just herself. He comes down to the door, not looking like he's slept much and all dishevelled. She hasn't slept much either and they are both in a bit of a state. She says to him, Stephen? not knowing what she is going to say after that but he just takes her hand and leads her in. Then he undresses her and fucks her, does it very gently and nice and after that he makes her tea.

There are words to be said she supposes, but she doesn't want to say them and nor does he. They are where they are and how they got there doesn't matter much. Except it does in a way. It is like the punctuation of their love affair. How it is framed makes a difference. At first she doesn't know what the difference is and then it comes to her. Rokas has joined them, they are a threesome again and, when they are in bed, Rokas is there as well. Stephen feels him there and she does, too.

She thinks at first it will all go away, that they'll build up a routine together and that Rokas will just fade out. But he doesn't. He is everywhere – and he can't be got rid of because the less

Stephen wants him there, the more he is.

Stephen holds his head. Why can't he just leave us alone, why can't he get on with his own life? It's all in your head my love, she says, there's no-one watching us, no spirit, no ghost, just your imagination. No, he says, you don't get it, Rokas is actually here, actually, physically. And he points. Points at the room and his arm swings round. Points at her. She knows then, just knows, that Stephen needs Rokas more than he needs her, that he can't exist without him, that Rokas is the mirror in which Stephen looks to see his own reflection.

Somehow they keep on and, since he wants children as she does, she doesn't take any precautions and hopes with a bit of luck she might get pregnant, have a little baby to look after. And when that happens, it'll all be fine.

She misses her period a month after they get together and, even though it's too soon to get excited, she knows she is pregnant. She tells Stephen, thinking he'll be pleased, but he only says, Whose baby is it? What do you mean, we've been screwing every night since we met, whose baby do you think it is? He says, It doesn't feel like my baby. I feel I'm sharing him with Rokas. It might even be his entirely.

Well, Christ, I've hitched myself to a crazy man, she thinks. She doesn't know what to do. Stay with him or clear out. She stays. She sees his madness and she looks away.

One evening, they've just finished eating. She's cooked him something good, she thinks, made a real effort with it, and they are sitting around the table in the flat. He takes out some wood he's brought home and begins whittling on it. He has this big Porphyrian knife he uses for his carvings and he is gouging away with it, so she asks him what he's making. Rokas, he says, and when I've got him just right, so no-one can mistake him for anyone else, I'll make a fire and burn him. Good, she says, it'll do you good. Get it out, get rid of it all. Get rid of what? he replies. Get rid of Rokas, of course. Oh, I can't do that, he says, not now he's growing within you, that would require a bigger bonfire altogether.

She's scared. She puts on her coat. She doesn't know where she's going, she just walks and before long finds herself outside the polotti hall. She goes in then, though she knows it's no place for a woman, that polotti hall. But she goes in anyway. She is hardly through the door when this big man comes up to her and asks her if she wants a drink. No, she says, I'm not here to drink, I'm here to win some money on the polotti table. He laughs. No one believes women can play polotti. Strange, isn't it? Well, okay, that's fine she thinks, makes the odds better for me. She is steady on her feet by this time and now she is at the polotti hall she thinks she might as well make the most of it.

So the big man calls to the person who's hitting balls up and down the table and says, Hey, Jim, there's a little lady here wants to make some money at polotti. He gives her the once-over and says, Okay she can try, how much? 50 eurars, she says, straight game. Are you sure you've got it? I've got it, she says, have you?

They both put their money up. You hold it, she says to the big man. She has to trust someone. So the big man holds the money and they play. Jim is okay but he can't feel the table. Stephen would take him easily. She takes him easily. At the end of the game, she puts out her hand to the big man and he gives her the 100 eurars. Thank you, she says, and now I'm going home.

She starts to leave and then she notices a couple of men get up. She thinks they might follow her out. The big man thinks so, too. He says, Don't worry, I'll walk you home. She thanks him. Well, you have to trust somebody.

When they get close to her flat, she tells him he's been very kind, but she can't ask him in because her husband is the jealous type and won't understand. That's okay, he says, and walks away.

When she comes through the door, Stephen is still whittling. Where've you been? he asks. At the polotti hall. Look what I won. She takes out the 100 eurars. He looks at her and he looks at the money, and then he hits her across the face; he just flares up and hits her, and after that he goes to their bed and she thinks she hears him crying. But maybe he isn't crying, maybe he's being sick inside himself, sick to his guts.

The strange thing is that she knows then that he loves her, knows it for sure. He doesn't know what to do with his love, that's his problem. A kind of impotence, she supposes, but his love is real, she has no doubt of that. Just all choked up inside him with nowhere to go.

That blow on her cheek, the flat of his hand coming across and catching her square, but not full force or she wouldn't be standing up, makes her understand that they'll always be passionate, him and her, passionate in the way that the word is meant, all tangled up together, inseparable, no way out, no way in all that passion of finding release.

She sleeps on the sofa that night, and in the morning she tells him to leave. He doesn't argue about it, just says, I love you. I know you do, she tells him, but it's better this way. He nods. And then she says to him, she doesn't know why – she doesn't even know what she's saying – I can't have you killing it again. Such a strange word to use, *again*. Well, the whole thing is strange, but what is even stranger is that he seems to know what she means.

Suzanna: loves (continued)

She has a baby coming and what she needs is a mother to tell her it will all be okay. Helen opens the door to her, as she knows she will, puts her arms out and she just rushes into them as if she is 16 again. Helen seems to know her whole story before she even says a word, though Suzanna does tell her, both the good and the bad of it.

She can't stay there, not for long, because Helen has taken in three teenagers, all girls, and she and the baby, when it comes, will be the last thing she needs. Still, Helen gives her what she's always given her: a feeling that she belongs on this earth, that it is hers as much as anyone's and that, so long as things come from her heart, there's no right way and wrong way.

Helen hopes she'll get back with Rokas again – she doesn't say as much, but she doesn't hide it either – and Suzanna hopes this, too. He is my love for all seasons, she thinks, my love through thick and thin. I knew that even when I was with Stephen. I've always known that.

She goes to see Rokas, her heart thumping inside her as she walks, wondering how he'll receive her. He has every right to throw her out. Part of her thinks he will, and part of her, the part that remembers him for what he is, knows that he won't.

His house is in the old part of town, in a street of poor cottages, stone walls with tin roofs most of them, ramshackle and unsightly to those whose eyes were open in earlier days. Rokas' is similarly decrepit but pleasant somehow, even to her, even in the mood she is in then with her heart going like the clappers.

She knocks on the door and waits. He takes his time, big heavy steps taking an age to put her out of her misery, or into it. Then there he is. He doesn't say anything, just leads her into his one large room in which the necessary objects of his life are scattered: a bed covered with knitted blankets: a wooden table on which a torn crust of heavy bread is half-eaten and a bottle of beer opened and half-drunk: his old half-stuffed sofa: a corner where he works, sectioned off by a clothes line draped in sheets: and, on one side, but without a door or anything like that, a sort of kitchen area with an iron stove and a frying pan with the charred remains of fried egg still in it. She remembers how his place has always been a bit chaotic, but now she has the sense that the room and Rokas are returning to some sort of natural state, though she doesn't know what she means by that, not really, except that things have changed since she left.

He sits her on the sofa and they look at each other, neither of them speaking for a while. 'I've missed you,' he says. 'Are you coming back?'

She tells him she will if he'll have her. Then she corrects herself. 'If you'll have *us*.' He takes her in his arms then and she knows she's come safe home.

They don't make love after that, not physical love, but when she holds him she knows they are lovers in the real true sense, and she breathes out again and lets the world, which she's been sucking towards her like she's some great black hole in the universe, go on its way as it will.

'Seen anything of Stephen?' she asks one evening.

Rokas looks at her. 'Not at the factory. He might be on some special project for Porphyrian.'

'What sort of project?'

Rokas shrugs. 'No idea.'

'Must be important if it's for Porphyrian.'

'If it is for Porphyrian.'

'You should have a drink with him one evening, find out if he's okay.'

Rokas says he will, but she knows he won't.

Stephen no longer comes to the bar to hear her play. Where is he? How is he? She scrolls back in her mind to what passed between them. She looks for clues. What did he see in me? Just desire? Nothing more? That I was with his best friend? Did that make it exciting? Perhaps that's what it was, she says to herself but, at the same time, she feels there was something else, something that went beyond what was real, as if the idea that he must have her was more important to him than the having itself.

And then when she did open herself to him there was all that dither. She imagines his wanting as a bubble coming out of his head and then the bubble bursts and he finds himself with a real woman, a real prize that he's stolen from his friend, a real fucking which he has to do with Rokas looking on. And which he can't, the poor man, not really.

She feels calm thinking about it, but greyed out at the edges, as if the sky is low and dull and she's beneath it, wondering if it will rain. What must that have been like for him? All his wanting and then his moment of having so brief. So brief! Or *half-having* it was really and, before the moment has even elapsed, the not-having. It must have felt as if the not-having was his destiny, and the rest just an interlude, the most he could hope for. Well not-having is something she knows about and she knows how sad it is, no other way of looking at it, just sad.

She goes up to the polotti hall once to see if he is there. She is going to go in if he is and ask him to come to the bar one evening when she is playing. She puts her head in the door and sees him at the table, hustling. He looks rough, unshaven. There are bottles of home brew on a table beside him. She doesn't know if he is winning or losing. She doubts if he knows. She doesn't go in. Perhaps she should have, but he is in his own world, forgetting as much of his other lives as he can, and he doesn't want her bringing them back to him.

Then just when she's given him up, there's a knock on the door of her flat and there he is, back as if nothing much has happened. A bit redder in the eye, a bit wary perhaps, the sudden almost bashful looking-down that she doesn't remember from before, but otherwise the same. The same and not the same. His smile still has the old wild charm to it but, at its edge, an almost defiant tilt; nothing much at all, but what she sees it as – what she knows it to be – is a memento of his humiliation. It makes her want to stroke it away, to take him in her arms like a baby and tell him it is okay, really it is okay, it was just a moment, nobody died.

He doesn't say, either then or later, where he's been or why or what he's been feeling; he just comes back. She doesn't know if he thinks he's wrestled with his demons and come out ahead, or just buried them deep. Whatever, they are a threesome again, a little tentative at first but together – that is the main thing. He comes to the bar as he did before and chats to Rokas pleasantly enough from what she can see. They even go to the polotti together. The big man is there who helped her. She points him out to Stephen, and he goes over and buys the man a drink. She is proud of him in a way for behaving so well.

Stephen takes up with Angie on and off, and they are just as they'd been before, except she has a life inside her that is growing, Rokas has what Rokas always has, his papers, his journey, and Stephen has all his Rokas stuff and his passions and his knots and everything else. She has no doubt these will come out somehow. Everything leaves a trace or, perhaps, uncovers a trace: exposes what is hidden and hangs it out in the open to fizz.

Still, were someone to ask her, she would say they are happy, that they are friends again and that they have a baby on its way with two fathers to welcome it into the world. This seems okay to her, unusual perhaps, but okay and, as far as she can tell, okay to Rokas and to Stephen. They are happy, as happy as they can be, really they are.

And then Porphyrian comes.

Porphyrian

Porphyrian's Touring Tiger advances down Stanley Street with a motorcade behind it. His flags fronting the bonnet flutter like the fingers of devotion. The crowds lining the pavements chant the god-name as he passes: *Porphyrian Porphyrian*. Behind his bullet-proof window, Porphyrian waves, a discreet and understated wave. A faint expression plays on his lips, though what the expression is, whether of mild pleasure or of its opposite, even its extreme opposite, is impossible to tell.

In a fit of exuberance, a family man with several children throws his very special hat in the air – and why not? Not every day God is in town. The hat rises majestically, displays its imitation sable to all who look up, gets caught on a sudden gust of wind, flies over the bridge on which four splendid horses expose their eight enormous balls as they have done for every minute of every day for the last few hundred years, and disappears into the river, down which it floats until caught on a sandbank, where it will become a nesting place for the last surviving family of Ferruginous Duck[7].

The man gazes after his hat and is overcome with yearning, with loss – it was a present from someone, a lover obviously – so that when Porphyrian looks in his direction he sees, not joy, not exuberance, but sadness. This causes him to reflect. He inclines his head towards his mistress whose thighs on the leather upholstery touch his own and says, 'My dear, there is sadness even here, where I have fed them and clothed them, provided education and pleasure, and given them life.'

To which she replies, 'Do not expect gratitude.' She is a tall woman and 20 years younger than he is.

The car drives slowly through the town. It passes the old opera house, where someone has put up faded posters from the last time the place was packed, the time when the great German tenor, Möbius, sang all the favourites to rapturous applause and expired on stage after producing an effortless top C in that most famous of arias, *To whom out there it may concern*. 'He sang in many splendid cities,' declared the Trumpeter, 'but will die in only one!'

The opera buffs are gathered in a clump beneath the posters and hold aloft two placards. One reads, 'Let your money sing.' The other is a cartoon showing coins tumbling out of a sow's ear and into a silk purse. The purse is singing: *To whom out there it may concern*. Porphyrian hums to himself, a song from his youth.

The crowds thin as the car passes the Corinthian pillars of the house of the Conways, but are no less enthusiastic. They wave the official photograph of the young, future-gazing Porphyrian, full-haired and strong as a light heavyweight, not to be tangled with.

Porphyrian reflects on the singers of days gone by... *Tenors get women by the score*, he recalls, now where did I read that? Good though. True, too, I should think, when they go down on one knee and serenade. Weren't the Conways the power about the place long ago? Now look. Just a museum, mock up of the old chemist shop I shouldn't wonder, the flesher's, the candle-maker's, all that.

And me? Is that what they think of me: a museum piece? Porphyrian's jaws hang loose in reflection, his mind flashes backwards – scenes shot in mist and in the dark – his teeth snap shut. 'Driver! Pearl Street!'

So he interrupts his dreams – and is interrupted in turn by his mistress, who has picked up his transmissions thigh to thigh. She turns so that her hand brushes as if by accident his upper leg. She looks up into his still blue eyes and smiles.

They come eventually to the gates that lead to the factory, where they are greeted by thin sunshine sparkling on highly polished toecaps and a synchronised salute from a guard of 10 who have been practising hard. A few minutes later the cavalcade reaches the front entrance. The official photograph of his youth gazes out from left pillar and right. A red carpet runs back to the arriving car. The carpet is lined by the chief officers of the company, with Rokas and Stephen to the side.

Porphyrian steps out, stared at by his younger self, receiver and transmitter suddenly juxtaposed. Time is tricky, he thinks. He reaches back for the hand of his mistress and helps her down. The mistress looks about her as if taking the measure of her underlings.

'Hello, Stephen,' says Porphyrian turning his gaze.

Stephen doesn't know why he's been singled out. He is suddenly fearful. He nods his head, a nod which would have been a bow if he had let it continue.

Porphyrian moves into the factory, passes down corridors. The rest follow. The lights dim, the show begins, Porphyrian centre stage.

The company's finances, its numbers which capture in their sterile fingers the great conglomerate's beating heart, its past, its present and its future, have been processed into arrows, their lines of flight piercing the dusty dark. They start in an unseen corner, they rise, higher, ever up, go stratospheric and… what is this? how can it be?… they seem to pause, to hover, and then – as if reprimanded for their presumption by some Greater Power above – to plunge. And so a gasp from those below, a question that dares not speak its mind, but a question nonetheless: who, when the arrows fall to earth, will be impaled?

Porphyrian faces his audience. The light returns. 'The Pistolette is dragging us down,' he says. 'You've seen the figures. I love the Pistolette. It puts power in the hands of women, physical power I mean, equal power, and I won't apologise for that. Yet, now, because of a few saboteurs, I, you, all of us, are under attack. Not from the press – they are holding their tongues – but from the public. "Porphyrian has sold us this Pistolette," they think, "and innocent people are dying". Many have stopped buying from us. Many have stopped trusting us. "If Porphyrian and his companies have killed this many, what's to stop them killing this many more?" And once trust goes, so does the company, so do all of you who work here, so do all those who depend on us. We must reverse this. It is not yet too late. We need to understand what has caused this disaster. We need to make changes and, if there are those among us who have made mistakes, we need, for the sake of us all, to bring them to book. But my first task is to listen. I will listen to you all, but I shall listen most particularly, as is only fair, to the man who designed the Pistolette.'

As he leaves the room, Porphyrian cups his hands to his ears and turns his beguiling, dangerous eyes to the giant who lingers at the back. The giant observes, with as much detachment as he can manage, the pinpricks of fear in his stomach.

The Trial of Rokas

Proudly Rokas stands in the dock. From where does his pride come? Is it rooted in blood or in spirit? If in blood, from where does his blood come? Rokas doesn't know. He thinks his mother was a bear. And if in spirit, from where again? For the embodied, like Rokas, this is a greater unknown.

Still, he knows this: in times of trouble it is to mother you turn. He turns to his. He feels her soft fur warming him now as she warmed him once before when he was most in need of it. He tastes her milk on his lips and smacks them. Thus fortified, he straightens his back another notch. How tall he is, how incomprehensibly tall. He looks down on those seated before him, looks from such a height that it might almost be as if his spirit has risen to the ceiling and surveys the doings beneath and his lifeless body with equal and eternal equanimity.

They are in a small and sparse room. To Porphyrian's left sits his mistress, to his right, Stephen. Rokas notices a resemblance between Stephen and Porphyrian. Is this a resemblance of the spirit, he wonders, is this the family to which Stephen belongs? He entertains the possibility that it is, that it isn't. 'Hmm,' he thinks.

From behind a table, Porphyrian speaks. 'Be at ease,' says Porphyrian. He pauses, eyes Rokas reflectively. 'Sabotage is a serious business. Deadly. Expensive. Hence this... this...'

'Trial?' softly, inquisitively, interjects Rokas.

'If you like. Yes, you could call it a trial, trying to us both no doubt, but I'd say this is more like a conversation, an exploration. You can sit if you like.'

Rokas, like the trees in the forest, prefers to stand.

'Well now, Rokas, you will understand that my first task is to get to the bottom of what's happening, to get behind the special pleading and the excuses, and to find the truth.'

Rokas thinks, Who knows the truth? Is it: a) Porphyrian. b) Rats. c) Those out there it may concern. 'I'll do my best to help,' he says.

'Thank you. So, first of all, is it your belief that the Pistolette is being sabotaged? Might it be technical deficiencies, might it be inept programming? What's your opinion?'

'We haven't found technical issues of any sort.'

'Have you looked thoroughly?'

'We've investigated the Pistolette from top to bottom. There's nothing wrong with it. The Pistolette works fine.'

'So?'

'So I believe it's sabotage. The fact that *Porphyrian* is the trigger word suggests motive.'

'Indeed,' says Porphyrian, 'indeed it does.' He pauses, drinks from a glass, puts down the glass and sits back in his chair. He regards Rokas in silence. A question comes to him. He attempts to find the answer in Rokas' face. He lets the question frame itself. 'You told me once that you would only design guns for self-defence.'

'I did, sir.'

'And I respected that. Have you ever been asked to design anything else?'

'No.'

'Yet now the Pistolette, which you designed for the protection of women, is killing people, killing them at random, killing the innocent as well as the guilty. What do you think of that?'

'I am deeply troubled. I believe this will weigh me down when my time comes.'

'You believe in Judgement?'

'I believe that my spirit will live on after my body passes away and that, in its next lives, will carry with it the unresolved burdens of this one.'

'And you worry that the Pistolette is an unresolved burden... well, I wouldn't know about that, but isn't it the case that these deaths aren't the fault of the weapon but the fault of those who use the weapon? Anything can be used for bad ends as well as good. Is this not so?'

'I comfort myself with this thought.'

'So what is it about the Pistolette that troubles you?'

Rokas doesn't answer.

'Well, perhaps if I may suggest… ' says Porphyrian. He pauses in case Rokas wishes to interject. He does not. '… Isn't it the conflicts within which trouble us all, much more than anything which happens without? You, my dear Rokas, are a man who wishes to save lives but a man who works in the service of an arms manufacturer, indeed an arms manufacturer of ill-repute, a manufacturer, some say, of untold evil.' Porphyrian smiles. It is a smile of self-deprecation, not intended to be taken seriously. 'This must create tension within you, does it not?'

Rokas shakes his head from side to side in oblique acknowledgement.

'Well, we are all conflicted, who isn't after all, we are all human… but when the conflicted man is a designer of guns… he works hard, does his best, but underneath, deep in his unconscious, the contradictions, the opposing forces of red and blue, battle away inside… they must, mustn't they, don't you agree?'

Rokas says nothing.

'So then,' continues Porphyrian, 'this Pistolette is sold to many hundreds and thousands of women. They love it. They see it as a boon, as something they need; in this society, something that is needed more than ever. The designer is pleased. He has done women a favour. He has protected them. He is a man who wishes to save lives, so of course he is pleased. And yet… out of all the products being sold every day, the saboteurs choose this one to sabotage. Just this one. Which makes me ask; is there something in the design of the Pistolette which cries out to the saboteur, "sabotage me, sabotage me"?

'And of course there must be. How else can the sabotage be

explained? Why else is the saboteur enticed?

'And from where does this fatal flaw in the design of the Pistolette come? It comes, it can only come, from the contradictions hidden deep within the designer, a designer who only wishes to develop guns for self-defence! How laudable this is. Laudable, but surface-deep. If we probe further, as we must, do we not discover, my dear Rokas, that our designer knows that there will always be deaths from what he does, inevitable deaths. Guns are guns after all... and that the only way to avoid deaths from guns is to have no guns at all. A gun-free world. A world without those who manufacture arms. This is so, isn't it?'

'This would be one solution certainly, but... '

Porphyrian puts up his hand. '... So our designer has, deep within him, the unconscious, unknown, never articulated desire to see our company, like all other arms manufacturers, come to an end. Not articulated, deeply subconscious, but there it is right enough, working away down below. And so, and so, this man designs in such a way as to encourage the saboteur to sabotage. What better way to bring down the company? Perhaps even,' – Porphyrian pauses as if the thought has just struck him – 'perhaps the designer even does the sabotage himself... Or perhaps not. Who can say. But what can be said is that this man, this designer, is – unknown even to himself – a dangerous man...'

Porphyrian pauses, watches. Reflectively, almost inclusively, he adds, 'You see, Rokas, how easy it might be for me to presume that, in our little armaments company you are, how shall I put it, a loose cannon.'

'I am loyal to you, Mr Porphyrian. I always have been.'

'I am glad to hear this, truly I am. But let me ask you one last question. Have you ever been approached? You know many of the company's secrets. Has anyone tried to woo you away? Or offered you money?'

'No.'

'No?'

Rokas thinks. He wonders what Porphyrian knows. He assumes Porphyrian knows everything. He says, 'I was approached once some years ago. I told the man to go away, that I wasn't interested. He never bothered me again.'

'Why didn't you tell us? At the time.'

'I didn't tell you because it wasn't important. Nothing happened.'

'But, if it wasn't important, you would have told us.'

'You are a busy and powerful man, Mr Porphyrian. I wouldn't bother you with things that didn't matter.'

'No, you wouldn't, I suppose. That's right, I can see that... but let me think this over. We can meet again when I've come to a decision. Lives are at stake. We mustn't rush to judgement.'

Without further word, Porphyrian leaves the room, his mistress following behind.

Rokas imagines rats escaping from a water maze. He wonders if all the rats escape. He watches one gasping for air. The rat watches him. They say hello over the thought waves.

Rokas escapes

On the departure of Porphyrian, Rokas remains, his weight sinking into the carpet, his body erect. He asks, 'What shall I do?'

'Run!' Stephen comes towards him and grabs his arm. 'Run, my friend, run now. Run while you still can.'

'Do you think he'll decide against me?'

'He already has. Porphyrian doesn't like risks, not if he can avoid them. You're a risk.'

'Am I? Why am I?'

'Wrong question... Because you might be. That's enough for him.'

'And if I stay?'

Stephen shakes his head, says nothing. Nothing needs to be said.

'What about Suzanna?'

'You can leave her to me. I'll look after her, don't worry.'

'And the baby?'

'I'll look after the baby, too... it is mine after all.'

Rokas smiles at that. It's something he's forgotten. 'You're a good man,' he says and he puts his arms around Stephen to thank him and he kisses him on both cheeks because he doesn't believe he'll see him again.

Rokas doesn't go back to Suzanna, doesn't feel her in his arms one last time, for his sake and for hers. He returns to his flat, draws the curtains and packs a small hold-all. In it he puts only those things he cannot live without: some food, Suzanna's picture, his papers, a collapsible hunting rifle and a few books. He leaves through a hatch in the roof and, crouching low behind a dummy gable, comes out at the end of the street. He steps down on a window ledge and a drainpipe and, aping unconcern, hops a tram to the outskirts. Once off the tram, he walks reflectively, expecting a bullet in his back.

Porphyrian's proposal

'Come in, come in.' Porphyrian grasps Stephen's hand in his and doubles his other palm over. Stephen feels energy, alternating currents of warm and cold. 'We have much to discuss,' says Porphyrian and, seeing Stephen's uncertainty, adds, 'Ah, but we have. Come, sit down.' He opens his palm towards the centre of the room.

Stephen moves over silk carpets, past ornaments in ivory and bronze, towards an ornate wooden chair with a steep, carved back depicting, so he thinks, columns criss-crossing city streets. Power is in the air and Stephen inhales. He enjoys the breath of it; and within himself, like an old friend who hasn't been around for a while, desire stirs.

'You were an *Academy* boy, were you not?' asks Porphyrian.

'I was, sir, yes.'

'I knew it. I can always tell.'

Stephen senses opportunity. He senses danger. He is a hustler and knows the signs. He waits. The hustler knows how to wait.

'I'm 70, you know,' says Porphyrian.

'That's hard to believe, sir.'

'Well it is and it isn't, but thank you anyway. I'm 70 and I have no children. Neither my wife nor my mistress were able to give me any. That's how things turned out. No use complaining, but it is a sadness.'

Stephen locks his face in neutral. Waits.

'I don't want to see the business I have created squabbled over by pretenders, run down by incompetents, broken up, sold off, turned to ashes. I want it to live on after I have gone. When you are 70, you think about such things.'

Stephen nods in acknowledgement.

'So for some years now, I've been looking around to see who, within my company, has the loyalty, the brains and the guts to become my heir. I haven't seen many. Running this company provides all the compensations a man could wish for, but it is not for the squeamish. The things I've had to do in building this enterprise have not always been pleasant, sometimes most unpleasant – it's one of the crosses I've had to bear – but the question I've always asked myself is this: is our society better off with Porphyrian, or without? And when I look around at things as they are – not as they might be one day, not as they could be in Rokas' perfect world, but as they are now – I say, yes, society needs Porphyrian. Without Porphyrian what is there but chaos?'

Stephen listens, anticipates, calculates, but keeps his counsel.

'I had high hopes of Rokas, you know. I trusted him. I empowered him. I thought his scruples would melt away as he grew. Well, we all make mistakes... but I didn't expect betrayal. That's the last thing I expected. And now he's gone off to the forest where he'll lie low for a while and then sell himself to the highest bidder. He'll get a good price if we don't stop him; those with scruples always do.

'But that's Rokas. We'll come back to him. What about you, Stephen? I've been watching you for some time. You have the brains undoubtedly. I've seen how you work in the factory, little tweaks here, little tweaks there. You listen to the machines. You understand them as I did years ago when I was starting out. You remind me of myself you know, a fixer, a man who can get things done. And you have the bottle, of course you do, you were one of the first of my *Porphyrian Pups* – you won't flinch when it comes to it. But loyalty, Stephen, that I don't know. Perhaps you have it, perhaps you don't. I shall have to put you to the test, you understand that don't you? I can't consider you for what I have in mind without first testing your mettle.'

'May I ask what exactly you have in mind?'

'I'm thinking of moving you up the organisation, preparing you – I make no promises, be clear about that – preparing you for the day I step aside. I want to give you a chance to prove yourself.'

'Thank you,' says Stephen. 'This is unexpected.'

'Is it? I don't think so. Not really. You've been reading the signs I'm sure, the promotions, the pay-rises. And from the moment you came in, you expected me to offer you something. I'm a hustler, too, you know.'

Stephen laughs. 'I imagine you're pretty good.'

'Not bad,' he says. 'But it's a pleasure to see you laughing again, Stephen. You had a hard time of it with Suzanna, didn't you?'

'I did.'

'I worried about you for a while, wondered if you'd come through. Are you over it now?'

'I think so.'

'Do you want her back? She's carrying your child, I imagine you do.'

'I do.'

'But Rokas stands in your way.'

'She loves him.'

'And you love him too, do you not?'

'I do. I suppose I do.'

'But while Rokas is around, Suzanna will never come back to you. Isn't that right?'

'Rokas has gone.'

'Come, come, Stephen, you don't believe that. Rokas will always be in her head as long as he's up in the forest. In your head, too.'

'Yes.'

'And if you were to do anything to remove him, he might be in your head forever. Then again, if you don't, he will hang over both of you until you can stand it no longer. It's a quandary.'

'It's a quandary I shall have to live with. Rokas is a friend.'

'So he is, so he is. And so you set rules, boundaries: beyond this line I will not go. Is that it?'

'Yes, sir, more or less, I suppose it is.'

'Very commendable. Of course where the line is drawn depends, doesn't it? Circumstances, inclinations: all these change. To win back a wife or child, for example, or indeed to protect yourself, there might be things you'd do...'

'Maybe.'

'There would be, of course there would. Lines are moveable. Always have been. I daresay there are things you did as a young man, you might not do so readily today. Or perhaps, should the circumstances arise, you might jump to them. It's hard to know, isn't it?'

Stephen says nothing.

'So, let us imagine... let us pretend for a moment that Rokas is no more. Suppose he died, let us say mysteriously, no one knows how. Can you not then conceive of a moment when Suzanna might want you again? The child will need a father, she'll know that. And fathers can be lovers, too.

'And if you progress in this company, as I believe you will, you will have great wealth, great power. Power you know is sometimes irresistible to women. It makes them forget things they believed themselves incapable of forgetting. It is possible, indeed probable, that before long Suzanna will think, "I live in a dangerous world... without Stephen, what will happen to my baby, what will happen to me?" And from such unworthy thoughts, Stephen, love grows. I'm 70, I know.'

Stephen, his eyes opening to the future, imagines.

'I've sent helicopters out to look for him. They might catch him if they get lucky, but I doubt it. Rokas'll be hiding with the Tribals by now. He'll only show himself to someone he trusts. To you, Stephen. He'll show himself to you. I want you to find him. He is a criminal.' Porphyrian looks intently at Stephen and, without changing the set of his eyes, strikes the table. *Bang.* Stephen flinches, startled in his gut, swamped by the vibrations of the table and of the man. 'He knows too many of the company's secrets. I want you to flush him out, Stephen. Understand?'

The room has gone cold. Stephen awaits another word. The room needs it. He needs it. Porphyrian leans back, speaks softly, persuasively, 'And should he die in an accident in the forest, or should the men in the helicopters be too quick to use their guns... ' He looks at Stephen knowingly. 'But if... ' Porphyrian pauses once more, '... if you do manage to return him to me, I will look after him.'

Stephen gathering himself says, 'You mean you'll kill him.'

'No. Not if you don't want me to. I will deprive him of oxygen, take away his work, take away the things that make him what he is. Then you can observe Suzanna and see her love for him wither. She won't stay his for long, believe me... or don't believe me; imagine it for yourself. You can read the future as well as the next man. Better, I hope, if the day is to come when you succeed me. '

'And if I don't go after him? If I don't bring him back?'

'Ah,' says Porphyrian standing up and putting his arm around Stephen's shoulder as he shows him to the door, 'you see loyalty, my dear Stephen, real in-the-guts loyalty, the kind of loyalty that I expect of you, is a rare and precious commodity. It is rare and precious because it has consequences... consequences if you give it... and consequences if you don't. But I'm sure you know that.'

The door closes behind him.

Stephen and Suzanna

Stephen's feet take him slowly along.

His desires are like marked cards that have been fingered once too often: sullied, exposed to the gaze of every passer-by and yet, inexplicably, hidden from himself. He doesn't know which moves him more, Porphyrian's temptation or his threat. Or neither: to be done with him altogether, to be free. But where, how? What would he do? – ambush passers-by for the price of a drink?

He walks, he hardly knows where, each step a working and a reworking of his future. He thinks of Suzanna and his need for her blessing.

His feet carry him over the cobbles of Paulician Street with its humps, its windings, its stoops and its ancient peeling lampposts. He passes the old houses at the top of the hill, and descends by those whose paint is less fresh or without paint at all, whose wood and windows show their disappointment. All the doors of the houses are set back up stone stairs. One or two people are sitting out under the light of their own cigarettes, even though the temperature is a few degrees below. He nods to them and they nod or wave in reply.

He stands under a lamppost and lights a cigarette of his own. A single snowflake flutters downwards and lands on his boot. Soon it is snowing heavily, crystal webs of pristine white spun by some cold god above and let to fall. Unless booted out. The devil comes in many colours, thinks Stephen. The flakes swirl about him and settle on his hair and coat. He moulds a snowball in his hands and throws it aimlessly. It rolls, grows bigger under its own velocity and stops. Snow descends upon it and soon its separate form is lost, swallowed up in the greater white around it.

Rokas is gone, swallowed up in the forest. But what is *gone*? If he were to make love to Suzanna again, if Suzanna were to have him back, not now but later, perhaps years later, would he be gone then? Or watching? And if he was dead… ? What then? And if he'd had a hand in that death, even a distant hand, hardly a hand at all… ?

'Stephen? Is that you?'

Coming down steps towards him, wrapped in fur, is the mother of his child to be. 'It is you. I looked out and thought it was. So I came down.'

'Come and have a drink,' he says. 'There's a place on the corner, isn't there?'

'Yes, but I've never been inside.'

The bar is a drinker's bar, men mainly and silent when they come in, as if the regulars don't like to speak in the presence of strangers. Heads turn towards them and then turn away. Stephen greets the man behind the bar cheerfully and smiles around him. He calls out to Suzanna, 'What would you like?' She comes close to him and says she doesn't want to stay, she doesn't like the place, let's go. 'That's all right, barman,' he says, 'we've changed our minds.' The barman raises his eyebrows and, in resigned silence, shares the moment with his regulars.

Stephen takes Suzanna by the arm and walks out into the falling snow. They bend their heads and hurry together, back up the street to her place.

'Thank you,' she says when they are through the door. 'Not exactly welcoming, was it?'

'Not exactly.'

He follows her up three familiar flights of wooden stairs. She chatters as they go up, telling him who lives where, the snorer on the first floor whom you can hear at the top, the one who never goes out, the one who never does her share of cleaning – as if she hasn't told him all this before.

At the top of the stairs is a landing lit by a skylight. She lets him into a large room nestling under the slope of the roof. It has two windows built into it on which the snow is starting to stick.

He looks at the knots in the wooden floor, the rugs, the prints of dancing women that cover parts of the wall not covered by books. A skirt hangs over the back of a chair. A bead necklace curls on a small table. He sees a thick leather belt. His. Rokas'. The man who has gone.

Suzanna sits at her piano. She puts all 10 fingers on the keys by way of announcement, *taraa*, and plays.

The music pulls her in and Stephen, too; it takes him back to the days he spent with her in this same flat, the days when he was the future for her and not, as he is now, just another lover turned friend, somebody who was for a moment interesting but is no longer. Future become past... and why? Because of Rokas. Because he writes himself across her skin, and on her lips and in her eyes and will do so forever until she yearns for him no longer. Until he is dead and also departed.

He sees yearning now in her face and he thinks there is sadness, too, something in the mouth, something in the eyes. He listens as the sadness seeps into the music, and the longer she plays the sadder and slower it becomes until, like a plough-horse slipping and straining through a sodden field, it sinks to a halt.

'What is it, Stephen? Why have you come?' she asks.

'Rokas has left.'

'Left! What do you mean?'

Stephen tells her about the trial, how Porphyrian took against him. 'He ran. He had to.'

She absorbs this, that he is gone from her, that she is once again alone. She says, 'Good. I'm glad he's safe.'

'He may not be. Porphyrian has sent helicopters after him.'

'My God! Will they kill him?'

'If they find him before he reaches the Tribals, they'll kill him. That will be their instructions. If they don't find him, the Tribals will hide him.'

'So he can lie low and then try to get away south. If anyone can get through, he can.'

'Do you think so? Not many could, but he might. Perhaps. I don't know. That's if he tries.'

'Why wouldn't he? It's his only chance.'

Stephen looks at her, at her baby which is beginning to show.

'You mean he'll stay for us… but that's madness.' She stares at Stephen. 'You must find him and persuade him. Please, Stephen, you must. If he remains in the forest, the helicopters will get him in the end. They will, won't they? And he can't come back here…' Tears come to her eyes and she holds on to his arm so tight he can feel her nails in him. 'You must find him, Stephen… for me.'

'And if I do, what shall I say to him? Keep running, kill yourself in that wilderness… Why should he listen?'

'Won't he?' She pauses, weighs it up. 'But if I tell him… if I speak to him, he will, I know he will. I'll go to him. I'll go tomorrow, before I get too big to walk.' She looks up, implores. 'And you'll take me… '

Stephen imagines Rokas gone, and he without a hand in it. 'If that's what you want.'

'And if he won't go on his own, I'll go with him. We'll get away together, all three of us.' Stephen's heart leaps. 'I mean,' she adds, 'Rokas and me and my baby.' Stephen feels her words as a slap across his face.

The slap wakes him. 'No,' he shouts, 'what are you talking about?' He grabs her by the shoulders. 'You can't go with him, you must know that. You'll never make it. You think the forest is easy, no more than a stroll through the trees? It isn't. It's nothing like that. It's immense beyond imagining, unending, interminable. Rokas might be able to get through. On his own. Might, though I wouldn't bet on it. You can't. Not in your condition.'

She brushes his hands away. 'We'll go tomorrow. You'll find him, Stephen, I know you will.'

Rokas' fourth short story: Pursuit

Call it a family tradition if you like – the poaching I mean. I learnt from my father, and he from his. Meant that we've always lived that little bit better than the others in the village, more meat in the pot. Not better than the new man, of course. Colonel Johnson he called himself. He owned the land on which we did the poaching so he was always going to do better than we did.

Kept us strong, the extra meat. That's why the Colonel liked to give me work when I wanted it. Knew I'd pull my weight. He was always very welcoming when I showed up with my cap in my hand asking for something.

'Ah, it's you, Morton, come for some work, have you?'

'Yes, sir, I have, sir.'

'The higgling a bit slack just now, is it?'

The Colonel knew I did a bit of buying and selling. I went round the farms with my old horse and cart and saw what they had. Then I took what I picked up to the town and sold it on. Higgling is what we call it round here. The Colonel must have heard the word. Perhaps I told him. He liked to use it whenever he could, though it sounded odd coming out of his mouth. I dare say he thought it made him part of this place, though he only came to the village after the war ended. He bought the whole estate on the cheap, if you ask me. The previous owner, nice man he was, lost all his sons in the fighting, all in the same year too, 1915 – and just about everything else he had he gave away. Wanted to do what he could, wanted to help those who were still over there. Out of grief, I suppose.

Nice man, the previous owner, as I say. If he'd caught me poaching, I doubt he'd have done anything. Probably told me that if we were short, I'd only to ask. But I would never ask. I don't beg, I don't. We've always looked after ourselves, and I didn't intend to go round begging, not then, not ever.

When the war was over, he sold the lot. It's my belief that when he looked out at his fields and his river and his trees, he just wanted rid of them as fast as he could, as if it were those that had been the cause of his sons dying. The fight had gone out of him, I suppose. Couldn't see the point of it.

That's when the Colonel showed up. I don't imagine, what with the war going on so long, that many people had much to spare, not even those with the estates; but the Colonel had plenty. He just bought the whole lot over. Perhaps he'd done his share of higgling in the war. I don't mean eggs and chickens either. Big stuff. Uniforms for the army, or maybe guns. He wasn't short of a bob or two, I can tell you that.

So anyway, I'd say to him very respectfully that, yes sir, things were a bit slack just then, and he'd tell me to go and see his wife. She was the one who looked after the estate, the books and that sort of thing. She did a good job, so people said, even though she was in a wheelchair and never left the big house. Thank you, sir, I'd say and off I'd go.

I liked working there now and again. Gave me a chance to get a look at the lie of the land – in the daylight I mean. I'd work quietly, thinking of all the rabbits I was going to take that night. Or, if it was the right time of year, a deer or a trout. I like a nice piece of trout straight out of the river.

One day, the Colonel decides he's going to go in for shooting: pheasants and partridge mainly. So what does he do? He gets himself a gamekeeper, a Scotsman. This Scotsman was a thickset, rough sort of man and as silent as misery. Didn't give you the time of day if you met him on the road, no more than a growl anyway. I knew if he caught me, that would be it. He wasn't the type to try and prove anything. He'd fire off that 12-bore of his and claim he was just doing his job.

Jenny wanted me to give it all up.

'We've enough with the higgling,' she said. 'A trout or two isn't worth dying for, is it, my love, not now, not after everything we've been through,' and she came to me with tears in her eyes begging me. I held her in my arms, her black hair which came down to her shoulders getting all wet with the crying.

She was still a beauty, my wife, even after everything she's had to put up with. Jenny was the best thing that ever happened to me, but I couldn't give up the poaching for her. I wasn't going to get driven off by some Scotsman and, besides, it was a family tradition. We'd been doing it for generations. It was our right.

At first, what with the birds that were now all over the estate, the poaching was as easy as I'd known it. Those birds were so tame, I didn't have to do much more than whistle and they'd jump into my bag. But then the Scotsman tightened things up. He put some village lads on night patrol and kept such a close eye on them himself that they couldn't look the other way every time I whispered their names. I also noticed a man-trap he'd put down, nearly stepped in it, so cleverly hidden it was among the leaves. It was Tess, my collie bitch, that saved me, whimpering and shivering so I knew something had to be up.

One misty night, sometime after dusk, the keeper came round to our cottage. I was out. I'd taken a rabbit, netted it on the edge of the copse above the 10 acre. We're a team, Tess and I, she working the bracken and me waiting with one hand on the netting. The rabbit came right in, and I had my knife in it before it could squeal. It bled all over me, but I've had worse than rabbit blood on my hands.

When I came back, I knew he was waiting for me. Some things you know. I stayed hidden in the trees with Tess beside me. Good dog is Tess, never barks, never wanders. I smoked my pipe so that when he came out, he'd understand I was on to him. He did eventually. Must have been midnight by then. He'd have smelled the tobacco all right, even over the damp and the dead leaves, and known. But he didn't come looking for me. He knew better than to do that.

Jenny didn't tell me what he'd said to her, but when I came through the door I could see she'd been crying. He was a single man, about my age I suppose, and he had his eye on her. I asked her, of course, but she just shook her head. So you see, I had to get back at him. I couldn't just let him get away with upsetting my wife. That's not how it works around here.

I didn't make plans, that's not my way. Scheming and puffing up and going all red in the face is for those who don't have their feet on the ground, who don't have a past to fall back on. No, I just knew my time would come. It always comes if you're patient. No need to go charging off and get yourself blown apart by a 12-bore. I waited. Didn't stop me getting my share either. Jenny makes a great rabbit stew even when she doesn't like where the meat's come from.

I kept up with the higgling and Tess kept Jenny company while I was on my travels. If I was a fair way from home and things weren't going well, I'd ask for a day's work on one of the other estates round about. That way I got to know who was who and what was what. You never know when a chance word here or there will come in handy. I always made myself likeable too when I was away from home, and didn't do any poaching either. One of the things my father taught me, that was: don't go out after dark on land you haven't grown up on. Good advice.

I was in a pub maybe 30 miles away when a weaselly sort of a man comes up to me. He says, 'You travel around a fair bit, don't you. You know the Blidwell estate then?'

'I might, why? What's it to you?'

'Goings on there from what I hear.'

'Goings on? What do you mean? What goings on?'

'The Lady stuck in her wheelchair in the big house. When the cat's away…'

'Yes?'

'That new keeper providing the entertainment, that's what they're saying. In the boathouse.'

'That's what they're saying, is it? And what sort of entertainment is this keeper supposed to be providing?'

Here he gives me a wink and says, 'Girls what else.'

'Girls!' I say, not believing a word.

'They've got one called Miss Ellie or some name like that, tasty little thing by all accounts, performs with a python.'

At that I look him in the eye and he turns and runs. My head was all over the place then, full of fumes. I downed my pint and had another. Then another one after that, and I'm not a drinking man. Lies all of it. Ellie hadn't been anywhere near Blidwell for years. If she had, I'd have known. Some things you just know.

I went out the pub and looked around. I thought I'd ask Mr Weasel a few questions, but there was no sign of him. I knew I had to get home sharpish. Even though it was dark, I harnessed the horse to my cart and set off. She was an old horse, so we were less than half way by the time I had to stop again and give her a rest.

If I didn't know it before, I knew it then: that it doesn't matter how much you try to give it the slip, the past just keeps coming back. It's like when you're walking through a wood, you get the sticky willow on your trousers and you pull it off and pull it off, but it doesn't make any difference: there's always a bit you've missed, the bit that doesn't know when it's not wanted. Yes, I've done bad things, hurt some people, but that was years ago, when I was younger. Who hasn't gone off the rails a bit, one time or another? But I thought I'd put it behind me. Paid my dues. But to use Ellie like that, poor, beautiful, sad Ellie – it just wasn't right.

When I did get home finally, I asked Jenny what'd been going on. She didn't want to talk to me. Well, she was often a bit withdrawn was Jenny, that was just how she was.

The biggest shoot of the season was about to start. Late October, that's when the Colonel gets all his friends up to blast away, and not just the fancy ones either. I went up to the House. There was a heavy mist hanging over the fields, you couldn't see 100 yards: but good enough for shooting.

'Need any beaters, sir?' I asked the Colonel.

'Things a bit slack again, eh, Morton? Well, we always need good beaters. Go and see McNab. Tell him I sent you.'

The Scotsman took me on. He didn't have much choice, coming as I did from the Colonel. Before I left the cottage, I tied Tess up and asked Jenny to keep an eye on her. Jenny told me it was all right, that nothing had happened, that there was nothing to worry about, but she was just trying to protect me. I could see that. And even if it had been – nothing to worry about, that is – I knew which way things were going. I've been around. So I also knew that there comes a point when things have to be done, when you can leave it no longer, when it won't go away of its own accord. Women don't understand this, but men do. It's what makes us men.

I didn't have a plan, but I knew that there, in the thick of it, when everyone was thinking about the birds, and the guns were all pointing in the air and firing off, I'd have my chance. A moment would come. It was bound to.

For the first day, I kept my head down, did nothing except my job. I tapped against the trees, beat the undergrowth, made rooting noises, just like all the other beaters. In a long line we were, driving the birds onto the guns, driving them to oblivion, to the fate they had been born to. I was waiting for the feeling, you see, that moment when I knew the time was right.

On the last shoot of the afternoon of the second day, the feeling came to me. We were walking through Baguley Wood which is on a slight slope and comes out onto sparse grazing land, pock-marked by furze and rocky hollows. I knew it well. I'd had good pickings in that wood on many a night. The gentlemen, if that's what they were, with their loaders beside them, were waiting just below the wood in their tweeds and plus fours, their expensive guns tucked all nonchalant under their arms. They were expecting good sport. It's what they'd come for, what the Colonel had promised them.

The line of us beaters was stretched across the wood. We were marching as best we could through the bracken, beating, calling, just as we'd been told, with the Scotsman keeping to the side, just on my right, shouting out, 'Keep in line, keep up,' and swinging away with his stick. The mist was sitting on the tree tops, the smell of cordite was all over everything, and the birds were coming out, fast and high. The Scotsman was loving it. 'Keep up, keep in line,' he yelled again and he beat about him like it was some poor girl he'd got in the boathouse.

I was going to use my knife on him then, but I noticed a switch that had been torn off an ash tree and was lying on the ground, its pointed end signalling to me. I bent down as I passed and picked it up. It was sharp enough. It would do. In the wood accidents happen, plenty of them. I moved over to the side, meaning to stick him when he came close to me, and it was then, with the guns sounding in my ears like it was Ypres or Passendale and the birds thumping to earth dead or dying like men cut down in the act of escape, that I let the switch fall and turned away.

I began to run. I knew what I had to do. I would take my darling Jennie and we'd just go, keep on going, go to places where they'd never catch up with us, where they couldn't use Ellie against us, where we'd find peace at last.

I ran as fast as I have ever run through the undergrowth, ducking under branches, pushing through the brambles and thorns until my foot suddenly seemed to be pulled away from behind me. I crashed to the ground and it was only as I struggled to rise that I felt the pain of a pair of steel jaws closed around my ankles.

I have no idea how long I lay there. It might have been hours, it might have been days. When I woke, my leg was covered in blood and the ground around me stained with it. What I saw in place of what should have been the moon and the night stars was the Scotsman looking down and the Colonel behind him.

'Not a nice thing to happen,' said the Scotsman shining his torch into my eyes, 'particularly with that weak heart of yours. After a shock like you've been through, easy to have a seizure.'

'There's nothing wrong with my heart,' I gasped turning my mind away as best I could from those steel teeth biting down to my bone.

'Hasn't he got a wife?' the Colonel asked.

'You can leave her to me,' the Scotsman replied and those were the last words I heard, the last words that I took with me on my journey.

It was no kind of ending, nothing right about it at all, the bastards.

Among the Cathars, Languedoc, Mid-13th Century

Riders again traverse the dusty landscape, eight in all. In their search for the brother and sister, they look for the footprint of a single horse heavily laden, or that of a horse accompanied by a man on foot. An eagle soars above them, wonders if there is a kill below and flies lazily on. It is early in the day, the sun only half up and a good time to be in the hills. The men have started to loosen their leather jackets. Two carry theirs across their saddles. They travel slowly, savouring the air, still cool. They are swarthy men, solid, silent, except for one who is younger and yellow haired. His skin is smooth and he might almost be thought a boy were it not for a certain knowingness in his eye. He keeps his distance as he rides.

He knows he is not like the others. When he was growing up, boys pointed at his fair hair and his ears which stuck out from his head and they said, You, what kind of place do you come from? When he asked his mother, she pointed a finger towards the north. As soon as they could, they would return. Accordingly, the boy with the strange hair and the ears has the instincts of the outsider. It is no surprise that he thinks his own thoughts, that he observes and does not attach. The actions of others, be they right or wrong, are not his concern.

He wonders as he rides where his sense of being different from the others will lead him. Will it – and the thought rises unbidden – turn him into a heretic? He has listened to the Perfect Men but decided nothing. Will it lead him to the stake? Perhaps. He shrugs.

The idea carries no weight, a background murmur only against the present rhythm of his horse and the sound of his horse's feet on the rocky trail and the call of birds and the smell of the air. These are what determine his life and the idea that he might one day be hunted himself disappears into that same

Did they dig a tunnel? Enlighten me, please.'

'The gate of their cell was unlocked.'

'And the jailer heard nothing?'

'He was dead when we found him.'

'Dead!'

'His throat had been cut.'

'Do we know by whom? The prisoners? An accomplice?'

'Either is possible. He might have been helping them escape.'

'Why would he do that?'

'Perhaps he had been bribed. Stefan had sold his sheep. Who knows where the money went.'

'But if he was helping them, why is he dead?'

'The dead tell no tales,' says the First Inquisitor. 'Who knows this better than the Church?'

'Dear God, the ways of the world!' The bishop crosses himself. Then sighing, he says, 'May I take it that all our lost property will be recovered?'

'It will, my lord.'

They watch the bishop leave. The First Inquisitor says, 'They seem to have escaped the castle through Torturers' Gate.'

'Yes,' replies R.

'For which not many have keys.'

'Indeed my lord.'

'Could the gate have been left unlocked?'

'It is possible. Sometimes, when in a hurry, even the best may forget.'

'Even you?'

R looks down. 'I have used the gate. I may have failed to lock it. Perhaps.'

'But perhaps the assistance they received was deliberate. Could they have been helped by one of our own, do you think? Is such treachery conceivable?'

'There is little in the way of treachery that cannot be conceived.'

'And you, have you conceived of treachery?'

R considers the fat man below him who holds his life in his hand. He wonders what treachery is, whether such a crime exists. A man may serve many masters. And himself.

'I imagine that there is only a thin line between the traitor and the good men among us. There but for the grace of God...'

'Indeed. And for those who cross the line?'

'There can only be one truth. That truth must be defended.'

The First Inquisitor laughs to himself. Only one truth! Ha! Is it possible R believes such a thing? He looks up at his face and sees more than he expects: a mask. He understands for the first time that this man has become dangerous. Perhaps, and he pauses in front of the idea, even murderous. Perhaps even that, he says to himself and then he wonders for a moment why the idea troubles him so little. The things a man will swallow, he thinks. Then to R, he says, 'We charged you, did we not, with the defence of the girl?'

'Yes, my lord.'

'Were you zealous in your attempts to defend her?'

'I did what I could.'

'Were you perhaps too zealous? Did you do more than you should?'

'I hope not. I pray that I am always conscious of where my duty lies.'

The First Inquisitor considers whether to pursue this and knows he won't. Where does R's duty lie? Where, come to that, does his own? To the Church, of course, but what is the Church? To the bishop, the bishops in conclave, the Pope? Without doubt. To believe anything else is heresy. And where does the power of the Pope and his legions, of which I am one, come from if not from the Word of God? Unless the Devil made this earth and the people in it, as the heretics like to think. He smiles at the thought and says to R, 'There but for the grace of God go us all.'

R crosses himself and bows deeply. Today he serves this

master. Tomorrow it will be another. Vibrations pulse across his chest and down his legs. He stays bowed as if fearing that, should he straighten, more will be revealed than he as yet understands.

The horse meanwhile is striding out, carrying Suzanne on his back half-asleep and pulling Stefan, who has him by the tail, along with him. The horse has caught the smell of food and stables. The smell must be coming from the town. Stefan, who smells nothing, sees austere walls rising up at the top of a steep hill. A hard town to take, he thinks. A good place to hole up…

And later, when the same sight greets the riders who pursue them, it engenders the same thought. The riders click their tongues, dig their heels into the flanks of their horses and let the wind play with the rims of their leather hats.

The streets of the town are narrow, and the cobbles hard on the feet of those who have travelled far. Brother and sister walk, one on one side of the horse, the other on the other, both holding the saddle. They see a man in blue robes coming towards them. He stops. He looks at them closely. No words are spoken but what they have in common passes between them. The man moves away and they follow him.

'Come in,' says a woman, 'welcome. You'll be safe here.' A table is in the middle of the room and round it sit five men. There is food on it: bread, cheese, some salted fish. An open hand stretches out, indicates. 'The food is for everybody,' says the woman. 'If you're hungry, eat.'

The two of them eat and the act of eating drives everything else out of their consciousness. They believe they are among friends. They believe they are no longer the hunted. They close the corners of their eyes out of which they have watched day and night. They shut down their imagination and no longer hear that scrape on the rock behind them nor a horse's sneeze. Instead, they chew and smile at those around them and compliment the woman on the food. How good it is to taste fish again. Mmm. Yet the riders are coming closer. They have entered the town. They know the language of the region and how to dissemble.

It is a strange place this town, a place where heresy flourishes, where the power of the Church, even though supported by armies, is not what it is elsewhere. The town, better than any sermon, illustrates the danger of turning the other cheek. It underlines the wisdom of the Pope. How right he is to seek out this heresy and destroy it. First this town, then another – the contagion is infectious. It will spread. Soon it will be unstoppable.

The strangeness of this town, where people do not think as they have been taught to think, shows in its faces. The townsmen and women breathe deeply, as if they are breathing a different kind of air. They savour their freedom to breathe the air they choose, they savour each breath, the more so because they do not believe that freedom like theirs can last. So they smile, so they laugh. So they make love with abandon before the Papal Emperor in Rome strikes them with his fist.

The town, for all that it is free, is therefore a fragile sort of a place. People look at their truths as if through a mirror and see over their shoulder the long and admonishing Papal finger. Try as they might to shut their eyes and their ears to what is behind them, the admonishing finger still taps on their noses. So for all its smiles and laughter and making of love, when the town sleeps, a blanket of inevitability creeps over it, which the inhabitants draw across their shoulders with a sigh.

Suzanne and Stefan are led to a bed in a room off the kitchen. They lie down in each other's arms. Their sleep, like that of the riders now bedding down in a stable, is the sleep of travellers who have journeyed far.

Not everybody sleeps. A man on a horse which looks too small to carry him is picking his way through the night. The man's head is bowed, as if perhaps he is dozing while his horse plods on. Every now and then, he jerks himself upright. Flowers that come out only in the moonlight, or for him, acknowledge his passing. Stars, dying like old men in the night, watch but make no sound. By dawn, the town is in the distance. Now he dismounts, stares at the town as if trying to interpret its contents from the little he can see of its steep streets and lies down with his cape around him. He is in no hurry.

As he rests contentedly, the riders wake, knowing they are in a hostile place. They do what men like them do when they cannot see what happens next: they give themselves time. One of them goes to buy bread. One passes the flagon around. They drink. They sleep. Later they find a tavern. They sit at a table and a woman serves them wine.

The tavern is full. Men and women are laughing and drinking. One of them has been to a village, where he witnessed a burning and a miracle. The listeners gather around as he tells his tale.

'Why, if I didn't see her soul float up out of her body and hover over it, reaching out to wipe the sweat from her own face.'

'And then?'

'Then the soul went over to the priest and squatted above his head.'

'It never.'

'It did. I saw it and I wasn't the only one.'

'Did the priest see it?'

'The priest went on praying, but half-way through he stopped, looked up as if he'd felt a drop of rain and wiped his eye.'

The listeners laugh. The riders laugh, too. They raise their cups to the storyteller and offer round some cheese they've carried with them. One of the riders says, 'Talking of miracles, in our village an old woman was frying fish by the stream when a spirit tickled her under the chin and made her flip her pan in the air. All the fish flew out and landed back in the water. They're still there, swimming around, fried on one side.'

This is greeted by good-natured incredulity. Another flagon is put on the table. By morning they will be strangers no more.

A girl comes over to the group of riders and beckons to the fair-haired young man among them. She is dressed in a blue robe fastened at the waist by a metal chain. On it are circular links fashioned with crosses of a type the boy hasn't seen before. He gets up and she indicates that he should follow her into a corner. The men he is with hoot and guffaw and make remarks.

'Why do you stay with them?' she asks him.

'Why should I not?'

'Because you are cut from a finer cloth.'

The boy blushes. 'Different maybe. No better.'

'You have spoken to the Perfect Men.'

'No.'

'No?' She smiles.

'Maybe,' he says. 'So what?'

'Then why do you pursue those two?'

'You mean the brother and the sister?'

'Yes, I mean them. Why do you pursue them? Do you want them to be burnt?'

'I don't think of that. I just do my work.'

'And when these same men come after you, what will you say then?'

'Why should they?'

'Because you will be suspected and they will follow you. The Inquisitor will say, or if not him, then his henchman, you know the one, he whose head touches the roof, "Remember that young man with the fair hair and the ears which stick out; he has gone over to the other side. Go, track him down, bring him back to face God's justice." Then they will come for you and you will think back to this time when you came for another.'

'But what am I to do?'

'Leave.'

'But if I leave, they will wonder why. What reason could I give?'

'Give none. They are occupied with other matters. Now is your opportunity.'

The door of the tavern rattles and shakes. Whoever is trying to enter is pulling the wrong way. One of the hinges comes away. Before the door is ripped off completely, the woman whose tavern it is, opens it. She greets the stranger. He comes in bending low. When he straightens he looks around him like the ghost of the apocalypse come to feed. There is silence.

'Ah, you there,' he says jovially to the riders at their table. 'I know you. May I sit?'

The riders try to disown this man who threatens their anonymity. They look to the others around them as if he is nothing more than the lunatic he appears to be. The others make room, and R lowers himself onto a bench. First, there is silence, as if all sense a presence in their midst that is alien. The world this personality inhabits is strange to them. It seems to have no anchorage in anything they understand nor any inlets which they might safely explore. Those who are native to the town, one by one, make their excuses and move away. Soon R and the riders are alone at the table, while the rest of the tavern pretends to pay them no attention.

After a while, R tells the riders of his journey, how he can never find a horse large enough. He points disparagingly at his frame and the men around him do their best to appear amused. They are not used to being subdued, and they don't like it. They become angry. As a way of breaking free of the shackles that have been put around them, one says, 'What is the purpose of your journey?'

To which R replies, 'The same as yours.'

'As ours?' The men are nervous. They look around.

'Why, yes, to find the heretics, to bring them back.'

'But we're not here for that,' say the riders, 'we're passing through. We have family on the other side of the hills.'

'Oh,' says R, lowering his voice, 'so sorry, I didn't mean to… ' He looks across the room to where the fair-haired man is talking to the girl. 'You two,' he calls out, 'come and join us.' He beckons with a sweep of his arm. More gently he says, 'Come.'

They come. They sit down. All are uncomfortable except R. R swims on the unspoken currents, feels the energy beneath him carrying him along and laughs. 'Ah, if only we all said what we think, what fun we would have. Don't you agree?'

'We would have blood,' she says.

'Blood, fun, it is all one to me.'

'Is your blood as much fun as another's?' the girl asks.

'My blood is not in question, not here, not now. I believe I have an instinct for knowing such things.'

'I believe you do.'

'It's like this, you see… Some of the things we do, most of the things we do, only confirm our slavery. But other actions, such as the one I will shortly undertake, free us forever.'

'What action is that?' asks the girl. All listen attentively, all those at the table and in the room. Some take a step forward to hear better.

'What action?' R repeats the question and, in so doing, realises that the understanding which has welled up within him is blurred at the edges, is out of reach of words. It exists in the space beyond, a reality which is neither a this nor a that. How strange to be aware of such things, he thinks, savouring what turns within him. 'A new world is opening up,' he says. 'You will soon see.'

Each of the listeners interprets the remark according to his own hopes. The fair-haired young man with his ears standing out even more than previously says, 'A better world, do you think?'

'How do we judge? What's better for me might not be better for you.'

The girl says, 'Isn't a better world better for all of us?'

And R replies, 'It ought to be, but whether that's how it turns out is another matter. Nothing lasts.'

'You mean nothing gets better,' she says.

'I mean I don't know.'

He says this with a smile which acknowledges his ignorance. The room relaxes. The aura that has surrounded R has disappeared. He has become human. One of the townsmen brings him wine. Some who have left the table go back. Meanwhile, one man is taking his leave of the tavern. He says goodbye with a joke about a man and his wife and slips away under cover of raucous bonhomie. He walks up the cobbles. When he is at the corner of the street, he looks behind him. He hasn't been followed.

In the house of Baille, the townsman finds the brother and sister alone. He says, 'They're here.'

'They? Who?'

'The riders. The giant inquisitor also.'

'Him, too?'

'Yes.'

'But why?'

'It's strange. Before he was no more than a rumour. Yet now he is among us, drinking in the tavern, speaking, not caring who hears.'

'He helped us before,' says Suzanne. 'Perhaps he will help us again.'

'Or perhaps he regrets what he did and is here to bring us back,' says Stefan. 'I don't trust him.'

'He has been talking about a different world, about being free,' says the man.

'Ah, has he? So, it's a trap. He let us escape hoping we would lead him to you. Now that we have, he pretends he has joined the heretics.'

'Unless he has joined. Perhaps he means it,' says Suzanne.

'I see us burning on the pyre.'

'I will go to our mother's cousin. Perhaps she knows a better place to hide.'

'I'll come, too.'

'No, my brother, stay. I'll be safer without you. The riders are looking for a man and a woman. On my own, I won't be suspected. And besides, if I am captured, you at least will live.'

'I'll not live without you sister. I will come.'

'Stay, I beg you. We'll be safer apart. If our kinswoman can hide us, I will send word. If not, I will return myself.' She kisses him on the mouth. 'Wait until you hear from me.'

A man enters and whispers in R's ear. R listens, waves the man away. After a while he pulls his legs out from underneath the table and stands. He walks towards the door and, as he passes the fair-haired young man, indicates with no more than a tilt of his chin that he should follow. Outside, he says, 'Deny nothing. I'm not interested in your innocence or guilt. Listen to what I tell you.'

The young man is frightened. He seems to be in a world in which the truths about him have galloped ahead of anything he has done or said. It is as if he has been anticipated and taken to be what he has not yet become. He doesn't know how, or indeed whether, he can become again the person he imagines himself to be; so he shakes in fear.

'Go to the house of Baille. Tell them they must leave, that the riders are coming. Go now. Do not delay.'

The boy runs, hardly daring to turn round in case R's stare is at his heels. Of that he need not worry. R has returned to the tavern and sat down at the table. The riders are getting ready to leave.

'Where are you going?' demands R, his mouth stuffed with fellowship and good cheer. 'Stay, drink some more. You, woman,' he shouts, 'more wine for my friends.'

One of the riders whispers to him that the brother and sister have been found.

'One more drink to speed you on your way,' says R, slapping the man lustily across the shoulder. 'Here...' He grabs the flagon from the woman and pours into all their cups. 'A toast! Come, drink. To those with whom we shall shortly be reunited.'

They drink and, as they do so, the young man enters the house of Baille and finds the brother alone. 'Get out,' he says. 'Tell your sister to get out. The riders know where you are. They will soon be here.' With that, the young man pulls his cape over his fair hair and leaves. He will go north. In the north, among his own kind, he thinks he will be safe.

Stefan gathers what he has but goes no further than the door. He opens it and peers up the hill along the cobbles. The lane is deserted and he hears nothing, no footsteps coming to him from higher up. 'Where are you?' he asks himself, punching his fist into the palm of his hand. He walks around the table. He again goes to the door and looks out. Nothing. He should have gone with her. Why did he let her persuade him? Once more he circles the table. Once more he goes to the door, but this time, thinking he hears the footsteps of men coming closer, he slips away.

The lane curves upwards and he climbs. He pauses, listens again. Were those footsteps he heard or his own imaginings? Should he return? What if she is even now coming back to the house? Who will warn her? He turns back, then stops. She will be safe where she is. Someone will tell her that the riders have found the house. If I go back, what advantage will that serve? They will take me and torture me, and… Here he shakes his head in sad self-knowing. If they torture me, no secrets will be safe, nor her either.

So the brother does not return to the house and perhaps wisely, for the riders have come. They are sitting around the table, waiting. They will see what puts its head into their snare. As for R, he is in the tavern drinking. Soon he will return to the First Inquisitor and await the arrival of the riders. If they have what they came for, he will reward them. And if they do not, he will wonder aloud how it could be that the two got away. Please explain, he will say, how it can be so difficult to find a simple brother and his sister? I am told you even knew the house in which they were hiding.

R takes the flagon by its throat and drinks. His skin will be safe; he has no doubt of that. He knows now that when people look at him they feel but one thing and this thing drives out all else, all wisdom, even the canny wisdom of the common man. He tastes it on his tongue, this thing; he tastes power. It is chalky with tones of amaryllis. Power, he understands, is the pervasive force in the universe. When the great men laugh at his buffoonery, they feel their own. And with the lesser, he lets them be afraid of his. How it dulls their senses. The great and the small, chalk and amaryllis on their tongues, imagine him to be either this or that, but, as for other things, these they do not suspect, not even the most obvious of them all: duplicity. This escapes them entirely.

Who is immune he wonders? Who does he have to fear? The girl in the robe? Yes, her, but she is no more than a passer-by. Suzanne? Maybe. He can't tell. Stefan? He has fear aplenty but yet there is enough inside him to allow him to stand back and see. Perhaps he should not have saved them. He laughs. Does the actor not put on the show for fear of what the audience might

throw? Never. Let them throw whatever comes to hand. Life is risk. Only death is safe.

There is silence in the house of Baille. The riders have heard footsteps on the cobbles. A girl is coming towards them. The footsteps stop. They picture the girl looking around, imagining, calculating. She does not move. They hear a whisper. 'Stefan?' One of the riders says in a whisper of his own, 'It's safe. Come.' The footsteps retreat, gather pace, she is running up the hill and in the sudden commotion on the silent lane, the sound of her breathing bounces off the walls and speaks of everything that is to come: the faster feet running her down, the rough binding of her wrists, the long journey on horseback, the nights of use and abuse, the first crackle of flame, the cauterising of skin, the melting of fat.

The riders that remain in the house listen as the story is told, the future coming out in gasps, the faster footsteps and the slower, the shriek that speaks for all that is known to all and then the silence. They shrug. It is work. It has to be done. They have families and, if they did not take what was offered them, then others would. They put themselves in her shoes, each one of them, but they do not flinch. They do not expect things to be other than they are. The agent does not blame himself.

✠

A smell of burning wafts across the courtyard. It is a smell sniffed in anticipation and so appears in the nostrils of those who have come early like the scented air of imagination. Each breathes in according to his inclination.

For those who have been to such events before it is sweet, cloying even, and takes those who wish to be taken, or are unable to resist, back to the days when they themselves were no more than motes and sunbeams.

For those who are new to such occasions, the best comparison they can make is to the frizzle that comes from the cast iron of a frying pan. They say to themselves, It will be like… and then they pause. Like what exactly? What exactly will be burnt? Well, meat certainly but of what sort? Not liver. Nor mutton kidneys with their fine tang of faintly scented urine. They know that while offal will be included – the carcass will not, after all, be butchered – it is not the primary offering. What then? The leg, the rump, the loins of sheep pig cow goat? Perhaps all, amalgamated in the mind as a proxy for what is to come, as an approximation of what is beyond imagining.

The tall man is not in a hurry. Life, or more correctly the manner of death, may be the issue at hand, but he sees no need to rush. He, too, has come early. He wants to give himself time. With a wave of his hand, he dismisses the peasant who thinks himself in charge. He takes upon himself the construction of the bonfire. From time to time he issues a curt command, 'You! Straw!' or he points and says, 'There, kindling, more, more. No, not that wood, look at it man, smell it, too green by far. I want mature timber, that, by the wall, bring that and plenty of it.' Finally, all is complete. Almost complete. He himself clambers up the pyre and, holding the stake, twists it and drives it down so that when she is tied, her feet will be in the flames.

Afterwards, R stands back, mingles with the shadows cast by the morning sun. There is time yet.

Little by little, others of the town come in chattering, first those from the lower classes and then, as if dropping in on their way to some other more important engagement, the higher. The crowd builds, its noises louder but less distinct until, now and again, a raucous laugh rises above the din and makes itself heard. In the hubbub and broil, what may once have been worthy in the individual is now subdued, the loftier toppled by the lesser without a struggle, a reduction down to the thick gravy of the lowest common denominator, the crowd. R has seen all this

before. He knows the process. From the shadow of the wall, he watches while, elsewhere, another man, his head hidden in a cowl, also watches.

Suzanne is brought. She shrieks. She cries out for mercy. Then, as the people begin to bask in the warmth of the spectacle, she stills herself, allows herself to be bound without complaint and enters into some silent place of the mind. The crowd quietens, its common persona fractured by what it sees. Some find it in themselves to admire, others to feel cheated. At a signal, a torch is thrown onto the pyre and the flames take hold. Those who have not smelled this smell before, smell it now and lock it away for the next time, or for their own private imaginings once the ashes have cooled. The woman makes no sound. As the flames gather around her, she is silent. As the first flesh comes away from the bone, still she is silent, trying as best she can to put herself beyond pleasure and pain. Does she succeed in this? At least she does not cry out.

For those in the front row of the audience, the small facial movements of the victim are there to be interpreted, the lines across the forehead, the sudden, stifled flinch as the fire sears again. We may suppose – how could we not – that even as Suzanne tries to push aside pain and pleasure, even if she succeeds, she will not be immune entirely from the temptations of thought. And when she thinks, what else can it be but her loves who come to her: her brother, her mother, her father, her sisters and the dear body, now ash, of he whom she cast still living from her, whom she allowed to be taken and for whom she will mourn long after all other faces will have been and passed away, long after life will have left her body.

R observes the events before him. He gives them his full attention but yet is not caught up in them. He does not love the woman nor hate her. He does not take her pain into himself, nor does he deny it. He does not judge her as better or worse. Alone, perhaps, of all the crowd, he sees without obstruction and so sees what is there to be seen: her spirit, reluctant, departing the body, arched in flight, its hands trailing back from where it emerged, its hips pressed forward. He sees it come towards him, reach out and press its lips to his forehead. Not its lips. Her lips. He feels the kiss of the spirit of a woman he hardly knows and looks around. Who else might have seen? he thinks. Why am I the one?

☦

He hears, from behind, the voice of the First Inquisitor. 'There have been complaints you know.'

R turns, but reluctantly. He prefers the world he has left. 'Have there?'

'Too fast, they say. Of course I don't agree. I don't hold with suffering for its own sake, but then again, there's no doubting that the performance benefits if we can, what shall I say, stretch things out.'

'Indeed.'

'And the needs of Mother Church… I wonder… perhaps those who say that our message, too, is best stretched out, may have a point.'

'They may.'

'But you don't agree do you? I can see you don't. In spite of appearances, I do believe you value mercy.'

'I no longer know what I value.'

The First Inquisitor looks at him. 'Be careful. A certain amount of reflection is allowed, but there are limits.'

'I will be careful, my lord. I thank you for your concern.'

'All of us stand on the brink between this world and the next, but only the Church shows us the way across.'

'I believe as you do, sire.'

The First Inquisitor smiles, rather in the way that an indulgent father might smile at his son. 'Good. Then do as I do. Never forget that even inquisitors may fall from grace.'

'I will follow your example in all things.'

'At least we captured the woman. A pity, though, about him, don't you think? What was his name, ah, yes, Stefan. Do you believe we will catch him?'

'The riders are looking. It is probable. Not many escape the course of justice.'

'Or the will of God.'

✟

R stands alone. The crowd has departed. The flames have died back. He moves towards the pyre remembering how her clothes caught, how her fat bubbled through her blackened skin and spat, how her eyeballs popped. He wonders why he harks back to this woman particularly. He has been to many burnings before. The consumption of her body went entirely as expected; there was no surprise in what he witnessed. Nor outrage. This woman, Suzanne, was no more innocent nor more guilty than any of the others. Just a victim. Just fuel for the flames. So what is it about her that makes her linger? Why?

He scratches his chest as if to rid himself of an itch. He holds his arms in the air, clenches his fists and brings one of them down into his stomach with enough force to have dropped most men to the floor. He roars into the empty square. 'Go!' he shouts. 'Be gone, witch. Out.' But the witch, if witch she is, does not go. She lodges above his navel, lays herself down and spreads out. She exists within him as heat, as a warm glow, and it makes him uncomfortable. He tries a softer tone, though he is not used to softness. 'What is it you want?' he asks. She doesn't answer.

He steps forward and puts one foot onto the bonfire. The ashes are still hot and, within the ashes, pieces of wood, moved into action by his foot, flare up. He stands back and searches until he finds a length of unburnt timber. This he takes to the embers, places it like a bridge and steps onto it. When he is over the middle, he reaches down and picks up a small piece of bone that has escaped the inferno. It is part of her. He doesn't know which part.

He holds the bone in front of him like a cross and kisses it. It is a declaration, but of what precisely he doesn't know. Can it be love? Is this what people mean when they talk of love, this feeling spreading from his navel? Is this where his defence of this woman has led him? Is love the penalty? That he should love the dead: how cruel. How hopeless. What sort of life can he now expect?

R feels as if all roads before him have suddenly come to an end, but why this should have happened he doesn't understand. He has broken free of the court, he has taken risks, he has ridden out across that barren country, the flowers of the dark have glanced sideways as he passed, he has come to a town, he has sat in a tavern and all have attended to him… how free he has felt, how his power has flowed through him. Freedom! Power! Such pleasure in those, such sweetness. But now, look at him, a moment later and he is once more trussed up, and by what? By a dead woman. By a spirit who kissed him. By a bone, dry as dust and fracturing even now in his hand.

He laughs at the ridiculousness of it all. He tosses the bone away and looks up into the sky. I will leave this place, he thinks. I will travel. People will feed me. I will do for them the services they cannot do for themselves. The air will brush my skin, the grass my toes, the birds will slip their notes one by one into my ear, water will pass down my throat drop by drop and each one I will acknowledge. I will be large on the earth. I will live. As for love, pah!

R looks around. If there is a horse, he will take it. He knows that whoever might own the horse will shrink away from what confronts him. He knows this. It is one of the certainties that has come to him. He sees no horses. He walks along a street. Nothing. Nor in the next. There is only a donkey being led by an old man wearing a threadbare smock of the kind worn by peasants. On the donkey's back are two panniers, one carrying bread and the other straw. R puts his hand on the arm of the old man and separates him from the donkey. He takes off the panniers, removing as he does so a stick of bread and throws a leg over the animal's back. His feet touch the ground. He hits the donkey on the rump with the flat of his hand, and it moves slowly forward. The old man watches. When he reaches the end of the street, R dismounts. He walks back and gives the old man all the coins he has. Even as he is doing this, he doesn't understand why. He then returns to the donkey, sits astride it, clicks his tongue and leaves the town, bouncing up and down on its back and laughing as the beast decides it wishes to stretch its legs.

They travel slowly. From time to time R leans over the donkey's neck and sleeps. The donkey trudges on. Or stops. When it finds in all that sparseness and rock something to eat, it eats. R lets it have its head. He will go where the donkey goes.

Day turns to night, a bright star-filled night with nothing between him and the heavens. The donkey has brought him to a ridge overlooking a broad plain. On either side are rocky hillsides. He doesn't recognise this landscape from when he was here before, but the thought doesn't bother him. He gets off the donkey and lies down on the ground. It takes him a while to find a comfortable spot but, when he does, he settles back and watches the stars. He watches the moon. Presently, a veil comes over it, perhaps a passing cloud. He notices a heaviness in the air he hasn't noticed before. He stands up and looks down the plain towards the horizon. He sees the Divine hurling his spears, lighting up a chorus of startled sandstone faces with his flashes and thunderclaps. For the entertainment of them both. R laughs and holds both his hands up to the sky as if caught in the act of applauding. Hoorah! Hoorah! – except his hands do not come together. The act of raising them is applause enough.

When the rain comes, he leads the donkey away. He finds a cave and sleeps. The woman comes to him in his dream. She is walking through rain as if oblivious to it, shedding her clothes until she is naked. She lies down next to him, putting her hand to his face and pressing her body into his. She lets him warm her. She lets him dry the raindrops from her skin with his fingers.

'My love,' she coos, 'where are you going in weather like this?'

'I am going nowhere,' he replies. 'I am here with you, forever, for always.'

The softness of her flesh under his hands passes through his body and into his spirit. It overwhelms him. It drives out all other sensations, all thoughts. He has never felt such softness before. He has never before lived in a world where such softness exists. He rests his head on her breast and weeps and sows his seed on the barren rock. Then he sleeps soundly until dawn.

When he wakes, he finds the landscape has been greened by the rain. It lies before him, shining. The donkey jumps once into the air and brays harshly as if trying to remove some irritant from its innards. R throws a stone at it. He eats the last of the bread and walks beside the donkey for some miles, climbing with it to a vantage point from which he is able to see the town that spreads itself on the top of a steep hill. He sits on the donkey's back and steers it in that direction.

He doesn't know why he wishes to revisit the place where Suzanne was captured, but he knows that he does. In kicking on his beast, he declares himself happy to follow a path that is understood by some part of his mind or body but not by a part that can readily state the whys and wherefores. There are words for such an understanding in many languages, though not in his own. In his language there is only a shrug, an acceptance.

The town's lofty situation and its steep, austere stone walls give it the aspect of a fortress. Battles will, in years to come, be fought over this town, and it will not be found to be as impregnable as it seems from the outside – but that is in the future. R follows the path that leads upwards. The sun is now high in the sky, and R feels its heat. He dismounts and walks beside the donkey. He realises he has no further use for the creature and, with an affectionate pat for the time they spent together, he lets it loose.

The donkey finds some grazing and begins cropping quietly until whoever will come and assume ownership happens along. He doesn't have long to wait. A little girl with a garland of flowers in her hair comes tripping down the path, passes R who is labouring upwards, and spies the donkey. She goes to it and strokes its nose. She looks around and sees nobody except the figure of R, now almost at the town gate. R turns. He exchanges glances with the girl and watches as she leads the donkey away. When she gets home, her father will ask her, 'Where did you find that donkey?' and she will tell him that a very tall man gave him to her. Her father will ask her why, what possible reason could this man have, a donkey is a valuable beast, and she will only shake her head and say, 'But he did, Papa, he did.' And he will believe her.

R enters the town smiling. The sight of the girl and the animal has lodged inside him in that place where he will in future store fond memories. Still smiling, he enters the tavern. The townsmen within greet him warmly and without reservation, as if he is one of them. He doesn't know why they do so, but he is happy nonetheless.

The woman brings him wine, but he asks for water only. He tells her that he has no money. She says, 'Drink now for nothing and, when you have money, we will charge you double.'

'In that case,' he says, 'drinks for everybody.' The taverners laugh. They gather round. They sit at the table where R sat before and all of them relax and stretch their legs.

R, for the first time in his life, is happy not merely to be among good fellowship, but to be a part of it. He embraces it without restraint. He drinks too much. He talks too much. He laughs too much and the others drink and talk and laugh with him. Even the girl in the blue robe fastened at the waist by a metal chain of strange inscriptions joins in. She sits next to R and dabs wine from his chin with a cloth when he has swigged too mightily even for him. She is in high spirits.

Presently, R says to her, 'You are the girl who was here the last time I came.'

'I am,' she replies.

'You seem different. Then you were sombre and fearless and, if I deduce correctly, doing your best to seduce a fair-haired young man from the path of righteousness.'

'You mean from the path of the Church?'

'Yes.' He pauses. 'And will you do the same for me?'

'Would you like me to?'

R pauses. To hell with it, he thinks. 'I would,' and he takes the girl in his arms and kisses her on the mouth. The townsmen around him continue to drink as if they haven't noticed.

The girl laughs. 'We may be thinking of different things,' she says.

'We may or we may not.'

Just then the door opens. Stefan enters the tavern, takes in what he sees and comes to the table at which R and the girl are seated. He acknowledges them both and sits down next to R.

'Aren't you supposed to be on the run?' asks R.

'Yes and no,' answers Stefan. 'I am both hunter and hunted.'

'Who are you hunting, if I may ask?'

'Why you of course,' says Stefan.

'Me?'

'You.'

The girl with the blue robe says, 'He is one of us.'

'He is one of us and one of them. He is many things to many people, but who he is to himself, I do not know.'

'And who are you to yourself, Stefan? Do you know that? Do

any of us?'

'I know what it is that brings me to this tavern.'

'You mean me?'

'Yes, you. And my revenge.'

'Revenge… is that enough? It seems like thin broth to me.'

'No, you're wrong. It's hot and thick and nourishing.'

R feels a knife point in his side. 'You wish to murder me,' he says.

'I do.'

'What will my death bring you?'

'It will cool my blood.'

'And what will my death bring your spirit? What do you believe will happen to it in its lives to come?'

'Not much. The death of an inquisitor! What does that amount to?'

Ooch ooch ooch: the words sound in R's head though he doesn't know from where they come or what they mean.

Stefan inserts the knife and smiles at the doing of the deed: the breaking of the skin, the scoring of the surface of the meat – ah, the release, the letting out… and still more yet to come, the initial and the deeper penetration.

R sees Suzanne, her fat spitting through her blackened skin, her eyeballs popping. So unexpected a gift, he thinks.

The two men, like two friends, look each other in the eye for signs of sins and saintliness. R breathes in as the blade enters and twists. As it withdraws, he sighs as if after the act of love, 'Ahhh.'

Stefan stands up, says goodbye to the girl and is gone.

R empties his cup. 'More wine,' he calls.

The woman whose tavern it is brings another flagon. 'For a man who has no money, you certainly have a thirst.'

'I have thirst and hunger. Do you have food?'

'I'll bring you bread. Cheese also.'

'Wine, cheese, bread: a feast.' He pulls the woman towards him and kisses her. He slumps forward onto the table. The women and the taverners think he is drunk and carry on talking and laughing.

Much later, when one of the men punches him good naturedly on the shoulder, they find his body unattended, his spirit having slipped away unnoticed.

Northern Europe, Mid-21st Century

Rokas' fifth short story: Return

All the doors of the houses are locked. Such is the custom of the town, a gentle town but cautious.

Xavier is late. He is a visitor. When he reaches the door of the house where he is staying, he grasps the handle knowing, before he turns it, what he will find. It is his own fault. The young woman, with whom he is lodging, has warned him. 'We lock up here as soon as darkness falls. You may find this strange, many visitors do, but we have our reasons. So come back early and I'll have a fine plover pie waiting for you.' She must have noticed the look on his face because she then asks, 'Have you ever eaten plover?' He replies that he hasn't and she tells him, 'Oh, they're quite a delicacy in these parts.'

It may have been the thought of those little birds whose plaintive song, phee-oo, phee-oo, has always found a place in his heart – was he to eat them whole, heads and all? – that causes him to tarry. Or it may have been the snow, which is most unexpected this far south. Or it may have been the feeling that comes to him as he is still trudging through open country that something or somebody is following him.

Where this feeling of not being entirely alone comes from, he has no idea. He is sure there is no reason for it – the land is flat and white and, when he looks around, he sees nothing, nor anywhere for a pursuer to hide – but as Xavier well understands, reasons are one thing and feelings another.

Xavier trudges through the snow which melts on his boots and penetrates the stitching that holds the pieces of leather together. He is aware of the dampness in his feet, but doesn't mind. He sings as he goes along, a cheery sort of a tune, the sort of tune which he feels might encourage whoever is behind him to make himself known, so that they might cover the remaining miles together in good companionship, swapping stories as travellers on the road are wont to do.

No one shows himself and the bright light of the afternoon begins to fade. He imagines dusk gathering on the horizon and would no doubt quicken his steps if the pie he has been promised was more to his taste: beef or lamb, even pigeon.

Xavier likes his food. He has always eaten well; his parents were church folk. Even so, he tries not to take life's abundance for granted. Things change. Today's plenty might be gone tomorrow. This he knows. Though knowing, as he also knows, is not always enough. A life without a good meal to sit down to of an evening, or a good bottle of wine come to that – what sort of a life is that? Hard to imagine. Hard to contemplate. Who would want to spend their days in a place where plover pie is regarded as a delicacy?

He shudders at the thought and slows his steps. Better to be locked out. At least he will be spared having to hear the crunch as he bites off the poor little creatures' heads. And yet the young woman in whose house he is staying does not seem unhappy. Hard to explain, but so it is. Life is full of mysteries, he concludes, and begins to hum to himself a popular folk tune of the region, one he heard earlier in the day: a song of love and yearning and regret made more poignant by the beauty of the singer's voice and the blindness of her eyes. When he stood before her to pass over a coin, she seemed to flinch as if she didn't know that what he was offering was a gift. 'Here is a small coin,' he said, as he pressed it into her hand.

He notices an outcrop of rock ahead of him and decides that there he will stop and rest for a while. He has some bread with him and some strong peasant cheese, which he bought in the market before setting off. It will be enough. Or at least preferable.

When he comes to the rock, he finds an area that will serve as a seat and sits down. He takes out his bread and cheese and begins to eat, a mouthful of bread followed by a mouthful of cheese. Such simple food, but so good. When the pie is offered to me, he thinks, I shall refuse it. I shall say that so much food was thrust upon me earlier in the day, I can't manage another mouthful. The woman will understand. From somewhere behind him comes, or so he imagines, birdsong: tlee, treeolee, phee-oo, phee-oo.

Xavier's thoughts turn towards girls. When he isn't thinking about *food, he thinks about girls. Sometimes he thinks about Marianna, the girl he is going to marry. He pictures her sewing. She is always sewing. Or baking. Or making stews. Marianna is a home-maker, a nest builder. He thinks of her sleek black hair which clings to her scalp like feathers, and laughs. He opens his mouth as if to receive some morsel from her, a worm perhaps, and drops into it a piece of cheese.*

He wonders what it would be like to be with a blind girl. He would describe the world for her in all its detail, and she would respond with the only reliable instruments she has at her disposal: her hands, her lips. She would touch him all over, searching out the source of his magic and, in her feeling of him, he would understand her desperation, her need to swallow him whole in case he should escape her and be gone.

Xavier lies back in contemplation of blind love and hums once more the tune he heard earlier.

Something then makes him turn, though what it is, he can't say. He imagines for a moment that perhaps the person following him is Marianna, that she wants to find out for herself what he gets up to when he goes out on his journeys. He searches for her in the landscape but sees nothing. This doesn't trouble him. He is happy being alone.

He continues to stare out across the flat plain of snow behind him. The longer he looks the more certain he becomes that his instinct is correct; something, even if not Marianna, is out there. The gloom of dusk gathers about him and, as it gathers, the land which so recently appeared empty now confirms his suspicions seeming, suddenly, full of shapes, full of flitting here and gone, full of appearances too large for this world or too disproportioned, of gargantua and absurdia and all things weird.

'It is the dark,' Xavier says to himself. 'The mind plays tricks.' He shakes himself to clear his head of its phantasms, finishes his last piece of cheese and is preparing to be on his way when he feels a hand on his cheek. He jumps back in alarm, forcibly detaching himself from the hand, if such it is. He shudders and prepares once more to leave with as much speed as he can muster, when he feels the hand again. This time, perhaps because he is half-expecting it, he doesn't jump away. He lets

the touch linger. It is soft, pleasant, like the inquiring hand of a girl who wishes to absorb into herself the sensations she feels on his skin. There is nothing but curiosity in the touch, no malice in it, no hint of evil, so he remains beneath it, in its orbit, perhaps even under its control, though he can see nobody to which the hand might be attached, nor indeed anything.

It is a dream, he thinks. I am dreaming. He lies back on the flat rock and lets the hand go where it will. It travels down his face and rests on his chest, its fingers playing in the hair it finds there. He thinks that perhaps the hand's further movement might be restricted and so, carefully, not wishing to scare it away, undoes the buttons of his clothing. He lies on the rock with his front bared to the sky, his eyes closed and his body quite warm enough in spite of the snow on the ground all about him.

He must then have fallen asleep – if indeed he hasn't been asleep earlier – because night has truly set in by the time he gathers himself. 'I can't stay here forever,' he declares and, buttoning himself, gets to his feet and walks. His mind is easy now and, if there are phantasms out there, he is content to regard them as friends from whom he has no secrets.

Presently, he reaches the village. He walks down the main street in silence except for the sound of his boots on the stones. A single dog wakes and barks. Then another and soon all the dogs of the village are howling. 'Soft, my friends,' he whispers, 'be soft, people are sleeping.'

When he reaches the door of the house, he finds, as he knows he will, that the handle will not turn. He tries it again. I can't spend all night outside, not in this cold, he thinks. He turns the handle once more, this time applying all his strength. Still it doesn't move. He rattles the door frame. Perhaps it is the act of rattling which starts it, or perhaps some deeper frustration, but anger now begins to rise within him. He kicks the base of the door with his toe. 'By what right is she keeping me out?' he asks himself. 'Haven't I paid? What is she afraid of?' The door stares back at him impassively, or rather, as it seems to Xavier, provocatively. Fuelled by its mute resistance, he leans his shoulder into the wood, pulls back and crashes against it. The lock snaps.

'Thank heavens,' he says to himself. His anger leaves him as quickly as it has arisen. He brushes himself down with his fingertips, pushes the door back quietly so as not to create any further disturbance and creeps across the threshold. He feels for a lamp that he knows is kept on a ledge by the window and bends down to light it.

The glow of the lamp casts a flickering light across the room. In the corner, he makes out the figure of the young woman with whom he is lodging. She is standing. He has no doubt that she has watched, terrified, as he beat down the door.

'I'm sorry,' he says. 'I have broken your lock. I will repair it in the morning.'

'If you can, I would be grateful.'

'I hope I didn't frighten you.'

'You did. Nonetheless, it is better that it's you who enters than a stranger. I have prepared a pie as I promised. Would you like it now?'

Xavier, after all the damage he has caused, feels he cannot refuse. 'If it's not too much trouble,' he replies.

'No trouble at all. Please sit.' She points to the wooden table in the centre of the room. After a while, she comes out with a plate on which is a large portion of pie, so carefully cut that the faces of the plovers are looking up at him with their beaks open as if they are in their nest awaiting the return of a parent.

Xavier is overcome with sadness. 'I have nothing to give you,' he whispers to the dead and hungry birds.

As the woman bends to lay the plate before him, her blouse brushes against his cheek. He feels the curve of her breast beneath.

'Eat,' the woman urges. 'The plovers this season are particularly delicious.'

Xavier lifts up his fork and prepares to plunge it in...

The Journey

Stephen waits for her at the edge of town. At first she isn't sure it's him, something about him, the way he's standing perhaps, an alertness she hasn't noticed in him before; something is different. She approaches him warily, though he follows her with his eyes up to the moment she comes close and stands staring at him. 'Stephen,' she says, almost enquiringly, and then the difference comes to her in the way that music sometimes comes to her, music she might play and play and never believe she has right and then one day, there it will be, coming from her fingers as it should be, as it has to be. 'Ah, Stephen,' she says, 'I see you now.'

He points to the endless woods and the hills that rise to the south. In the distance, a helicopter circles, fly-black and nosy, sniffing the treetops. 'Be careful,' he says, 'stay out of sight,' and he takes her pack from her and walks away fast as if, like the hunter she sees him to be, in pursuit.

By the time the sun is rising, they are climbing a steep path that borders a forest of pine and larch. Suzanna has filled her pack with the things she imagines will be useful: water, bread, nut paste hard-tack which is part food and part memento, and Chopin's piano music which she's squeezed in last because she's decided she'll believe in a future.

Stephen's pack carries only what survival demands in this wild and unpredictable country. In his inside pockets is a transmitter, a retractable garrotte and the Porphyrian all-purpose knife. Strapped to his back is a Porphyrian 220. And in his mind, folded and refolded: calculations, decisions. If Rokas runs, then the balls will roll as they will. He might make it, he might not. And if he doesn't, well... But he won't let her go with him. He won't let her walk to her death. He won't. Better to call in the choppers.

First, he has to find Rokas.

He waits for Suzanna to make up the ground between them. 'We'll head for the cabin but not directly,' he says. 'If we're spotted, I don't want to lead them to him. He may be there or hiding with the Tribals. It will take two days.'

'Two days!'

'It's longer but it's safer. Your choice.'

Two days away from Rokas, two days with him. Suzanna nods. 'I'm in your hands, Stephen.'

Stephen doesn't answer. He picks up their packs and walks on. Every journey has a history. Each person carries many sets of baggage, the baggage on his back and those laid down in the fossil remains of memory. No journey starts from here. So when Stephen places his boot on the ground, feels the give of decay beneath him, it is as if he is walking through water, looking down through ripples to destinies he can only calculate from the half-glimpsed and disappearing shapes beneath him. He is happy she is with him, just the two of them, as it was meant to be.

They walk tight to the trees. Suzanna's every instinct is to merge into what is solid around her, the trees and Stephen. She craves anonymity, fears the open and the visible. She wonders at this in herself, how she is now in hiding, body and mind, stooping within the flesh and bones that stand erect, as if her Self would find a place to hide within the alert and circumspect body. If Rokas could see me now, she thinks, and the little person within straightens herself at the admonition and stands tall.

Snow falls, fat wet flakes at first, which land on the walkers and the earth, live for a moment and dissolve into nothing more than damp, nothing left of their snowness but a trace here and there, a stubborn resilience, a determination to cling. As the land climbs, the survivor flakes are joined by others and others again, and soon the land and the walkers are white.

'As long as it continues, we are invisible,' whispers Stephen. He steadies Suzanna where she stands. 'Ssh.' Above them, the muted paddle of rotor blades rowing for home. 'How well our roto-silencers work,' he says in admiration.

Now they walk more freely in themselves, though slowed by the snow and the effort of snow walking. Suzanna looks behind her, sees their tracks visible for a few moments and then snowed under. 'As long as it continues,' says Stephen once more.

The line of trees they are following gives way to a shrouded landscape of crowberry, dwarf willows and birch. The weather thickens. Now whatever appears in front of them appears as a surprise. Stephen takes out his compass and a map. 'There are hills ahead. We'll go around and come back behind them, but first we must find shelter. It's too dangerous. I can't see what's beneath us. Stay close.'

They move forward slowly, hardly at all. After two hours they are sweating in spite of the cold. The tumbling, blanketing snow falls thick, wrapping them and the landscape equally so that all they see is white and, peering through its threads of white, the same floating falling blanket. It floats and falls, floats and falls.

Presently, they sense the darker presence of rocks ahead and Stephen moves towards them. He knows there could be a cave anywhere or nowhere. 'We need to find a cave,' he shouts. 'We need some luck.'

'You're always lucky,' she shouts back and Stephen opens his mouth and laughs as he hasn't laughed for months, and she laughs with him, laughter of the sort which comes when the body is too tired and the mind too hopeless to construct reasons not to laugh. And led by their laughter or by nothing at all other than Stephen's luck or blind fate, they find an opening in the rock and fall into it. By the light of Stephen's torch, they see two sides narrowing into what appears to be a deeper chamber and not a flake of snow within.

Their cheeks are pink. Their eyes are bright, bright with tiredness, bright with exhilaration – we made it, didn't we – and bright enough to be seen by the other across the few feet of cave as a small fire flickering in the dark, a glow of companionship, soul to soul. Whatever they will face tomorrow, they will not face alone.

They eat a little food in silence, roll out their sleeping blankets and lie down in the darkness with unseeing eyes. He lies on his side towards her, and she on her side away.

Stephen takes the garrotte and the knife from his trousers and puts them carefully behind him. He fingers the transmitter, traces the letter P inlaid like a curled baby hair on its wafer facade and falls into a deep, unmoving, unconscious sleep. Only when it lifts does he dream. He dreams of walking through a mountain – only a touch and the solid stone opens before him. He is amazed at the power in his fingers, incredulous. In wonder, he stretches out on a flat rock and is soothed by the soft hands of a woman who, like all women in all those dreams which visit men in the night, he both knows and does not know…

The dream-layers separate like strands of cloud before the moon but do not clear entirely. Stephen is asleep still and yet not asleep. He smells the hair of a woman, he feels her hip under his hand. His hand stretches, loosens her trousers and his own. He moves above her, asleep and not asleep within the sleeping blanket that is now falling slack behind him. He puts his hand beneath the clothes that cover her and feels her breast. How soft it is, how soft.

She punches him with as much leverage as she can generate, high up on the chest, just below the neck. 'Get off me,' she shouts.

Still his hand remains, still he stays above her. Hard to imagine he is still asleep. 'Don't do this, Stephen,' she says, 'don't.' Her voice is concentrated into a narrow beam which penetrates deeper than her punch; it carries into him and beyond.

'Agh… ' he begins and what he then intends to say or not say, to do or not do, is never said or done by him or understood by her because at that moment they hear a growl far back in some distant depth of the cave that might be coming, such is its primeval intensity, from a world elsewhere. It freezes them both.

At first the growl sounds more implied than real, a possibility only, and then it grows, grows angry, angrier and there is movement of stones on rock and the heavy rumbling of an animal disturbed.

Resumption

Suzanna and Stephen grab what they can and flee. The snow has stopped. The sky is blue. Stephen falls to the ground and sights his 220. The bear appears at the mouth of the cave, his arms stretched above him, his nose creased with fury. He roars and trees are shaken roundabout and snow comes loose. 'If he moves a step closer, I'll have to shoot him.'

'Don't,' says Suzanna. 'He won't come.' The animal continues to roar, watches them as they edge away, roars once more. Presently, he drops down on all fours and lumbers back inside. Stephen and Suzanna shiver. They clothe themselves, put on their boots and jackets, and pack up what they have. 'My music,' says Suzanna, 'my sweet, gentle Chopin; he must have fallen out.'

The anger she held against him in the cave has gone now, driven away by the bear and the cold and by her knowledge of all the knotted miles of passionate gut twisted up inside him. She takes his arm and they walk on in silence.

Stephen says nothing, doesn't know what to say. He takes out his map and studies it. 'We'll sweep round and through the valley.' He shows her with his finger. 'See. Should be good tree cover there. If we can reach the valley before the choppers return, they won't find us.'

They walk in silence, him ahead and her behind. They walk for an hour or two and reach the trees. They sit and share out food.

'Will they see our tracks?' she asks.

'They might, but I don't know what they would make of them. They're looking for one person. Double tracks might make them think it's Tribals.'

'Do Tribals leave tracks?'

'Probably not. I don't know. But they don't know either.'

'What will they do if they find us?'

'We are Rokas' friends. They won't believe we are out for a stroll. They'll make us tell them where he is.'

'We'll say we don't know. We don't.'

'They won't believe us. Better that they don't find us,' he says.

'How far are we from the cabin?'

'We could reach it tonight if we push on.'

The land undulates and then climbs steeply. They move through the trees, finding a rhythm over the pine needles and the snow and the fallen branches. The trees thin and they move fast, breaking sweat. At the top, the land flattens. It is stone, stumpy trees, white, no wind to stir up the snow, clear, sunlight. They stand in tree-shadow looking out. Both listen for the helicopters. They hear nothing. They don't know why they hear nothing.

'Perhaps they're not coming back,' says Suzanna.

'I wouldn't put much on that.' He points to descending layers of forest ahead of them. 'That's where we need to be. From there to the cabin isn't far. But we can't cross now, we've no cover. We'll stay here until dusk. Then we'll cross. With the snow-light and the moon, we'll manage. We'll be at the cabin tomorrow morning.'

Suzanna takes out her sleeping blanket and sits with her back against a tree. She gathers herself in and, somewhere between sleep and watchfulness, contemplates her baby. You'll be born in a different country, a warm, gentle soft country, she tells him. I will look after you better than any baby has ever been looked after, you will have the best daddy that any baby ever had, and you will grow up strong and happy. She smiles at the baby and she sees him smiling back. She kisses his nose. First, I'll give you a name. Alexander, what do you think of that? It was my father's name, the one who decided to die. She plays with his cheeks. Only kidding. Nobody can decide to die.

Stephen sleeps. He doesn't dream. His head is too solid for dreams. At dusk, they cross over the open country. By the trees' edge, Rokas greets them. He is standing with a Tribal. They ride on deerback to the valley.

Moments

Suzanna stares at the sky. The sky is hidden by trees but she stares at it anyway. 'Time to go,' she says to Rokas. 'What are you staying for? Do you want to grow old here?' She knows that he does. She's seen him with the Tribals, his life and theirs tumbling like drops in a waterfall, landing together, flowing together. He is where he wants to be, she knows that. 'Do you want to die here?' She knows the answer to that also.

Stephen sits by himself, his eyes quiet, his hand treasuring the transmitter in his pocket. Now is the time, he thinks. They will find us. Sooner or later they will, and then there will be death. Better that Suzanna lives even if she never forgives me... But she will. She'll have to. I will have saved her life and the baby's. His, too, if Porphyrian keeps his word. He takes the transmitter from his pocket, places it in his palm. It's this, or let her die with him in the forest. Is that what she wants? He opens the palm of his other hand and finds Porphyrian sitting there cross-legged, listening and smiling and shaking his head from side to side encouragingly.

Stephen looks up. Rokas and Suzanna are watching him.

'Tempted?' asks Rokas.

Stephen lays the transmitter on the earth, the curled *P* face downwards. 'I've thought about it.'

'Good. Do it. It'll put you in with Porphyrian. Then you can take Suzanna back, you can live together, have the baby, be happy. And I'll be away before the chopper comes.'

'Don't!' commands Suzanna. 'Don't play God with our lives, Stephen, don't.'

Rokas picks up the transmitter. He presses a small indentation on the casing. Nothing. He presses again.

'Thumb print activation,' says Stephen. 'No one can use it but me.'

'Then use it. Save yourself. Save Suzanna. And I will run like I've never run before.'

'Are you a runner, Rokas?'

'Use it, Stephen.'

Stephen receives the transmitter like a man might receive the elixir of life and other mixed blessings. He tosses it from hand to hand, weighs it in his mind, wrestles with the good and the bad. The devil comes in many guises, he thinks, and on the instant Porphyrian is once more in his palm, lying back on his elbows and smiling the way good fathers smile. 'Listen to Rokas, Stephen,' he whispers. 'It's the smart move, it's money in the bank. In fact, it's the only move, unless you want to see her dead in the forest and the two of you scrapping over her remains. She'll thank you for it in the end, believe me. I'm 70, I know.' And with a nod, or a wink, Porphyrian vanishes.

Stephen rests the transmitter on the precise spot which Porphyrian has vacated. He imagines Porphyrian beneath it and smiles. 'You know what I'd like,' he announces as if they are all gathered for a picnic and the transmitter is a feast of meats and wine and white napkins, 'I'd like us all to live together and be happy. Three is an odd number I know, but why not, who's counting?' Stephen laughs, but his laugh dies quickly in the cold air, becoming at its last gasp a sad puff of a breath, hardly a breath at all. 'The thing is,' he continues, 'I can't see it happening. I shuffle the deck and shuffle it again, but however many times I do it, I can't find happiness in the cards. Of all the actions I might take, not one leads to happiness. There is only the greater and the lesser unhappiness. So what I should do, the least bad thing I can do, is to call down the chopper, save you, Suzanna, and the baby, and perhaps we might make a life together, even a good life, who knows?'

Stephen turns from one to the other as if searching for the single magic thing that would make it all come right – and, not finding it, he shrugs and says, 'But the fact is, I can't do it. It'd be like sticking a knife in your guts, Rokas, killing you with my own hands. It's the only move that adds up, but I can't do it. It would make me no better than Porphyrian.'

Suzanna puts out her hand. 'May I, Stephen?' She takes the transmitter from him gently and lets it fall. She puts the heel of her boot over it. 'For all we know, they may have found the cabin already. They may be waiting for us up there.' She points upwards and, as she points, she lifts her boot and smashes down on the transmitter with all her strength. Then she grinds it into pieces.

Stephen gets to his feet. 'Now we will all die,' he says, and he takes her in his arms and kisses her.

The sub-surface undulations in Suzanna's face and in her body loosen and lie flat. The baby breathes a sigh.

Suzanna spends time with the women now in the great hulled canopy of deerskin and furs where the Tribals commune. They show her how to prepare the strange roots that hang from roof poles like onions. They show her the barks and grasses and leaves: which for flavour, which for fever, which for life. They show her how to hold the horn tools to pound the sacred root into drink and how to serve it and to whom as the tribe gathers each evening, chief and shaman and men, and passes slowly and sublimely into music and into sleep. And when she picks up a curved pipe of deer horn and magics from it curious sounds of yearning and death, which speak to them in some strange language unheard by them before, they let her play alongside their soft drumming and bow to her and smile.

She plays games of catch and dodge with the children. The women put their hands on her stomach, they stroke her hair, fairer than theirs by far, they laugh. She points up to a patch of sky visible through the trees and folds of rock and asks in sign why they are not afraid of the choppers. They look and laugh and are not afraid.

It is evening. Rokas and Suzanna and Stephen kneel. Around

them, a circle. The Tribals chant and pound roots and sieve them in water and take drink from their ceremonial *sharboo*. The drink soothes them all and sleep, merciful and releasing sleep, casts its cloak upon the three.

Rokas' sixth short story: Death

Uniforms lie in front of the old post office. They may once have been laid out in ordered piles but, since everybody is helping themselves, this is no longer the case. The man in front of me (about my size as it happens) picks up a pair of trousers, glances at them with disdain and throws them over his shoulder. He repeats this performance several times until I lose the taste for watching. Multiply such inane activity by the hundreds of soldiers who are doing likewise and you will realise that the ordered piles that may once have been have left no vestigial trace. They exist as conjecture only.

This conjecture is based solely on one piece of circumstantial evidence: the existence of a sergeant with a clipboard. He looks like the kind of man who might, at the beginning of this process, have made sure that the uniforms were laid out neatly, jackets here, trousers there, caps on this side, boots over there. He might even have subdivided them by size, starting with the biggest and working down, or the other way around. The presence of this sergeant with his creased trousers, his neatly combed hair and, of course, his clipboard, make me feel that in the beginning, or at least not so long ago, there was order.

Thinking this, I begin to pity the sergeant. I believe he tried. I hear him intervening, 'No, you, put that down, one uniform only, take only what you need.' No-one listens. Now's the time, they think, to stock up, get something for their brothers, their sisters, their uncles, their aunts and, of course, their children – what am I doing forgetting their children? They're little now but they can find a use for this jacket, surely. Why it's so big, it would make a perfect tent. They can sleep under it at night.

The sergeant shouts, his voice becoming shrill. He tugs at his hair. No-one listens. No officers back him up. They are helping themselves with all the rest. Some are even using their rank to move to the front of the queue. In the end, he stands aside and watches, still holding his clipboard but not bothering to record anything. What is there to record?

It starts to rain, a dull grey rain that looks as if it has set in. The clothes that are lying about quickly become sodden and the day dispiriting. I scratch around among the debris that is left and eventually manage to gather together some items that might do. Because it's raining and because everything I've found is a little big, I put them on over my existing clothes. The cap I've found has a hole that falls just above and between my eyes so that someone could, if they wished, lean forward and touch the bare skin of my forehead.

I hear a shout from behind. 'Eh, Petrusha, how are you?' My name is not Petrusha, but I turn round anyway. The man comes lumbering up to me. 'You remember me? Sergei. Of course you do.' He looks at my hat and laughs. His jacket has a ragged hole over the heart. I notice a trace of dried blood around it, unless it's paint. He puts a rough finger into the hole and hooks the fabric with it so that it puffs up. 'See,' he says proudly, 'no heart. I am safe. Lightning never strikes twice in the same place.'

Passages intersect. Junctions (of necessity) join. We have nothing in common, this man and myself, but yet we are linked by a moment he believes he shared with me. He doesn't refer to it. Peace, after all, has been declared. A new day has dawned and each of us, the whole city I mean, prefers to pretend that the past never was. It is better like that. All of us have touched and been touched. You me him.

The past never was but suspicion is ineradicable.

Who did what to whom? You can't help but wonder. It was that kind of war. It is that kind of peace. Our uniforms even now remind us.

Does the world try to tell us things? When a boulder topples for no apparent reason from a great mountain top, is it signalling the advent of the apocalypse, the small boulder in free fall a metaphor for a larger crumbling elsewhere? But then what about the other way round? Does a tsunami signal some minor disaster like the overflowing of a bath? Is there, to take the case of our uniforms, a wider message in my hat, in his jacket? But why wider? Why not just a message? Or perhaps no more than a suggestion, a supposition even?

'Petrusha,' says Sergei, 'come with me. I have an office now. Inside

my desk, I keep a bottle of the finest.' He gives me a wink. 'Don't ask me how I got it.'

I have the impression that though he issues an invitation, my ability to say no is constrained. I sense there would be consequences should I refuse, but this is only a sense. I cannot analyse any of his words and justify such a conclusion, and yet this is what I sense. I don't put it to the test. I accept.

We walk out from behind the old post office, him first and me behind. His feet make marks in the mud like the webbed feet of a dinosaur, each bone touching the ground and splayed out. It is a curious walk. I wonder for a moment whether he finds walking painful, so much weight supported on such broken arches. I begin to feel sorry for him.

'Don't worry about me,' he shouts over his shoulders. 'I have adapted to the pain. I don't feel it any more, not anyway as pain. If I feel it at all, it is as a reminder of why I'm here.'

'Why is that?' I ask.

'Because I was asked.'

'By whom?'

'By the person who gave me the whisky of course.'

'Who is that?'

'You will soon see.'

'See! Soon! You mean in your office.' I am by now alarmed. Is this a trap? I try to reach into my old jacket for my revolver, but my hand won't go in. The uniform I have just acquired is on top of the one I set out with and the entrances to the two, the old and the new, do not align. I begin to panic. Where is my revolver? Can I get hold of it if I need to? I try to appear casual in case he turns around.

We walk for a considerable length of time, at least an hour, him in front and me behind watching him grimace each time his instep comes down on a rock or sharp stone. Even so, we are moving at a good pace and must have covered several miles by the time he pauses. We are in a part of town with which I am unfamiliar.

'Is your office here?' I ask.

'Not far,' he replies.

'But this is not where offices usually are. We are in the suburbs. Soon we will be out of town.'

'Don't worry, my friend. You will find what awaits you worth the journey.'

At this my sense of unease, which had been in abeyance during the walk, reappears more strongly than before. I feel as if our meeting was no accident, as if I am being lured into something planned beforehand. Tremors run up and down my spine, but still I keep walking.

The streets of high-rise concrete along which we have been passing come to an abrupt end. The surrounding is suddenly rural. We are on a country lane with hedges on one side and a pleasant vista over rolling countryside on the other. Cows are grazing. We pass over a narrow bridge under which a family of swans are gliding by. A peasant in a smock is stacking hay with a pitchfork while beside him a girl is chewing wistfully on a straw.

I immediately notice that the girl is good looking in a homely sort of way – rounded face, intelligent blue eyes, fair hair twining around her ears and falling in strands across her face. She's wearing a loose fitting skirt that floats freely and a short-sleeved embroidered top. The man and the girl look happy together. The sun is shining.

I stop walking and, resting my forearms on the stone of the bridge, gaze at the sights before me. So pleasant is the view of the country and the two peasants making hay in the sunshine that I'm overcome by a desire to leave the lane and join them. While I'm wondering whether or not I should, how I might be received, if it would be right to intrude, the girl lies down on the haystack. As she lowers herself, her skirt rises up above her knees. The peasant seeing this throws down his pitchfork. She smiles at him. He takes a couple of steps and is beside her on the hay.

I am suddenly jealous. I should be the one to lie next to her, not that peasant. It's obvious, even from a distance, that he doesn't deserve her. 'No!' I shout, 'leave her alone, get off her,' but they don't hear me or, if they do, they take no notice. I shout again, but again no response. I wave my arms and yell as loudly as I can. To no avail. They entwine without me, as if I don't exist.

'Don't worry, my friend,' says my guide, 'they are young, they have each other. Be happy for them. You have enjoyed such pleasures in the past, I have no doubt. Come, leave them to it.'

Somehow I follow the flat feet ahead of me feeling, as I turn my back on the two of them, that I am turning my back on life itself. We continue walking for a further hour but the thought of the man and the girl won't leave me. My desire to return to the bridge becomes irresistible and I am about to do so when a voice says, 'Hey, Petrusha, it's not far now, just beyond the next corner, in fact.'

'That's okay,' I reply, 'I'm not going any further. Not now. Another time maybe. Thanks anyway.'

I begin to run expecting at any moment to feel a bullet between my shoulder blades. The bullet doesn't come. I rotate my shoulder blades in expectation, but still it doesn't come. I now run freely, and am soon at the bridge. The girl is there waiting. She is smiling. The peasant has disappeared. Sergei catches up with me and the three of us walk on together.

It is snowing now, quite freely, and the landscape of trees and grass and streams soon becomes entirely white. We walk for some time, blind to everything except each other and the snow until Sergei stops. He delves into his uniform and brings out a transmitting device. He switches it on, mutters something to himself, and continues without a word of explanation to the two of us.

This should have been a warning to me but I am, by this time, preoccupied with the girl. Somehow, even though she, like us, is wearing several layers of clothing, I become aware that she is going to have a baby. Whether I understand this from the quiet smile she wears or from her hand which rests comfortably on her stomach even as she walks, I don't know. All I know is that I suddenly feel protective of her. I feel the child is mine, though this is nonsense of course.

I don't know for how long the three of us proceed through the snow – I'm too absorbed by the presence of the girl to notice – but presently we start moving out of flat country into forest. The land climbs steeply and I offer the girl assistance in ascending. She takes my hand gratefully and also takes Sergei's, so that we form a chain as we make our way upwards.

When we reach the top, we find that the snow, from which we have been somewhat protected while among the trees, is now falling more heavily than ever. At first there is nothing we can make out but the fat flakes that drift downwards and cover our boots even as we stand. After a while, however, shapes begin to appear. We see trees, ghostlike behind the white, and gradually we make out what appears to be a line of soldiers moving towards us. We believe, though we cannot be sure, that they have rifles.

My immediate and powerful belief is that Sergei, inspired by jealousy perhaps, has betrayed us, that he has led us into this trap. I soon realise, however, that he is as disconcerted as I am.

'I will draw them away while you run for your lives,' he says. With this, and without any other last words, he sets off on his wretched feet as fast as they can carry him. He heads in the direction of a stand of trees among which he will be safe, and so good is his progress in spite of the difficulties underfoot that we start to think he is going to make it. The girl cheers, 'Come on, Sergei', and I cheer also. Hope rises within us until, muffled by the snow, we hear the sound of a single shot. We see him stagger and fall, the outline of his body tumbling down, sinking into the white cushion beneath him.

'No!' the girl screams. 'No, Sergei, no!' She rushes to where he lies and throws herself upon him, kissing him and crying uncontrollably. Presently, I hear a second shot and then silence, whereupon, realising that I cannot live without this girl or the baby she is carrying, or indeed without Sergei himself, I hasten to their bodies and to the bullet which is my destiny.

We lie in a heap, the snow sticking to us and piling up – so that anybody regarding us from some ethereal elevation beyond might wonder what this mound is and think perhaps of a tent pegged out as shelter for the lost.

The last lament

An eagle glides silently over the treetops, seemingly asleep on the wind, whistling now and again, a sleepy twee-oo, a killer about his business, unhurried in his concentration, effortless in his purpose, that swoop of death not solely his to command.

The Tribals kneel around the fallen bodies. They breathe deeply of the vapours that the bodies emit. They chant. They touch their foreheads to the snow. After some minutes, they lift their eyes and watch as two souls rise from the bodies and fly. Between them, holding their hands and looking up from one to the other, is a wisp, an intimation of what might have been to come.

A fourth soul lingers on the earth as if reluctant to leave. The man and the woman turn back from their departure. 'Come,' they call, 'Come, Stephen, join us.'

And Stephen joins.

Epilogue

Jimmy Sands was hanging from the rope for a long time before they found him. When they cut him down, they thought he had a smile on his face.

THE END

Notes

1. For further elaboration, see our *Self-Recycling Training Manual for Instructors,* ch. 4, Time and Other Passings.

2. *Porphyrian's Spring Clean*: a short but punishing civil war in which Porphyrian supplied both sides with tanks, mines, armoured personnel carriers, flame throwers, water cannon, lasers, death rays, cross-bows, knuckle dusters, blow pipes, kukris and much else besides. When the war ended, when both sides, the red and the blue, were exhausted, Porphyrian found that his eurars, like his munitions, had rocketed.

3. Question: why does Porphyrian allow Rokas to decide for himself the type of guns he will work on? He understands the absurdity of scruples, so why? Answer (1): patience. Porphyrian is a patient man. His patience is legendary. Answer (2): is it the flesh which causes inconsistencies? We often wonder.

4. From *Self-Recycling Training Manual for Instructors*, ch. 9: Preparing for the Thankless Task, transcript of interview. (Although incomplete and unauthorised transcriptions of this most important manual have been in circulation since 2023CE, there is no evidence that leaks of this sort have had any significant effect either on human belief or behaviour. Those who, before seeing the manual, are unaware of the *Life Beyond* dismiss all evidence – including the manual itself – as the work of charlatans, a fact to which the extract alludes.)

5. The *S-RTMI* encourages the use of such verbal caltrops in situations damaging to the individual or communal spirit. Where there have been acts, such as murder, which may take lifetimes to repair, we advise our Instructors to suggest thumping the chest three times followed by contemplative breathing. (For manipulation of nasal cavity, see illustrations.)

6. For discussion of the simultaneous nature of events both past and present, see article, 'A Number of Mountain Tops Viewed from Above' as appended to Ch. 4, Time and Other Passings, *Self-Recycling Training Manual for Instructors.*

7. The post-extinction consciousness of Ferruginous Duck, or its subsequent evolution, is not considered in the *S-RTMI.*

Also by Michael Tobert

Pilgrims in the Rough

The Mating Call of the Racket-Tailed Drongo

Photograph by Caroline Trotter

MICHAEL TOBERT lives in Scotland and has been writing ever since he stopped imagining he looked good in a suit. Now, he bakes the second best sourdough in the country and spends more time looking in than looking out.

**COSMIC
EGG
BOOKS**

If you prefer to spend your nights with Vampires and
Werewolves rather than the mundane then we publish the books
for you. If your preference is for Dragons and Faeries or Angels
and Demons – we should be your first stop. Perhaps your
perfect partner has artificial skin or comes from another planet –
step right this way. Our curiosity shop contains treasures you
will enjoy unearthing. If your passion is Fantasy (including
magical realism and spiritual fantasy), Horror or Science Fiction
(including Steampunk), Cosmic Egg books will
feed your hunger.